"In *The Rhythm of Fractured G*   with wisdom, tenacity, and grace as the characters within the pages traverse painful places in search of healing and wholeness. This third installment of the Sedgwick County Chronicles will inspire readers on their own healing journey as they meet new characters and revisit old friends."

AMANDA COX, author of *He Should Have Told the Bees*

"Amanda Wen brings richness into her careful and conscientious storytelling of people who struggle to journey through faith, injustice, and the search for redemption. The heart of the author is evident in her stories, and readers will be blessed just for entering into them."

JAIME JO WRIGHT, author of *The Lost Boys at Barlowe Theater* and the Christy Award–winning *The House on Foster Hill*

"Amanda Wen skillfully weaves little-known history and enduring truths into the stories of Siobhan and Deborah. Readers of any generation can relate to the struggles and doubts these women face. Ultimately, *The Rhythm of Fractured Grace* reminds us that Jesus alone mends what is broken and redeems what is lost—a hope we need now more than ever."

SARA BRUNSVOLD, author of *The Extraordinary Deaths of Mrs. Kip*

"Amanda Wen has become one of my new favorite authors, and this book just seals the deal. Handling a difficult topic with finesse and grace, yet with necessary truth, Wen pens a page-turning tale full of characters you will fall in love with. This novel is destined to be another award-winner."

DEBORAH RANEY, author of *Breath of Heaven* and the Chandler Sisters novels

the

RHYTHM

of

FRACTURED GRACE

Sedgwick County Chronicles

Roots of Wood and Stone

The Songs That Could Have Been

The Rhythm of Fractured Grace

the

RHYTHM

of

FRACTURED
GRACE

*Sedgwick County
Chronicles*

AMANDA WEN

KREGEL
PUBLICATIONS

The Rhythm of Fractured Grace
© 2024 by Amanda Wen

Published by Kregel Publications, a division of Kregel Inc., 2450 Oak Industrial Dr. NE, Grand Rapids, MI 49505. www.kregel.com.

All rights reserved. No part of this book may be reproduced, stored in a retrieval system, or transmitted in any form or by any means—for example, electronic, mechanical, photocopy, recording, or otherwise—without the publisher's prior written permission or by license agreement. The only exception is brief quotations in printed reviews.

The persons and events portrayed in this work are the creations of the author, and any resemblance to persons living or dead is purely coincidental.

Scripture quotations are from the ESV® Bible (The Holy Bible, English Standard Version®), copyright © 2001 by Crossway, a publishing ministry of Good News Publishers. Used by permission. All rights reserved.

Library of Congress Cataloging-in-Publication Data
Names: Wen, Amanda, 1979- author.
Title: The rhythm of fractured grace / Amanda Wen.
Description: Grand Rapids : Kregel Publications, 2024. | Series: Sedgwick County Chronicles ; 3
Identifiers: LCCN 2023034677 (print) | LCCN 2023034678 (ebook)
Subjects: LCGFT: Christian fiction. | Novels.
Classification: LCC PS3623.E524 R59 2024 (print) | LCC PS3623.E524 (ebook) | DDC 813/.6—dc23/eng/20230728
LC record available at https://lccn.loc.gov/2023034677
LC ebook record available at https://lccn.loc.gov/2023034678

ISBN 978-0-8254-4849-2, print
ISBN 978-0-8254-7159-9, epub
ISBN 978-0-8254-7158-2, Kindle

Printed in the United States of America
24 25 26 27 28 29 30 31 32 33 / 5 4 3 2 1

To the glory of God
In loving memory of my dad, Jim Peterson
Father extraordinaire, fixer of all the things,
and unwavering believer in possibility

CHAPTER ONE

THIS WAS NOT how Matt Buchanan's life in Wichita was supposed to start.

He stood on a street corner on the edge of downtown, his breath puffing up around his face, a slushy pile of leftover snow in the gutter. In his left hand, he juggled a crutch and a violin case. In his right, the opposite crutch and his phone.

Bending awkwardly around his crutch and a sore hip, he set the violin case on the sidewalk and flicked his thumb over the phone screen. The Uber driver was still over a mile away.

He regarded the tiny screen with a chuckle. Waiting on Ubers was supposed to have been left behind in Chicago. The crutches too, a relic from his high-school-football, torn-ACL past.

And his grandmother's violin was supposed to still be in one piece.

But thanks to that texting twentysomething and her beat-up bright-blue Nissan, here they all were. The damaged violin. The badly sprained ankle. His beloved almost-new silver pickup being patched up at the repair shop.

Thankfully, that was the extent of the damage. Most of his belongings had been in the moving truck his new job had paid for. He hadn't trusted them with the heirloom violin, though. Thought it'd be safer in the back seat of his truck than bouncing around with the movers.

Oh, the irony.

Less than a minute now, according to the app. Pain shot through his hip, making him wince as he bent to retrieve the violin.

Right on schedule, a red Toyota Corolla pulled up, and a petite platinum blond in buffalo plaid hopped out, then slammed the car door. According to the app, her name was Siobhan, but its helpfulness ended there, with no hint as to pronunciation.

"Let me help you with that." She wasn't asking, and a moment later the damaged old violin was in her slender fingers.

"Careful," he said. It came out more grunt than word.

Sharp blue eyes peered up in silent challenge, and Matt gentled his tone. "Sorry. I didn't mean to be rude. It's just been through a lot."

A keen gaze swept him up and down, then the woman tucked the violin in the back seat. "Looks like the same could be said of you."

He laid the crutches on the floor in the back, then hopped to the front of the car and lurched his way in, falling into the seat with another grunt and a shot of pain. How much longer until he could take more Advil?

According to his watch, an hour. Okay. He'd probably live.

"Chitchat or quiet?"

He glanced left to find Siobhan behind the wheel, those blue eyes studying him in a way that seemed to see everything but also seemed to reserve judgment. She was prettier than her app photo.

"Pardon?"

"You a chitchat kinda rider or a quiet kind?" She leaned forward to adjust the heater. "I can do whatever—just let me know." Her voice held a slight twang that sounded southern to him after so much time in Illinois, although it was probably just the normal Kansas accent.

"I never mind chitchat." He buckled his seat belt. Heated seats, if the pleasant warmth radiating through his stiff muscles was any indication. He leaned into the headrest and breathed a silent prayer of thanks for modern technology. "I'm Matt, by the way."

"Siobhan."

It sounded like *Sha-von*. He could've been given a whole year with the name and never stumbled upon that as a possible pronunciation. "Never heard that name before. Which I'm sure *you've* never heard before."

A corner of her mouth quirked. "It's Irish. Pretty sure it's the only Irish thing about me. No idea what my parents were thinking with that one."

He tossed her his best pastor grin. "Well, it's pretty."

"Thanks." She glanced toward his bandaged right leg. "That come with a story, or do I get to make one up?"

"Probably whatever story you come up with is better than the real thing."

"Try me."

"Car wreck. Last Thursday. Some girl decided her text was more important than the stop sign she blew through."

"Ouch." Genuine sympathy softened Siobhan's voice as they rolled up to a red light. "Gonna be okay?"

"Yeah, should be. It's a nasty sprain, but the doc says it's a miracle it isn't broken." He shifted to get more heat on his left hip, still a lovely shade of purple from the impact of the seat belt. "Not the best welcome to Wichita I could've had, that's for sure."

Siobhan turned left, gifting him with a glimpse of silvery river through barren January trees. "New in town, then, I take it?"

"Sorta. I was born near Augusta, but my folks split up when I was five. Mom and I moved to Illinois—more corn, less wheat, but otherwise not too different. I lived there most of my life. But a job opened up here, and I decided to come back."

"Wouldn't be the first to leave and then come back." Siobhan negotiated a left turn into a bustling district filled with brick streets and century-old architecture. "What's the story with the violin?"

He winced again, though not from physical pain. "It was in the truck during the crash."

"Any damage?"

"You might say that. It's probably a lost cause, but it never hurts to check. Which explains our destination."

"Speaking of which . . ." Siobhan pulled to a stop at the curb outside a small, unassuming storefront. McFarland Violin Shop, read the white paint on a window. A sign with a stylized violin hung from the eaves, leaning right in the stiff January wind.

And they called Chicago the Windy City. Ha.

"Thanks." He pulled out his phone and paid via the app. Five stars for Siobhan. A generous tip.

When he glanced up, though, his driver had left her seat. In fact, she'd hopped out and was standing at the passenger door, his crutches in one hand and his violin in the other. Wow. Maybe he should've tipped more.

"You didn't have to get out. I'm fine." His discomfort came through in his tone, though, as he heaved his battered body from the car.

Siobhan didn't say anything, but her lifted brow was comment enough. She handed him the crutches but held the violin firmly in her grasp. "Don't flatter yourself. I saw your request come through and decided to make a couple extra bucks on my way to work."

It took him a minute to realize what she was saying. "You work here?"

Finally a full, sunny smile. "Siobhan Walsh, luthier in training. We specialize in lost causes."

⇥⇤

Tucking the violin under one arm, Siobhan held the door for Matt, the bells jingling against the glass, and ducked into the little shop after he hobbled through. The small space was cluttered with instruments of every size, shape, and description, from basses and cellos standing at attention along a far wall to violins and violas hanging from hooks near and far. The comforting scents of wood and varnish enveloped her in a gentle hug.

Of all the jobs she'd pictured herself in, tucked away in a tiny shop learning how to rehair bows and repair stringed instruments hadn't even made the list.

But after her last job? Tucked away seemed ideal.

"Just me, Ian," she called toward the back, and a moment later her tall silver-haired mentor appeared, clad in his usual maroon shop-logoed polo, jeans, and messy apron, bow in hand. "But I brought us a project."

Ian eyed Matt over the rims of his glasses. "Not sure orthopedics is my specialty, love," he said in the clipped English accent forty years in the States had done little to soften. Ian McFarland hailed from the same hometown as Shakespeare, a fact highlighted by a sketch of the Bard's birthplace holding a place of honor on the walls, alongside old Wichita Symphony programs and vintage record jackets.

Matt leaned a crutch against the wooden counter and stuck out a hand. "Matt Buchanan. We spoke on the phone about my violin."

"Ah yes. The car wreck. Nasty business, that. Let's have a look."

Siobhan sidled around the corner to the cluttered yet comforting workspace and popped open the latches of the case. Whatever damage the violin had suffered in the crash was no surprise, since even the case was nothing to write home about. Rather than the padded rectangular cases or sleek carbon fiber ones the professionals used to protect their instruments, this one was violin-shaped, barely padded, and covered in dust.

Just as she suspected, the violin had suffered serious damage. Tuning pegs had popped loose, the bridge had collapsed, and the bow was snapped in half. But the lethal blow? A two-inch vertical crack down the violin's back. A post crack. Many instruments never came back from such damage, much less a student-quality instrument such as this. Unless it had historical significance or massive sentimental value, Ian wouldn't sign off on fixing it. Not that she blamed him. A steady stream of string players ranging from students to symphony professionals meant they already had a backlog.

But this violin called to her. Recent damage aside, it bore none of the hallmarks of something that had been shoved in an attic and forgotten for decades. It had been well loved. And apparently still was, if the shine in Matt's eyes was anything to go by.

"Well, the fiddle's definitely seen better days," Ian declared. "And to be honest, it'll probably cost you more to fix than it's worth. Perhaps I could interest you in a replacement?" He indicated the rows of violins along the wall.

Matt shook his head. "Whatever it costs, it's worth it to me."

Siobhan studied him. "Do you play?"

Amusement glinted in deep-set hazel eyes. "I can screech out 'Twinkle Twinkle,' but I promise you don't want to hear it. My talents lie more on the guitar end of the string spectrum." Then amusement shifted to curiosity. "What about you, Siobhan?"

She got that question on the regular, but it was a dagger nonetheless. One that brought memories of a stage and a microphone and a stadium-sized church. Of letting her song twine with God's during worship sets. Of the admiration in the eyes of the pastor seated on the front row, admiration that soon turned to something else entirely . . .

"No." She ducked her head to hide the faint patch of toughened skin on the left side of her jaw that would've called her bluff and quickly identified her as a violinist.

Matt sighed. "Look, I know you both probably think this is a waste of your time. And maybe it is. But this violin belonged to my grandmother. When she played, it sounded like angels singing, and I've never heard anyone play quite that way ever again." He shifted his weight on the crutch. "My childhood was . . . not the best. Grandma was pretty much the only stability I had. She died when I was twelve, and this is the only thing I have left of her."

There it was. The reason Matt was so passionate about fixing up this fiddle. Her heart twinged. Though it seemed her childhood had been better than Matt's, it wasn't without its broken moments. And when something good surfaced, so too did a desire to preserve that something—or its memory—at all costs.

Ian shook his head. "I'm afraid we've simply too much of a backlog to get this repaired in anything resembling a timely manner."

"That's no problem at all." Matt leaned forward. "I've got no deadline, and I'm fine with being bottom of the priority list. But it would still mean the world to me if you'd take it on. Please."

It was the "please" that did it.

Most of Siobhan's life, men never asked. They simply took.

But this one asked.

He gave a half chuckle. "Plus the other driver's insurance is paying for the repairs. I've got no real skin in this game."

She met Matt's grin with one of her own, then turned to Ian. "You keep saying I need to fix my first post crack."

Ian frowned. "This one's no minor crack, love. You know that."

"I like a challenge."

Ian considered her, his lips pursed in thought. "Then a challenge you shall have."

"Thank you," Siobhan said at the same time as Matt.

With a laugh, Ian dug in a desk drawer for a tag, scribbled Matt's name on it, and tied it to the violin's scroll, then slid paperwork across the counter to Matt. "Just a little information from you, if you please, and we'll get started."

The muscles in Matt's arms rippled as he shifted his weight, and she caught the barest glimpse of a tattoo peeking out from the rolled-up sleeve of his plaid shirt.

"Want me to call you a cab?" she asked.

"Uber came through for me earlier." A dimple appeared in his cheek. "Think I'll stick with them."

"Can't argue with that." Siobhan returned the damaged violin to its musty velvet nest. "I'll dig in to this in the next day or two and be in touch, all right?"

"Sounds good." Matt tossed a grin and a wave over his shoulder, then hobbled his way to the door, where another customer—a white-haired symphony cellist whose name escaped Siobhan—held the door for him.

Ian greeted the man, and Siobhan turned her attention back to the violin. It had seen better days, for certain. But she was determined to fix the damage. For Matt.

For herself too.

Her own damage was probably beyond the realm of possible repair.

But she was determined to fix this violin.

CHAPTER TWO

LITTLE BY LITTLE, despite the boxes still lining the walls and bookshelves only half-filled, Matt's office at Pursuers Church was starting to look like home. The collection of Fighting Illini posters and pennants. The autographed vinyl cover of Crowder's *American Prodigal* album.

And the football he carried from job to job, the one signed by his entire high school team, the game ball he'd been given after winning the state championship his sophomore year.

He hung on to the football for more than just the memories, though. That ball, those names, represented everything he'd been before. Jock by day, partier by night. The world was his burrito.

Until the third game of his junior season, when he tore his ACL. The defender's helmet. The pop in his knee. The wrenching pain. The sinking sensation his life was over.

And it was. His old life, anyway.

A quiet knock at the doorframe drew Matt back into the present, and there he was. Pastor Trace Jessup in the flesh.

Deep creases appeared on either side of Trace's trademark bright-white smile. "Matty B. As I live and breathe."

"T-Dogg." Even after all this time, the old youth group nickname still sprang to mind.

Trace wrapped him in a bro hug, the kind that left safe distance but still squeezed the air out of you, particularly if you were sore from a car wreck. And particularly if Trace's famous biceps had only grown larger with the passage of time.

"Becky said you were in, but I wasn't going to let myself celebrate until I actually saw you." Trace pulled back, brown eyes alight. "Every time I think I've got a grasp on how good the Lord is, he knocks another one out of the park and blows my mind again. Bringing you here to Pursuers was way beyond anything I ever could've asked or imagined."

Matt grinned. "You and me both, my brother."

"We've come a long way, haven't we?" Trace bent to retrieve a handful of books from one of the cardboard boxes lining the wall.

Matt took the books with a chuckle. "You can say that again. Gotta say I'm still getting used to you without the man bun."

Trace let out a belly laugh and ran a quick hand through carefully coiffed short dark hair, silvering at the temples. "That and the skinny jeans are two of the dumbest decisions I ever made."

Matt shelved the books, grinning over his shoulder at his mentor. Trace may have ditched the plaid flannel and long hair for torn jeans and a black leather blazer, but the same charismatic, Jesus-fueled energy radiated from him as it had all those years ago.

Matt's dad had been in and out of his life—more out than in—for most of his childhood, disappearing for good when Matt was eleven.

His mom had coped with a steady stream of transient men, most of whom never bothered even to learn Matt's name.

His beloved high school football coach had left for a college job after that championship season.

But Trace Jessup had stepped in and stayed. He was the steadying male influence. The father figure Matt never had but always needed.

The man who introduced him to Jesus and changed his life forever.

"Still can't believe this is real, Trace." Matt loaded another handful of books onto the shelf. "This office. This church. You and me. Together. On staff."

"We're gonna light the place on fire for Jesus, my friend," Trace declared.

Matt gave a wry grin. "Just as long as nobody figures out I don't have the faintest idea what I'm doing."

Impostor syndrome always picked the most inconvenient moments to surface, so Matt wasn't surprised it had pulled up a chair and plopped its feet on the coffee table. He boasted no seminary degree. Very little formal musical training. And other than some volunteer worship leading at his church back in Illinois, zero experience at the very thing he was now being paid handsomely to do. At a church of two thousand live attendees, with a sizable online congregation as well. He'd lead Trace Jessup's flock, a flock accustomed to powerhouse sermons and at least one new book every year from their fearless leader.

Was it just loyalty that had led Trace to offer Matt the job? Or did Trace actually think Matt could hack it?

A heavy hand landed on his shoulder, and Matt turned to look into Trace's suddenly serious brown eyes. "Hey. I wouldn't have gone to bat for you with the elder board if I didn't think you had what it took."

"What, a little-used marketing degree didn't impress the suits around here?" While it did accomplish his goal of escaping the endless cycle of trailer homes and lousy apartments that had characterized his childhood, working in advertising didn't feed his soul. Only music did that.

But the cash wasn't there to go back to college, especially since he was still paying off loans from his first go-round. Instead, he made do with YouTube tutorials and the generosity of the worship pastor at Sawgrass Christian Church back in Illinois. Only Trace reaching out on Facebook gave him the courage to apply for the opening.

"Not all of 'em, to be frank," Trace replied. "I told them all a seminary degree gives you is head knowledge, but I knew your heart. I've heard you play. I've seen the kind of songs you write. I know what Jesus has done in your life, and that was good enough for me. They eventually saw the light."

Matt's shoulders relaxed a fraction. "Sounds like you really fought for me."

"Oh, I may have said the words, but it was the Lord who got you here. And it's the Lord who'll equip you to do what he's so very clearly called and gifted you to do." Stepping back, Trace tapped the doorframe and flashed another smile. "I gotta jet. Staff meeting in ten. See you in there."

Matt nodded and applied a smile he hoped would cover the sheer terror washing through him.

Chill, he told himself. *You've got Trace in your corner. Trace and Jesus. What more could you possibly need?*

\>\<

Siobhan breathed deep of the wood-and-varnish scented air, did a couple shoulder rolls, and picked up the hair-thin knife Ian used to open violins. It looked like a butter knife—and in fact had once been exactly that—but Ian had thinned out the blade himself on a grinder. Typical Ian. Everything had to be just so.

A cheerful Boccherini minuet floated from the sound system, another Ian McFarland insistence. "Broken instruments need to remember what they're capable of," he always said, "lest they forget their purpose in life and refuse to be fixed."

Whether it worked for instruments or not, Siobhan had yet to figure out. But it hadn't worked for her.

She picked up the damaged instrument and scanned the seams for openings. As neglected as this instrument seemed to be, she'd be stunned if she didn't find one.

Sure enough, there it was, on the top near the tailpiece. She propped the fiddle on her apron-covered lap, then wedged the knife into the tiny opening and wiggled it back and forth the way Ian had shown her. Within seconds Boccherini was punctuated with the staccato cracks of separating glue. Enough practice on damaged student instruments had taught her the hard way the difference between breaking glue and breaking wood.

Would've been cheaper for Matt Buchanan to buy new. But he was attached to this one.

He claimed not to play, and she had no reason to doubt him, but the tiny ruts in the fingerboard indicated someone had put in some quality time with it. Were it still played regularly, she'd need to plane the strip of dark-colored wood. Maybe she'd do that anyway. Lord knew she could use the practice.

A pang tried to bubble up at the thought of her own violin. It sang hour after hour once. Resonated through a two-thousand-seat auditorium. Gave voice to her soul and wings to her heart.

Now it was shoved in the top of a closet, gathering dust. Doubtless it wondered what had happened.

No. Not what.

Who.

Siobhan pulled in a breath to steady herself. No. These thoughts weren't allowed here. McFarland Violin Shop was a place for fixing. For repairing. For healing. She could beat the crap out of a punching bag later if she needed to, but for now she needed to be as zen as possible.

Methodically she worked the knife all the way around the edges of the damaged fiddle. The corners proved more stubborn than most student instruments, but as much wear as this one had, there was a real chance this wasn't its first rodeo at the repair shop. She paused in her labor to reach for the little light they used for a better glimpse inside the caverns of instruments.

Her hunch about previous repairs proved correct, as evidenced by some stubborn globs of glue toward the fingerboard. The top had clearly been taken off before, a previous crack in the wood repaired, and whoever had glued it back together had a skill set that left much to be desired.

Her lower lip slid between her teeth, and she heaved a silent prayer heavenward—force of habit now. Actual faith had left her a long time ago, and—

There.

"Got it." Quiet triumph surging, Siobhan set the knife down on the wood-chip-covered workbench, slid the light out from the F-hole of the instrument, and wiggled the top plate off the violin.

Sure enough, there it was. Another glob of glue from a previous repair, and a fresh two-inch crack straight down the back. A serious injury for any instrument, but not irreparable. She'd simply need to shave the wood around the crack, then make a patch to cover. She'd watched Ian patch a post crack on a cello once, and after the repair it sang more beautifully than ever before.

Of course, that was Ian. She wasn't Ian.

But that had been a rare and precious cello. And this violin might have been precious to one, but it wasn't rare. That little square label should tell her exactly what she was dealing with. A Kay, more than likely. Eastman, perhaps. Or—

Or . . . no label at all.

"Well, is the top still in one piece?" Ian's shadow fell across the workbench, and Siobhan turned with a proud grin.

"So far so good."

Ian grasped the thin, painstakingly removed piece of spruce and studied the inside. "Certainly not the first time it's been cracked. And that's rather an odd-looking repair." He turned the top this way and that. "Never seen it done quite like that before. An amateur clearly. One who had no business patching the top of a violin."

"Why would someone do that to an instrument?" Siobhan peered closer. "Why not take it to the professionals? Even with a cheap instrument, there's no reason to try to DIY everything."

"Unless there wasn't much choice." Ian held the violin closer and turned it over again. "This glue formulation hasn't been used for over a hundred years."

Siobhan frowned. "Then maybe this isn't some student-quality fifties-era fiddle?"

"Student quality, likely." Ian set the fiddle on the workbench. "In any event, without a maker's label, it's impossible to know until it's played. But as to its age? Eighteen hundreds, easily."

"What do you think happened to it?"

Ian shrugged. "Hard to say. Nothing good, that's for certain."

"Would there be any way to find out more?"

Ian grinned. "I suppose you could always ask the handsome young bloke who brought it in."

Siobhan resisted the urge to roll her eyes. Any time a guy came into the shop without an obvious wedding ring, Ian tried to play matchmaker.

Fortunately, there was another source of information Siobhan could consult: her historian half sister, Sloane.

And they were entirely overdue for a coffee date.

"I've got my own sources." She slid her phone from her apron pocket and scrolled through her texts.

"Suit yourself, Siobhan," Ian replied jovially. "I've not given up on you yet."

That made one of them.

CHAPTER THREE

Sedgwick County, Kansas
April 1876

"Papa! Bee-bee! He asked me!"

Deborah Caldwell dropped her mending and glanced up at the door to their cabin, where her younger sister, Elisabeth, stood, cheeks flushed and eyes sparkling. It had been ages since the normally quiet Elisabeth had used the childhood nickname, a reference to the honey-producing insect that was also the English translation of Deborah's name.

"Who asked you what?" John Caldwell, in his rocker beside the fire, glanced up from the thick Bible he spent hours reading every evening. But the glint in his eyes, the craggy grin at the corner of his mouth, told the truth. He knew perfectly well that Isaiah Morton had asked for Elisabeth's hand in marriage. In fact, that had likely been the subject of Papa's hushed, hurried conversation with Isaiah after church this morning. Papa hadn't said a word, but Deborah was sharp enough to connect the dots.

Of course, no one would be surprised by Isaiah's proposal, nor would they be surprised by Elisabeth's eager acceptance. Anyone who spent more than a moment with Isaiah and Elisabeth could see the worshipful way he looked at her and the doe-eyed adoration with which she regarded him.

"Papa," Elisabeth chided, coming closer to the fire. "Don't be daft. Isaiah asked me for my hand."

"I see." Papa made a show of slowly closing his Bible and setting it on the small table beside the chair. "And what, pray tell, was your answer?"

Tears pooled along the lower rims of Elisabeth's blue-gray eyes. "I told him yes, Papa. Of course I told him yes. Ever since I met him, being his wife is all I've ever wanted."

"Oh, Elisabeth." Flinging her mending aside, Deborah leaped from her rocker and enveloped her sister in a warm embrace, ignoring the headache the sudden movement brought. Headaches had been a fact of life for more than a decade. "I am so happy for you. *So* happy."

And she was. Truly. A more perfect couple than Isaiah and Elisabeth could scarce be found, be it here in Sedgwick County or anywhere else.

But sadness twinged too. And more than a hint of envy.

"Thank you, my sweet sisterling." Elisabeth pulled back, eyes shining, her knit cap askew. Instinctively Deborah put it to rights, the lightweight fabric belying the heaviness of the seemingly routine gesture. Simple and flimsy though the cap seemed, it was the only barrier between the prying eyes of the world and the jagged, hairless set of stitched-together scars that marred Elisabeth's head of otherwise lovely deep-brown curls.

The same set of scars crossed Deborah's head. The marks of a tomahawk, the souvenirs from the childhood attack that had taken their mother, her brother, and two sisters. Though the fringed buckskin of their attackers and manner of their violence had led everyone to believe they were Sioux, Elisabeth had always claimed her attacker had blue eyes and white skin. Regardless, Deborah tried not to think about it, but the headaches, the scars, the ugliness . . . Some things were impossible to forget.

To forgive.

And yet, though Elisabeth's wound had been even more serious than Deborah's, she'd managed to attract the attention of a man. A husband. She had the promise of a life. A future beyond caring for their widowed father.

Not that Papa was a burden. Of course not.

But still, Deborah yearned for more. And now Elisabeth, the one person who truly understood what Deborah had been through, was starting her own life.

Deborah squared her shoulders. It would be all right. She'd survived everything life had thrown at her thus far. She'd survive this too.

Sometimes it felt like all she knew how to do. Survive.

"Well now." Papa rose and embraced Elisabeth. "Anyone with a nose on his face could see how much the two of you care for each other and how well suited you are. The Lord has indeed blessed you and young Isaiah, and

I pray he continues to do so." He pulled back, dark eyes darting around the firelit cabin. "Now, where is the young fellow?"

A knock came to the door, and Elisabeth's hand flew to her mouth. "Oh, gracious me. I—I think I left him outside."

Chuckling, Papa strode to the door and opened it to a similarly amused-looking Isaiah Morton.

"I never imagined my bride-to-be running inside without me." The smile spreading over his face, though, said all was forgiven.

"Oh, Isaiah, darling, forgive me. I was just so excited that you'd finally asked me." Elisabeth rushed to his side, her small fingers entwining with his longer ones. "I've been dreaming of the moment so much, I feared it was exactly that. A dream."

"No dream, my sweet." Isaiah tucked a finger beneath Elisabeth's chin and lifted her gaze to his. "Or if it is, it is one from which I never want to awaken."

Elisabeth's cheeks pinked, and she snuggled as close as propriety—and Papa—would allow. "What do you think of a Christmas wedding?"

"Christmas?" Isaiah blinked. "I thought you said you wanted to wed as soon as possible."

"I do, love. Of course I do." She brushed the tip of his freckled nose with a finger. "*But.* A proper wedding takes time to plan and put together."

"You want a *proper* wedding, then." Isaiah rewarded her with a teasing smile. "I see."

"Besides . . ." Elisabeth's voice took on a whispery quality. "Mama and Papa were wed at Christmastime. I thought it might be nice to honor Mama's memory in that way. Would that be all right, Papa?"

Papa cleared his throat. "I think that sounds wonderful. Your mama will be right proud, watching down from heaven as you wed this fine young man." He pulled his younger daughter into an embrace.

Deborah's eyes stung. What she wouldn't give to have her mother beside her. To walk her through the befuddlement of becoming a woman. To reassure her that she was still beautiful even though a third of her scalp had been torn off. To help her solve the confusing mix of emotions that would result from watching Elisabeth start a new life without her.

When would it happen for Deborah?

Would it happen at all?

The prairies of Sedgwick County were peppered with their share of men, to be sure. Those who'd fought for the Union, rewarded with their forty acres. Though some were married, just as many were still looking for a wife.

Even so, no one had looked at her twice.

Well. Some had. But it wasn't the look of attraction her heart yearned for. Instead, it was unabashed curiosity. Sometimes even revulsion.

She was used to those looks. At least, she tried to tell herself she was. But would she ever truly be accustomed to being a curiosity? The center of attention for the tragedy that had shaped her life, the moments she'd give anything to erase from history?

"I think this calls for a celebration." Papa clapped his hands together, the creases around his eyes deepening. "Deborah, fetch my fiddle, won't you?"

With a tight smile, Deborah reached for the scarred leather case, worked the latches, and opened it to reveal Papa's prized possession: his violin. Another miraculous survivor of the attack, though like Deborah, not without its scars. A crack down the front of the fiddle, painstakingly repaired by a carpenter who'd also made the journey to Kansas. The young man had never attempted such a thing before, but he'd managed to put the instrument back together. Papa claimed his fiddle sounded even better than it had before.

"This fiddle is a sign, girls," he'd told them time and again. "It's a sign God still loves us. Hasn't forgotten us. Our wounds are deep, to be sure. But he'll heal us."

And God had healed Papa. Pulled him out from the depths of despair and since then using him to reach dozens of settlers in this new land. So perhaps the violin was just the sign Papa needed.

But for Deborah, the violin was the opposite. God had taken four of her family members. Mama. Six-year-old Josiah. Two-year-old Mary Catherine. And baby Nancy, yanked from Mama's arms. All of them gone in a matter of moments. Deborah and Elisabeth left horribly maimed.

But that hunk of wood and strings, God had spared.

Careful providence? Or capricious cruelty? It was the question that had haunted the last dozen years.

In this, though, Deborah was alone. For if Elisabeth ever asked such a question, she'd never given it voice. Though her wounds were even worse, Elisabeth had endured the pain with incredible stoicism. She'd patiently accepted her suffering as her lot in life and part of God's plan, knowing that it would go on to produce perseverance, character, and hope. No wonder, then, that God favored her with Isaiah's love.

Papa plucked the strings to check the fiddle's tuning, then lifted the bow, and the violin's sweet song filled the small cabin. Elisabeth and Isaiah stared dreamily at each other, leaning close, their visions of the future so vivid they almost danced along with Papa's tune.

Deborah sat back down and looked away, jabbing the needle through the fabric with such force she pricked her finger. A crimson dot of blood appeared, and she lifted it to her lips to suck it away. Papa's knowing glance found her, but mercifully, he said nothing.

Oh, Lord, forgive my attitude. The prayer was a reflex, a knee-jerk reaction for a preacher's daughter. But had God even heard her? Did he care enough to answer if he had?

Elisabeth's engagement was a jolt. That was all. Deborah would get used to it. Last she heard, Isaiah planned to stay in Sedgwick County. Elisabeth wouldn't be far, and the sisters would remain close.

Wouldn't they?

Or would they drift apart, Elisabeth's love and care rightfully going toward her husband? The passel of little ones doubtless not far behind.

What about me, Lord? She heaved the prayer toward the God she both clung to and was still angry with. *Have you forgotten me?*

CHAPTER FOUR

HOT. RICH. CREAMY. Sweetly spiced. And just enough rocket fuel to get her through the rest of the day.

Such was the perfect chai latte, Siobhan's weekly indulgence at Frontier Coffee. Okay, more than weekly. But the only time she came in and sat down was during coffee dates with Sloane Kelley-Anderson. Siobhan marveled at the dark-haired woman across the table from her who shared half her DNA. Yet Sloane was someone she'd never even known about until four years ago. Her mother—their mother—Kimberly, had had another daughter. A daughter five years older, born from an affair and left on a city bus in Seattle, only to be randomly reunited in Wichita three decades later.

Well, Mom wouldn't say it was random. Neither would Sloane. Both were quick to credit God.

Siobhan would have too, once upon a time.

And now these occasional coffee dates had a third party, the tiny bundle sacked out on Sloane's shoulder. Domenica Rose Anderson came with her father's deep-blue eyes, her mother's dark-brown hair, and the fortunate ability to sleep through just about anything. So far, anyway.

"Talk to me about something. Anything." Sloane set her teacup down in its saucer and fixed keen brown eyes—their mother's eyes—on Siobhan. "My world has shrunk to nothing but diapers and feedings and laundry. If it weren't for meeting you here, I wouldn't even know what day it was."

Siobhan grinned. "Eager for maternity leave to be over, are we?"

Sloane's eyes softened. "I love Domenica. More than anything. But I miss . . . *thinking*. And researching. I even miss those field-trip kids."

"Going back full time, then?"

"Part time. Garrett's been working from home since the pandemic. He thought he'd hate not having an office to go to and coworkers to chat with, but it turns out he loves it. So we'll see how it works with me going in twenty hours a week and him being creative with scheduling."

"And if that doesn't work?"

Sloane chuckled. "You know Garrett. Not only does he have a plan B, he's got plan C and D lined up as well. As sweet as this little lady is, though, I think we'll be okay. But seriously. Tell me something about work. Something about your job. Surely you had an interesting customer or Ian had a good joke or something."

Siobhan lifted a shoulder. "Well, Ian did let me take the top off a violin yesterday."

"Yeah? That sounds exciting."

"Exciting, terrifying, take your pick. But I did it without breaking the thing."

Sloane nodded. "What's wrong with it that you had to take the top off?"

"Soundpost crack. The soundpost is the little vertical piece of wood inside a violin, and when it gets dropped or bumped just right or is in a car accident, like this one was, sometimes the pressure forces the soundpost into the back so much it cracks." Siobhan dabbed at a spilled drop of chai with her napkin. "Lots of times it costs more to fix than the violin's worth, so we don't do repairs on cheap student instruments, except I convinced Ian to let me do this one for practice. The guy who brought it in was super attached to it. Some kinda sentimental value."

"A guy, huh?" Sloane's eyes sparked with mischief. "Cute? Single?"

Siobhan rolled her eyes. "You and Ian both."

"So the answer to both those questions is yes."

"Look, you guys can play matchmaker all you want. I'm not interested." Siobhan lifted her chai. "What I am interested in is figuring out just what happened to that violin. Because Ian thinks it's a lot older than we first assumed. Maybe even as old as the eighteen hundreds. But without a label or anything to identify the maker, it might be a needle in a haystack."

Sloane grinned. "Needles in haystacks are my specialty."

"Only if you've got the time."

"I'll make the time. My brain needs something to think about besides baby care. No offense, sweetie." Sloane shifted in her seat and kissed the fluffy little head, then stopped, her gaze on something over Sloane's left shoulder. "You said the violin had been in a car accident?"

Siobhan nodded. "Guy said a texting teen ran a stop sign."

"Any chance that would result in an injury that'd require crutches? On a guy who's, say, six two? Light-brown hair? Who might be standing in line right now studying a menu?"

"Shut up. He is not." Siobhan threw a glance over her shoulder. Sure enough, there he was. Tall, leaning on one of his crutches, the lines of his well-fitting olive-green Henley accenting broad shoulders and muscled forearms.

The sight caused a spark to surface. One she knew well, by the name of Attraction.

She hadn't felt that jolt of warmth in quite a while. And the last time she'd felt it, the flames had fanned into an inferno that nearly destroyed her.

Nope. She had to snuff that out now.

Attraction led to nothing but trouble.

⤜⤛

Matt noticed Siobhan's smile before he noticed the rest of her. Bright, dazzling, and unguarded, he almost didn't recognize it as belonging to the violin repairer at first. Not until he caught a glimpse of platinum-blond hair and plaid shirt—purple this time, not red—did he realize he knew her. By then the smile had frozen and the light in her eyes had dulled, but she rose from her chair and met him in line.

"This place any good?" he asked her.

"It is if you like chai." The smile was back, with the barest hint of latte foam on her upper lip.

Matt balanced his crutch beneath his arm and fished his wallet from his jeans. "What about the coffee drinks?"

Her jaw tensed slightly, and her smile faded at the edges. "Wouldn't know. I quit coffee years ago."

"Ah well. I'm always up for trying something new." Shuffling to the front of the line, he ordered a chai. "Put a couple shots of espresso in it though, if you would."

"You got it," the barista replied. "For here or to go?"

Matt glanced around. He'd been planning to sit for a few minutes, but the utter lack of available tables made him rethink his plan.

"You're welcome to join us." Siobhan jerked her chin in the direction of the nearby table where she'd been sitting with her dark-haired companion. "That's my sister, Sloane."

Sister? There wasn't much resemblance between the curvy, dark-haired woman who gave a cheerful wave and the willowy blond Siobhan. His face must've registered his surprise, because Siobhan offered another half smile. "Half sister, actually. We just met a couple years ago."

Matt tossed Siobhan a curious glance as he hobbled his way to the table, thankful it wasn't too far. "I'm here for the story behind that, if you care to tell it."

"I'm adopted." Sloane's eyes shone warm behind black plastic-framed glasses. "I found my birth mom online a couple years ago and got a sister in the mix too." She gathered a large bag from beside her chair and stood, careful to not jostle the baby sleeping on her shoulder. "And with that, I'm off for a feeding."

Siobhan tilted her head. "But she's asleep."

"I know." Sloane's grin was slow and lazy, her wink conspiratorial. "But it was either that or blatantly announce that I'm leaving the two of you to get acquainted, and I decided a manufactured excuse would be less awkward. Your mileage, of course, may vary."

Well. Maybe they'd only known each other for a couple years, but there was clearly a warm relationship here, as evidenced by Siobhan's good-natured eye roll and easy smile.

"It was lovely meeting you, Matt." Sloane shouldered the diaper bag.

"You too, Sloane."

She departed at the same time a steaming chai with a heart in the foam appeared in front of him. Experience told him he shouldn't sip it—not right away, anyway—but the aroma was so enticing he couldn't help himself. While his tongue did protest the heat, the perfect combination of sweet spice, bubbly cream, and dark espresso silenced its complaints and made it beg for more.

It was official. If heaven served chai lattes, the ones from Frontier Coffee would definitely be on the menu.

He lowered the cup to find Siobhan watching him, lips curved, eyes sparkling. "Pretty good—am I right?"

"A hundred—no, a thousand percent. This just might be the best chai I've ever tasted."

She settled back in her seat, long fingers wrapped around the white china cup, her smile almost smug. "I know my coffee shops."

He leaned forward. "Clearly you're a trustworthy source. What other treasures does Wichita have to offer?"

Long-lashed pale-blue eyes flitted upward in thought. "The pizza place around the corner is pretty good."

"Pizza, huh?" He fought a grin. "Please tell me they don't claim to be Chicago-style."

"Not to my knowledge. They're mostly brick oven, I think."

"Brick oven's fine. I'm just kind of a pizza snob. There's nothing quite like a four-meat deep dish from Gino's East."

"Yeah, you're not gonna find anything like that here," Siobhan replied. "Although you will find great Mexican, Vietnamese, and Lebanese."

That was an interesting ethnic combo platter. He tilted his head to the side. "Any Ethiopian?"

"Nope."

"Sad."

"Right?" Siobhan gestured emphatically. "Ethiopian is delicious, and until Wichita gets an Ethiopian restaurant, its dining scene will always be incomplete. The ethnic cuisines we have are phenomenal, but I wish we had more. Until then, there's a place in Kansas City I go whenever I'm up there."

"Kansas City, huh?" Mischief surfaced. "Guess I'll just have to make a little road trip when I get out of this ridiculous boot and don't have to depend on Uber for everything."

"Uber is the worst," Siobhan deadpanned. "Those drivers. Can't trust 'em."

"Not for a minute." He glanced up to find those mirthful glimmers in her eyes again.

What was it about this woman that made it impossible for him to stop smiling?

"Chicago to Wichita, that's kind of a big change." Siobhan set her enormous mug back into its saucer. "What convinced you to give up all that deep-dish goodness and move here?"

"Work. An opportunity I couldn't afford to pass up." He took another sip of heaven-sent chai.

She tilted her head to the side. "What kind of work do you do?"

"I'm a worship pastor."

"I see." Her shoulders stiffened, and she avoided his eyes. "I hope that goes well for you."

"So far so good." Had he misread her signals, or had a chill settled over the table the moment he'd mentioned his job?

"Hey, not to change the subject," she said, "but . . . that violin you brought in. Do you know anything about its history?"

Matt shook his head. "All I really know about it is that it belonged to my grandma. Mom's mom. When my parents split up, Mom and I moved back to Illinois and lived with her parents for a while. Mom was . . . well, she was pretty young when she had me, and she was kinda unstable for a while."

A shadow crossed her face. "Yeah, I get the whole young-and-not-totally-with-it mom thing."

Their eyes met, and he read all the things she wasn't saying. Though their experiences might not be identical, there was common ground. The knowledge provoked both sympathy and kinship.

"Thank God for Gram," he continued. "She was there for me way more than Mom was those early years. She used to practice after she put me to bed. I remember falling asleep to violin music every night, feeling safe and warm. She wasn't classically trained or anything—I think she mostly taught herself—but she could play by ear like nobody's business. Hear a thing once, and it was locked in her memory. And all of that is *way* more information than you needed, since you asked about the violin."

A sweet smile curved her lips. "You're fine. Instruments are more than just hunks of wood and metal. They're friends. Family members even." Something bittersweet flickered in her eyes, but she blinked it away before he could process it. "Do you know where your gram got the violin?"

"Hard to say. She passed away when I was twelve. I want to say maybe it belonged to her dad, but I'm honestly not sure. I can give Mom a call and ask."

Siobhan waved a hand. "No big deal. I'm just curious, is all."

"Gotta admit I'm curious myself." And he was. About the violin, sure. But mostly about Siobhan. Why she'd stiffened when he'd mentioned church. Why so many micro-emotions flitted across her face during seemingly run-of-the-mill small talk. Why she appeared still like the surface of a windless lake, but why his gut told him those waters churned mightily beneath.

Siobhan set her chai on the table and pushed her chair back. "And speaking of violins, there's a passel of them back at the shop that aren't going to fix themselves."

He rose with her. "Quite all right. I've got some work to do myself."

She fixed him with a look that was hard to read. "I'll do some more digging around on my end about your gram's violin. But do let me know if you learn anything."

"I absolutely will. You've got my number, right?"

She pulled her phone from the pocket of a black leather jacket and tapped a couple buttons. "Yep. And now you've got mine."

His watch vibrated against his wrist, and digits flashed across the small screen, accompanied with a violin emoji. "Cool. Now I can bug you for a ride anytime I want. Like . . . maybe to check out one of those restaurants you suggested."

She shouldered her bag. "Long as we're going Dutch."

"Fair enough. Tomorrow night?"

She paused, head tilted. "Sure."

And then she was gone, and he was reeling. Her reply and the no-nonsense look she'd speared him with made it clear he'd been friend-zoned from the outset.

Which was fine. Good, even. Trace had always talked about aspiring to the example of the apostle Paul—remaining single so he could be fully devoted to his mission without the added responsibility of a family. Trace's example, and a couple relationship disasters in his college years, inspired Matt along the same path.

Friendship with Siobhan was all he'd been aiming for. He certainly didn't have the bandwidth for any romantic distractions, especially right now, stepping into his new and demanding role at Pursuers. The friend zone was doubtless where he needed to be, for a variety of reasons.

So that sting of disappointment at the walls she'd so quickly put up? At her abrupt departure?

Just a momentary bruise of his ego.

He was sure of it.

CHAPTER FIVE

THE PURPLE-HAIRED CASHIER turned the tablet at the register toward Matt that Friday night. The light from the neon wedge of pizza on the brick wall behind her glinted off a silver nose ring. "Your total comes to thirty-three dollars and eighteen cents. Will that be cash or card?"

"Card." Matt lifted his Discover toward the screen.

"I'm sorry." Siobhan held her phone in one hand, digging a card from a sleeve on the back. "It's separate checks."

The cashier blinked. "Separate? Okay, not a problem." She turned the tablet back and tapped the screen.

"Are you sure?" Matt studied Siobhan. "It's the least I can do, given that you drove and didn't even charge me for the ride."

"I don't when it's a friend."

"And I like to treat my friends when we go out," he replied. "Besides, the aroma in this place is making me feel like I'm right back in Chicago, and I have you to thank for that, so . . . please. My treat."

He wasn't sure what kind of response he was expecting from her, but the fire in her eyes and the stiffened shoulders wasn't it.

"I don't need anyone to pay for me," she hissed.

Matt glanced behind them, but the only people in line were a group of teenagers, three of whom were posing for a group selfie and the other two still studying the menu. He returned his attention to Siobhan.

"I'm sorry. I meant no offense. If it's that important to you, then by all means."

"It is." She turned to the cashier. "Separate checks. Put the appetizer on mine."

"Can do," the cashier replied.

As Siobhan led him toward a table by the window, gently shoving chairs aside to make room for his crutches, she softened. "I'm sorry. There's a chance I overreacted back there." She pulled the stool out for him before perching across from him and setting the metal number on their table.

"You don't need to apologize." He leaned the crutches on the brick wall beside him and hoisted himself onto the stool with a grunt of relief. Two more days and then, with any luck at all, the ortho doc would release him from these ridiculous contraptions.

"I feel like I do." She leveled him with an honest gaze. "I have . . . a lot of baggage. And part of it has to do with money. And dating."

He offered what he hoped was a reassuring smile. "Then maybe this'll help. Because I'm not thinking of this as a date." Man, he hoped he sounded more convinced than he felt.

One delicate brow inched upward. "You're not?"

"Nope. In fact, I don't date."

"Not at all?" Her shoulders lowered a fraction. "What a coincidence. Neither do I."

Matt lifted the large red plastic cup in front of him, filled to the brim with soda, and grinned. "Well, then. To our first not-a-date."

She clinked her glass to his. "I'll drink to that."

→←

Siobhan watched Matt sip his soda, then lower the glass to the table. He must've taken more of a swig than he intended, though, because a drop leaked from his lower lip.

"Good *night*." He wiped at the offending drop with a thumb, hazel eyes gleaming with self-deprecating amusement. "I promise this isn't my first time drinking from a glass."

"Sure. Keep telling yourself that." Siobhan handed him a napkin from the dispenser.

"Thanks." He dabbed at his lips with the cheap square of flimsy white. His cheeks darkened a shade, and the crease framing his smile deepened.

He was kinda cute, in a wholesome, boy-next-door sort of way. With those broad shoulders and muscular build, he'd doubtless been an athlete in high school. Probably homecoming king too. The sort of boy who could get any girl he wanted and wouldn't have to work too hard to do it. Heck, he'd even tried that with her and that sneaky attempt to buy her dinner.

But maybe that had been without an ulterior motive. He'd insisted he didn't want anything from her, and though her judgment of character had failed her in the past, there'd been a sincerity in his eyes, a richness in his voice, that made her at least entertain the possibility he was telling the truth.

"What?" Light-brown lashes blinked, and his brow creased. "I'm not still drooling Dr Pepper, am I?"

She propped her chin on her hand and met his gaze. "If this isn't a date . . . if you don't want anything from me . . . then why'd you want to pay so bad?"

"Well"—he smoothed out the napkin and slid it under his soda as a coaster—"because for the first time in my life, I can."

It was his repurposed napkin that made the statement ring true. Most people would've tossed it to the side without a second thought, but he'd been careful to reuse it. It was an echo from her childhood, in the fuzz of memories that was Life Before Todd, when Mom was just starting out in real estate and home was a cheap apartment with funny-smelling carpet and competing stereos from the parking lot. In those memories, nothing was wasted, everything could be reused, a penny saved was a penny earned, and all that jazz. Todd the heart surgeon arrived about the same time Mom's career took off, and penny-pinching rapidly became a thing of the past. But Siobhan remembered. She recognized the signs. And Matt's napkin folding was one of them.

"I take it financial stability is something of a recent development?"

"That's a nice way to put it." He chuckled, then folded his hands. "Grew up poor as dirt. Trailer parks mostly. Sometimes we crashed with my mom's friends when the leases didn't line up right. When I got older, a couple teammates let me stay with them sometimes. Then my coach."

He delivered his monologue without shame or pretense. He'd just stated facts. Nothing more, nothing less. What a refreshing change.

A piping-hot basket of mozzarella sticks arrived, and she reached for one. "Sounds like you had quite the childhood."

"I did."

"And you're . . . so open about it."

One plaid-covered shoulder rose and fell. "It's part of my testimony."

Oh. Right. How silly of her to forget. He was a Church Person, and honesty was never just honesty with them. There was always an agenda. A means to an end. She should've seen it coming.

"I never had a dad," Matt went on. "At least, not one I had any kind of relationship with. And I won't lie—it was rough for a lot of years. But then I met Jesus, and—"

Siobhan held up a hand, the old tension clawing at her chest. "I'm gonna stop you right there."

He drew back, blinking. "I'm sorry?"

Siobhan pulled in a breath. It wasn't him. He didn't do it. No sense turning an innocent bystander into collateral damage.

"Look, I . . . respect faith," she said. "I know it helps a lot of people. But you might as well save your breath, because that sales pitch is wasted on me."

"I'm not trying to sell you anything, Siobhan."

There was that earnestness again. That honesty she ached to trust but didn't dare. Not when she'd been burned so badly.

"But I'm not going to apologize for it, either." The firmness in his voice drew her gaze, and there it was, matched in the set of his jaw and the sheen in his eyes. There was no anger there. She hadn't offended him. But he wasn't backing down. "Jesus is the most important person in my life. The one who made me do a one-eighty and start living a life that actually matters. Without him, no telling where I'd be."

Matt paused, fingers tented, those creases appearing on either side of his smile. "There's an old hymn with a line I like. 'I give thee back the life I owe.' That's all I'm trying to do."

"And in thine ocean depths its flow may richer fuller be." A melody swelled in her heart, one that transported her to a stage. The drums at her back, the vibrations in her feet. The click track in her ear, just loud enough for her to stay with the band. A microphone. An endless sea of faces. But the one she sought, the one whose approval she'd have done anything for—had done anything for—sat in the front, eyes gleaming with an expression she'd mistaken for holy ardor.

"You know that one." Matt's voice sliced through the memories.

"Yeah." She yanked the gate shut over them with a nearly audible clang. "I, uh . . . sang it in choir. High school." It was true, but she barely remembered that setting. This one, though . . .

He studied her with new light in his eyes. "I didn't know you sang."

"I don't. Not really. Not anymore." Change the subject. *Change. The subject.* She fixed him with an artificial smile, one she hoped wouldn't invite further inquiry, and asked the first question she could think of. "So tell me about this new job of yours. You said you're a worship pastor, right?"

That should do the trick. Church guys liked nothing more than to talk about work, and worship guys liked nothing more than to talk about guitar gear. She could let him talk. Tune him out while she got her bearings. Insert appropriate reactions at the appropriate times. Stuff her memories back down where they couldn't hurt her.

Sure enough, hazel eyes lit, and the crease around his mouth deepened as he reached for a mozzarella stick. "Yes, ma'am. First-time worship pastor, and it's at Pursuers Church."

Pursuers. The name slammed her in the solar plexus and nearly made her choke on her iced tea.

Wichita had close to half a million in the metro area and a church on practically every corner. Sometimes two, if it was a busy intersection. Why, then—why in the name of anything and everything, why, why, *why*—did the cute guy across the table from her, the one dunking a mozzarella stick into the marinara sauce, have to work *there*?

"It's been around awhile." He held a hand over his mouth as he chewed. "Although it's undergone a serious rebrand. Used to be an unaffiliated Christian church meeting at a middle school, but then Pastor Trace arrived and the place exploded."

Yes, yes, she knew the story. Heard it at least a dozen times. How struggling Timber Ridge Community Church met the force of nature that was Pastor Trace Jessup and transformed themselves into Pursuers Church— single-minded in pursuing the lost, the seeking, and the not quite sure.

The unchurched and de-churched became re-churched, re-sanctified, re-committed, re-all the things, thanks to the relentless pursuit of Pursuers.

Souls weren't all they pursued, though. Siobhan was living proof.

"Trace has been there a little over a decade now," Matt continued, his excitement clearly building. "And the place has really grown. Four services every Sunday, almost two thousand in attendance on an average week, and we're looking at land in hopes of a new church building in the next few years."

That part was new. Guess Pursuers had continued madly pursuing even after they'd showed her the door.

"And Trace . . ." Matt's eyes took on a shine. "Man, I can't say enough good about that guy. I owe him so much."

"Yeah?" It came out like a croak, but Matt didn't seem to notice.

"He's the one who introduced me to Jesus. Way back in high school, when I was speeding down the highway to nowhere and he was just a youth pastor with a man bun and skinny jeans." Matt chuckled. "And now look at us. Both working at one of the fastest-growing churches in Wichita. Never would've dreamed that up in a million years."

"Sounds like Trace has done well for himself," she managed.

Matt must've picked up on the tightness in her voice, because his gaze turned curious. "You know him?"

Oh yes. She knew him. Knew the sound of his voice. The feel of his hands. The lecherous look in his eyes. The sick truth behind the slick facade.

"I . . . know who he is." That statement was far truer than Siobhan would ever like to admit.

"I'd love for you to come check out a service," he said. "Y'know, once I get my legs under me."

Laughter escaped in a bitter bark as she reached for the last mozzarella stick. "No. Thank you, but . . . no. Church and I are just . . . we have a complicated relationship."

She expected an argument. A sales pitch. But instead what she got was a sympathetic glance. "I get it, Siobhan."

Pizza slid in front of them, steaming and fragrant, and she tore her gaze from his with another chuckle. "Somehow I doubt that."

"No pressure. Really. Just an open invitation. Whenever you're ready."

And that day would be exactly the twenty-first of Not On Your Life. But she wouldn't tell him that. Matt didn't deserve a heaping helping of her bitterness along with his pepperoni and sausage. He may be allied with Pursuers, but he wasn't one of them. Not yet.

He would be before long, though. Pastor Trace had a way of making everyone around him act just like him.

A shame. Because Matt Buchanan—sweet, unassuming, eager, and kind, if a bit naive—was exactly the kind of guy she'd have gone for before Trace Jessup ruined her.

No matter. Matt was headed down a different path.

One that would inevitably ruin him too.

Chapter Six

THE WORDS OF Trace's prayer to end the Monday morning staff meeting echoed around Matt's head as he left the conference room—finally free of crutches and in a walking boot—on his way back to his office.

His office. *His.*

He still couldn't believe it. Couldn't believe anything about this job, frankly. Barely two weeks in, he'd led his first worship service Sunday morning, and the feedback from his fellow pastors at the meeting just now was overwhelmingly positive. He was using his skills, making an impact, and leading others to Jesus.

Dream come true? Answered prayer?

Likely both.

He'd reached the hallway outside his office when a leather jacket–clad arm landed heavy around his shoulders.

"Hey. Got a minute?" Trace's brown eyes peered deep into his, lips curved in an earnest smile.

"Of course." Matt gestured into his office—not entirely devoid of boxes, but he was making progress—and Trace took a seat on the couch that had been delivered last Thursday.

"Y'know, God's done a lot for me since I started here at Pursuers." Trace laced his arms behind his head. "It'd take a year to list all the ways he's blessed my ministry. But I think bringing you here . . . that just might be the best thing yet."

Matt sank into his desk chair, blinking at the onslaught of praise from his mentor. "Well, thank you. Truly. That's a pretty good way to start a Monday."

"Almost as great as how I started mine." At Matt's questioning frown, Trace's eyes gleamed. "I listened to the playback of yesterday's worship set, of course. And like I said in the meeting, it was incredible."

"Thanks, man." Maybe Matt would have to listen to the playback himself, because his memory of his first Sunday leading worship was foggy at best. Just an ocean of darkened faces and raised hands. The lyrics on the screens at the back of the auditorium. The cottony feeling in his mouth. The click track in his in-ears, keeping him grounded. The cool steel of the guitar strings beneath his fingertips. And under all the discomfort, the terrifying exhilaration of a roller coaster in free fall, the feeling he'd always learned to associate with taking the leaps of faith God so frequently required of him.

"I'm serious." Trace leaned forward, his tone conspiratorial. "That was the most inspiring, Spirit-led service I've been a part of in years. The sermon I gave was one of my best, and I have you to thank for it. All those new decisions for Jesus yesterday? I have no doubt in my mind they were because your worship primed the pump for them to hear my message."

Matt's neck warmed. "That's good, because I felt like I needed a puke bucket the whole time."

Trace erupted in his trademark boisterous laugh. "Like I always said, Satan wouldn't bother you if he wasn't afraid of you." Rising, he patted Matt's shoulder. "It'll get better, my brother. I promise."

"Thanks." Matt's watch buzzed against his wrist, and he glanced at the small square screen to find a text from Siobhan.

Despite their rocky beginning and her intense prickliness any time he mentioned church, they'd been communicating regularly since their pizza non-date last week. Texts, mostly, along with a few memes. It always warmed his heart when a funny meme she'd sent filled his screen. There was a special magic in shared amusement, one he'd not felt quite to this degree before. A warmth too, knowing he was in her thoughts just as she occupied a chunk of space in his.

Making progress on your violin, she'd sent. *Want to stop by the shop later?*

"That's a smile I haven't seen before." Trace's voice was close, and Matt jumped. He'd forgotten his boss was still standing there. "If I didn't know better, I'd think it was a girl."

"Nah." Matt tapped the screen to close out the message. "Well okay, it is a girl, but it's not like that. My grandmother's violin was damaged in the accident, and Siobhan's repairing it."

Trace leaned against the doorframe. "Siobhan, huh? That's an unusual name."

"I think she said it was Irish."

"We used to have a Siobhan on the worship staff here. Years ago. She sang. Played violin."

"Really?" Surely that wasn't his Siobhan. Not that she was his, exactly, but just . . . no way. She repaired violins. She hadn't said anything about playing them. And she didn't sing.

Or . . . wait. She had mentioned being in choir in high school, though that didn't necessarily make her unique.

Her name did, though.

"She was part of why we changed the way we staff the worship ministry." Trace stood to his full height. "Used to be we'd hire musicians whether they were believers or not, and we used to get excited when they weren't. We could provide them with steady income and a steady dose of the gospel. Lots of souls saved with that approach, actually."

Matt ordered his spinning thoughts to slow so he could focus on Trace's words. "But you don't do that anymore?"

Trace shook his head. "Siobhan was . . . she was too far gone. There was no reaching her. And after that we decided to only hire people we were sure were true believers."

Too far gone? Matt bristled at the description. Surely Trace couldn't believe Siobhan was beyond the reach of God's grace.

But Trace knew her far better than Matt did. He knew the whole story. Matt didn't.

For all Matt knew, it wasn't even the same Siobhan.

That was a question he could easily get an answer to, though. "Trace, do you know—"

"Pastor?" The new administrative assistant—Kayleigh?—knocked on the door and leaned in, curled brown hair tumbling over her shoulders. "Sorry to interrupt. Your ten o'clock is here."

"Thanks, Kales." Trace smiled over his shoulder, then turned to Matt with a hearty clap on the shoulder. "Duty calls, my brother."

"Catch you later." Matt lifted a hand in farewell, but Trace had already rounded the corner and disappeared from view.

A girl named Siobhan. A singer. A violinist. Too far gone. Surely . . . surely that couldn't be his Siobhan, could it? He couldn't picture it. Not in the slightest.

And why did he keep thinking of her as *his*? They weren't dating. She wasn't interested, and he was determined to follow Trace's path of single-minded devotedness to Jesus and the mission of Pursuers.

And even if a romantic relationship was something he wanted or felt called to, he definitely wouldn't want to date someone who was so openly reluctant to talk about matters of faith. Jesus—his faith, the church, his walk—all of it was everything to Matt, and if that wasn't something he could share with Siobhan, there was a natural line beyond which the relationship couldn't cross.

But friendship? No matter what, friendship was something he could have. Something he welcomed.

Especially friendship with Siobhan.

Absolutely, he tapped out in reply to her text. *Can't wait.*

⋊⋉

The twang of a slightly flat open E string against a perfectly tuned open A filled the tiny practice room at the shop. Siobhan drew the bow across the strings with her right hand while turning the small ebony peg with her left. Almost there . . . no, too far . . . *there*. Perfect.

This was the last step on her latest project, a refurbished violin they were planning to sell. An advanced student model, it would be perfect for any of the plethora of serious high school violinists running around Wichita. She'd grown attached to the red-brown maple fiddle over the weeks she'd worked on it, and now it was ready to join its cohorts on their display wall and online inventory, awaiting a match with the perfect owner.

Just one step remained—playing it. Training the molecules, as Ian liked to say. It was true, though. An instrument that wasn't played regularly didn't sound nearly as good as one that was, and that would mean a quicker union with that perfect buyer. But Ian had only a functional knowledge of the violin—his expertise was in repair, not performance. This meant that all the molecule training was up to Siobhan.

She made sure, though, that Ian was the only person who ever heard her play.

Absently, she strummed the strings with her left hand, willing away memories. What should she play? Bach was always a good choice. Or maybe . . . ooh. The Mendelssohn concerto. Yes. The soulful E-minor tonality suited today's mood.

It had been a while since she'd played it, a fact her fingers drove home with a couple errant early shifts. But gradually it came back to her. Her heart soared along with the melody as Mendelssohn's music transported her to the one place she felt at peace. Alone. In here. No audience. No cameras. No microphones. No in-ears.

No Trace Jessup in the front row . . .

But since when did Mendelssohn's concerto include a woodblock part? Her bow stilled on the strings, and the orchestra in her head fell silent.

Oh. Wait. No. That was the door.

Someone was knocking at the door of the practice room.

Frowning, she lowered the violin and opened the door. How long had Ian stood there knocking? How deep in the music had she been?

"Sorry, Ian." The door creaked open. "I think this one'll be just great for—"

But it wasn't Ian.

It was Matt.

Matt. Standing there. In the hallway. Sandy brow creased, the door casting an angled shadow on his stubbled jaw.

"I . . . thought you couldn't play," he said.

She snapped her gaze away from his. Loosened the bow. "Never said I couldn't play. I just said I don't."

"It's a shame." His quiet voice tugged at her heart. "I mean, I'm no expert or anything . . . but to me you sounded beautiful."

The word caused a different voice to spring into her memory. *Siobhan.*

Sweetheart. That was beautiful. So beautiful I can't keep my eyes off you. Can't keep my hands off you . . . Your playing is dangerous, Siobhan. Absolutely dangerous.

Jaw tight, she set the violin in its case and slid the bow into the pocket. *Gentle. Don't vent your anger here. Not on an instrument, for Pete's sake.*

"I'm better at fixing than I am playing." Her voice sounded odd. Oh well. Let it. Maybe him misinterpreting her reluctance to perform as a simple lack of confidence was better for all involved. Would the tremble in her hands give her away? She stuffed them into the pockets of her quilted vest all the same.

Matt's lower lip had slid between his teeth. "Hey, weird question . . ."

Oh no.

"Trace says there was a woman named Siobhan who used to sing and play violin on the worship team at Pursuers. Years ago."

All the memories she tried to suppress when playing flooded over her. The sea of faces. The bright spotlights. The cameras. The microphones. Trace.

"He did?"

"Yup." The look in his eyes was penetrating, but somehow still kind. "And . . . I'm guessing there aren't too many other violin-playing Siobhans running around Wichita, Kansas. Although it's entirely possible I'm wrong."

Her shoulders slumped. "You're not." But oh, how she wanted him to be.

"Seems like something you maybe would've mentioned." He sounded hurt.

She latched the violin case and zipped it shut. "Look, Matt. My time at Pursuers, it's not a part of my life I like to talk about. Or even think about. That chapter is closed."

"But I can't understand why you wouldn't even mention it to me. Especially since I just started working there."

"Exactly. You just started. You're excited. It's a new job, new city, fresh start—it's a huge deal for you. I don't want to do or say anything to put a damper on that, and if I were to share my experience there, then it would."

Matt blinked at the onslaught, questions dancing in his eyes. She had to shut him down. Shut the questions down. Shut everything down. It was bad enough she was friends with yet another pastor from Pursuers. She couldn't let that part of her life taint this fun new part.

"Besides," she added, her voice quiet. "I like being friends with you. And I don't want my past at Pursuers to come between us. So please don't ask me to talk about it. Not yet. Not now."

He nodded. "All right. If you don't want to talk about it, we won't talk about it." He paused and shifted his weight. "But if and when you ever do, please know that I'm here and I'm ready to listen."

Her throat thickened. "Thank you."

"Of course." There was a frisson of something between them, hovering in the small space of the practice room.

But frissons weren't allowed. Not anymore.

And especially not with pastors at Pursuers.

Apparently Matt had the same realization she did, because he took a step back. "You said you found something out about my grandma's violin?"

She resisted the urge to sigh with relief. "Yes. Follow me."

He stood aside so she could leave the small practice room, and she escorted him down the hall toward the storefront.

"Is that it?"

His openmouthed stare at the disassembled violin on her workbench brought a grin to her lips. "Yup. Bit of a mess right now, but I've got it under control."

"Oh, I trust you." He met her gaze with an uncertain smile. "At least, I think I do."

"That's fair. Anyway, here's why I asked where the violin came from." Siobhan held up the back piece of the violin, angling its unvarnished curved inside so Matt could get a better look. "That's the new crack from the accident. But see this other one that's been repaired?"

Matt leaned in close. Close enough for her to feel his warmth. To catch a whiff of outdoors and cologne and the wintergreen gum he was chewing. She jerked away. No. No frissons. No attraction.

"Pretty hard to miss," he said with a resonant chuckle.

Siobhan took the smooth piece of wood and slipped back into the security blanket of professionalism. "That crack, and the glue they used to repair it, tells us two things. One, that something significant happened to this instrument, and two, it's a lot older than we thought."

Matt leaned closer. "How old?"

"Eighteen hundreds probably."

"Wow, that's incredible. I had no idea." The light in Matt's eyes was so warm and inviting it might as well have been an embrace. "That old violin must have quite the story."

"Every instrument does." She ran a fingertip over the rough, chipped edges of Matt's violin. "Every dent, every ding carries a story with it."

"Kinda like people." Matt's voice was soft, his expression kind. No judgment there. Just curiosity.

"Yeah. Guess so." She put the violin back and avoided those sweet hazel eyes. He wanted to know her story. That was plain as day.

And part of her ached to share it with him.

But sharing it—especially with him—would ruin everything.

Chapter Seven

May 1876

Deborah entered the cool shade of the cabin and exhaled her relief. Barely even lunchtime, yet the sun was already blazing, making the time she'd spent in her garden uncomfortable. The harvest would be worth it, though. She could almost taste the string beans, onions, and peppers as she untied her bonnet strings and pushed back the fabric, relishing the fresh air against her damp forehead.

As she stepped forward into the kitchen, her foot encountered something soft. Warm. Blinking to adjust to the dimness of indoors, she looked down, and . . . oh. A little girl. In the kitchen.

A little girl in her kitchen.

"Beg pardon," she said, but the tot gave no indication she'd even heard Deborah. She looked to be about three or four, her hair a riot of strawberry-blond curls and her play centered around a little doll wearing a calico dress. The child looked familiar, but Deborah couldn't place her.

"Oh. There's Deborah now." Papa's voice from in front of the fireplace. But he wasn't alone. A tall, thin man sat in the rocker opposite him, his hat in his hands. Ah yes. Levi Martinson from church. This must be his little girl whom she'd just stumbled over.

Deborah's heart twinged. Mrs. Martinson—rest her soul—had always been a sickly sort, but this past winter she'd finally succumbed. Though Charity's death wasn't a surprise, it had still dealt a blow to the small pioneer community, leaving Mr. Martinson a sudden widower and little Nora motherless.

Quickly, Deborah replaced her bonnet. "Papa. Mr. Martinson. How do you do?"

"Miss Caldwell," the man said quietly.

"Once again allow me to express my sorrow over the loss of your wife."

Mr. Martinson gave a gallant nod. "Thank you." With his light-brown hair, longish nose, and prominent cheekbones, the man had an intellectual look about him, the sort who seemed like he'd be more at home in front of a classroom or behind a pulpit than coaxing a living from the unforgiving prairie. And though he'd always been on the thin side, he was even spindlier of limb than she remembered. Likely he hadn't been eating much since Charity's passing. Papa had gone through a phase like that.

The rocker creaked as Papa shifted his weight. "That's . . . precisely what Mr. Martinson is here to discuss."

Seeking counseling, no doubt, from someone who could provide advice from the perspective of both a learned preacher and a man who'd walked the same road long ago.

"Of course. Carry on. Please forgive my intrusion." She turned back toward the kitchen.

"You needn't leave," Papa said. "In fact, your presence here is most welcome."

Deborah blinked. "Oh?"

Papa pursed his lips, his telltale gesture when chewing on a thought before putting it into words. "Since his wife died, it's been . . . difficult for Mr. Martinson, to say the least. Even when Charity was ill, she could still care for Nora adequately. But since her untimely passing, Mr. Martinson— Levi—finds being both father and mother simply too great a load to bear."

Is that how you felt when it happened to you? The question burned in Deborah's chest, but asking it—especially now—would prove futile. Her father never discussed the horrendous incident that took the lives of his wife and three of his children. He referenced it only during the regular visits to Dr. Maxwell necessary for both Deborah's and Elisabeth's continued care, and then only from a purely medical perspective. How to care for their scalp wounds was at the forefront, but on how to care for their soul wounds, Papa, the shepherd of their small flock, was curiously silent. The only person she'd been able to talk with, the only person who'd ever even discuss it, was Elisabeth.

"To put it quite simply, Deborah, Levi needs a wife. A mother for

Nora." Papa looked at her expectantly, almost eagerly, while Levi Martinson didn't look at her at all. His gaze was somewhere between his worn Stetson and the wood-planked floor.

Wait. Did he . . . did they . . . was this . . .

"Me?" The word came out a combination of a whisper and a squeak.

"I can only imagine how difficult it is watching Elisabeth prepare for her wedding." Papa's brown eyes were kind through his spectacles. "I overheard you tell her how afraid you were that it would never happen for you."

She shook her head. "I was merely in a childish mood, Papa. The Lord has a plan. I know that." Though how a massacre and a mangled scalp fit into that, she had yet to figure out.

"He does indeed. And sometimes that plan takes turns we can't imagine." Papa's earnest expression turned to a full-on smile that crinkled the skin of his cheeks and carved deep wrinkles beside his eyes. The smile fixed first on her, then on Levi Martinson. "Levi has come to ask me for your hand in marriage."

"He has? You have?" Levi still wouldn't meet her gaze, but a small nod confirmed his intention.

"He's observed what a hard worker you are, what a strong and determined young lady you've become, and he desires these traits for both his home and his daughter."

A home. A daughter. A husband. A marriage.

But not the sort of marriage she'd envisioned. The sort she ached for. Starry eyed and dizzy in love, like Elisabeth, with perpetually pink cheeks and an ever-present smile and Isaiah looking at her like he couldn't fathom looking anywhere else. Like nothing at all in the world existed besides Elisabeth.

Levi was looking at her now, she'd grant him that, but it was the same expression with which she perused bolts of fabric at the general store in Jamesville. Sturdy. Practical. Economical. *Yes, this one will do.*

But what alternative did she have? With Elisabeth gone, it would be Deborah and her father whiling away their days in separate worlds. His world was the church, the parishioners, his fervent mission to spread the gospel wherever and whenever he could. Hers would be the home, a small prairie cabin that would soon be, for all intents and purposes, a home for one. The only time she ever felt close to Papa was when he played the violin by the fire at night, but even those evenings were becoming more and more rare.

"What about you, Papa?" She fixed her gaze on her father. "Who'll care for you if Elisabeth and I both wed?"

Papa's cheeks flushed an uncharacteristic shade of crimson. "Ah. Well. As for that . . . the widow Johnston and I, ah . . ."

"Abigail Johnston?"

"Yes." Papa's eyes took on a sheen. "We've had to keep things quiet for propriety's sake, and my calls on her have always been in the presence of others, but . . . well, you see, my dear daughter, neither of us meant for anything to happen, but the Lord's ways are not ours, and he has blessed the both of us with a late-in-life love."

Deborah drew back. "You're marrying too, then?"

"Yes. As quickly as propriety will allow."

The room rotated. Papa had been calling on the kindly, soft-spoken widow ever since her husband's passing a year prior, but Deborah never had an inkling that there was more than simply a pastor-and-parishioner relationship. And she was happy for Papa. He'd been so lonely for so long. He deserved every ounce of happiness God cared to bestow on him. They both did. Elisabeth too.

Elisabeth was getting married.

Papa—*Papa*—was soon to wed as well.

And suddenly it all made sense why Levi Martinson was sitting in their cabin. Why Papa had so eagerly acquiesced to the young widower's request.

He didn't want Deborah to be left alone, that was certain.

But neither did he want his scarred spinster daughter to be part of his new life. She was the final reminder of the tragedy. The last item to stash neatly away so he could move forward and never have to think about the attack again.

What little choice Deborah had in the matter suddenly vanished like morning mist.

"Well, Deborah? What do you think?" Papa still looked eager, and Levi still stared at the floor between his boots as though he wished the earth would open up and swallow him whole. Far from the proposal she'd always imagined, where the young man looked at her like every hope he had in the world hung on her answer.

She couldn't blame Levi. The bluish half-moons beneath his eyes, the gaunt cheeks beneath a thin beard . . . oh, bless the poor man, he looked utterly exhausted. He likely didn't have the inner resources to feel much of anything about the arrangement he proposed. If she rejected his offer, she suspected he'd simply give her a nod, replace his hat, gather up his daughter, and find a way to keep trudging onward.

Alone.

The same way she would.

Because really, with Papa and Elisabeth both moving on with their lives, what would be left for her here?

Levi's proposal wasn't the one she'd envisioned. Far from it.

But it was a proposal.

A route to the life she'd always dreamed of. A wedding. A marriage. A family.

Nora toddled in from the kitchen, clutching her doll in one hand, and Levi lifted her onto his lap, his lips brushing her disheveled curls and his eyes flickering with a glimmer of life. He faced the little girl outward, and she popped her thumb into her mouth and peered at Deborah, her large deep-blue eyes wide with something that looked suspiciously like hope.

Hope. Here, at last, was hope. For Nora. For Levi.

And for herself.

"Yes," she heard herself say. "I believe I find this arrangement suitable."

"Wonderful." Papa clapped his hands together, a broad smile spreading across his face. "Yes, this is truly, truly wonderful. God be praised."

"God be praised," Levi echoed, a deep relief underpinning the words. His lips curved in a faint smile, but his eyes—also blue, though a paler, cloudier shade than his daughter's—radiated the same hope as the little girl's.

She returned his hopeful gaze with a smile of her own, and a deep sense of satisfaction warmed her heart. She and Papa had been in these dusty, faded shoes once. No mother. No wife. No clue how to move forward.

But now, rather than the one needing the solution, she was the solution. She'd provide this little girl with a mother. This desperate man with a wife.

She, Deborah Caldwell, scarred and broken though she was, was an answer to the same sort of prayers Papa had no doubt prayed a decade ago.

This wasn't the wedding she'd dreamed of. It wasn't exactly the life she'd imagined.

But it was a life that teemed with potential. An honor—a daunting one, but an honor to be sure.

She would take this life, then, with both hands, and do the absolute best she could with it.

CHAPTER EIGHT

LAZY SNOWFLAKES DRIFTED down outside the fogged windows of the coffee shop, glimmering in pools of light from the streetlamps. Siobhan let out a contented sigh and lifted the blue stoneware mug of chai to her lips. Matt was right about the ambiance—busy enough to make the place feel alive, but not crowded or crushing or noisy. He'd told her about this place last week, one of the few coffee shops in Wichita she'd yet to try, and he was delighted to have been able to play tour guide for once.

He sat across from her, a steaming mug of hot cocoa in one hand, and let out a chuckle. "You've gotta be kidding me."

"What?" She followed his gaze out the window, where a car crept by well below the speed limit, its driver gripping the wheel with both hands and staring out the windshield with a look of grim determination.

"People here are really this scared of a little snow?"

She grinned. "Yep. It's ridiculous. Anytime there's a little winter in the forecast, the local media spends a week scaring everyone half to death, and all the stores run out of bread, milk, and toilet paper. Schools close, and everything gets canceled if we get more than a couple inches."

Matt's jaw slacked. "Two inches? That barely even gets noticed in Chicago. It takes a foot or more before anyone even seems to notice."

Mingling with the amusement in his eyes was a hint of wistfulness, though. She rested her chin in her hand. "Do you miss it?"

He took a slow sip of cocoa before replying. "Sometimes. Some things. It was the place I lived the longest, so I guess it was the closest thing to home I've ever had. But I've got a pretty good feeling about here too."

"Oh?"

A corner of his mouth quirked, and the creases around his eyes deepened. "I love my job, of course. But now that I've found decent pizza, a couple great coffee shops, and some fantastic new friends . . . yeah. It's starting to feel like home."

Oh crap. Attraction stole across the table, swift and sure. She tried to fling up her shield against it, but in her haste it wasn't perfectly placed, and tendrils sneaked past, wrapping around her heart and causing at least part of it to feel warm.

Warmth.

For the first time in years.

No. She couldn't. She *couldn't*.

She tore her attention from his boy-next-door smile and fixed it instead on the foamy swirls in her chai. Maybe this would give her a minute to straighten her shield and ward off any further attacks. "Glad to hear it."

"What about you?"

Her shoulders tensed. "What about me?"

Matt's index finger made a slow, lazy circle in the center of the tabletop. "Okay, maybe it's an occupational hazard of being a pastor, or maybe it's because I've experienced enough loneliness to know what it looks like. And if this is too intrusive a question, tell me and I'll back off. But does this place feel like home for you?"

"I've been here most of my life. Other than college and luthier school, I've never lived anywhere but here."

"That's not what I asked."

It wasn't, and she knew it. And she still must not have her shield in the right place, because Matt's question hopped over the edge of it and unlocked the vault in which she kept her memories. They spilled out, one tumbling over the other. Cookouts with the worship team. Late-night prayer sessions with her women's Bible study group. Board-game marathons and Super Bowl parties and taco bars and all the other things churchy people did in the name of Doing Life Together.

All of it—all of it—was gone. Torn away in a single instant. The people she'd done life with hadn't given her the time of day for over three years.

They'd unfriended her. Deleted her. Erased her. It was as though she'd merely been a design scratched in beach sand, washed away the second the tide came in.

At the time, she'd thought the loss of the man she thought she loved would be the most painful part. But it wasn't losing Trace. It was the deafening silence from the people she'd considered her friends. Her family. Her brothers and sisters. The people who were supposed to be there for her. The place that was supposed to be her home.

Apparently the much-touted unrelenting grace of Pursuers Church had its breaking point.

Matt was still waiting for an answer, and she applied a smile and picked up her mug. "It used to. Now I've just . . . found it best to keep my social circle small."

"Well." His voice was just a shade above a whisper. "I'm really glad you could make room for me."

The kindness in his eyes was like cold water after a long run. Try as she might, she couldn't tear herself away from it. She didn't want to need it, but she needed it anyway, and there it was, and she couldn't stop herself from drinking it in.

"Yeah," she managed. "Me too."

The strum of a guitar behind her jolted her out of the moment, and she turned. On the small stage at the back of the shop sat a woman with long dark hair, tied back with a flowered scarf that draped softly over her shoulders. A flowing top, distressed jeans, and ankle boots completed her look.

"Evenin', y'all." The woman's voice held a trace of Oklahoma twang. "I'm just here to worship Jesus. You're welcome to join me if you like, or feel free to keep doin' what you're doin'."

Siobhan's heart clutched as the woman's eyes closed and her fingers found the frets of the polished guitar. D. A. E. F-sharp minor. The same chord progression upon which countless worship choruses had been built. Siobhan had improvised melodies over those changes more times than she could fathom. Involuntarily, her fingers tightened around an imaginary bow. Curled around the neck of a nonexistent violin.

"Hey, that's a cool voicing." Across the table from her, Matt's eyes fastened on the singer. Not her anatomy, though. Not even her face. No, he studied her left hand, curved gracefully around the neck of the guitar. "I wonder how she's . . ." He squinted and raised his own left hand, arranging his fingers into the right shape. "Oh, yeah, okay. I see it now. That's a good idea. I'll have to try that one."

Siobhan tuned out Matt's half-whispered monologue and returned her attention to the singer. That was her, once upon a time. On the stage. In her element. Sometimes singing praise with her voice, sometimes with her violin. Eyes closed. Spirit soaring toward the heavens. Communing with God in a way she never had before or since.

And completely clueless that everything that seemed so real, everything she'd built, was a mere facade about to crumble to dust.

><

Matt shifted in the wooden chair and reached for his mug of cocoa. The singer wasn't bad, but she wasn't anything to write home about, either. Nothing to distinguish her from any of the other Taya-from-Hillsong wannabes. There was a woman like her at nearly every church. Decent guitar player, good enough singer, heart in the right place, and pitch in the right place most of the time.

Had Siobhan been this girl too? He couldn't picture it. With her plaid shirts, rugged boots, and quilted vests, she didn't look the part. Her eyes were closed, but her jaw was tight. Her expression drawn. She didn't look like someone lost in worship but someone lost in something she'd rather forget.

"Siobhan?" The unusual name harmonized with the gentle strum of the guitar, a musical phrase in and of itself.

She didn't respond.

"Siobhan?"

Her eyes opened, the purest pale blue he'd ever seen, but fixed on some distant point somewhere far above his head.

He leaned closer. "Are you all right?"

"You asked if this place felt like home." Wherever her attention was, that's where her voice was as well, husky and distant.

"I did."

"It used to. I had lots of friends. Family, even." She reached for her straw wrapper, twisting it into a tight spiral. "I was once the It Girl at Pursuers. I was part of two women's Bible studies. I was tight with the worship team. The staff. Lots of them are still there. They're the people you see at work every day. They used to be the people *I* saw at work every day. They were the people I'd laugh with, the people I'd pray with, the people I did life with, the people I would get together with late at night and see just how many songs fit this same stupid four-chord progression. I had a home. It was Pursuers Church. And then . . ."

Her attention dropped to the twisted straw wrapper.

"Then what?" The story she wasn't telling him hovered between them, fog-like. If he could just peer through the murk, if he could just see what she wasn't saying, then maybe it would make sense. Maybe she would make sense.

"Then they fired me. Kicked me out." The words fell through the fog, flat and heavy. "And I lost everything. Not a single one of them reached out to me. It was like I'd never existed at all."

His gut twisted. Lots of those people were still at Pursuers. Siobhan said so herself. Which ones had hurt her like this? They all seemed friendly and all in for Jesus and everything they should be. But the pain etched across the face of the woman he shared a table with was undeniable.

She'd been fired, though. And in all the times Matt had known Trace Jessup, he'd never known the pastor to fire anyone.

She was too far gone, he'd said. *There was no reaching her.*

So what had she done to receive such a brutal exit to a place that prided itself on welcoming everyone?

"I know why they reacted that way," she continued. "And they honestly believe they did the right thing."

Perhaps they had. Doubtless in their minds they'd felt it was the only viable option. If Matt knew Trace at all, that decision would've been one of the most difficult—the most painful—his pastor had ever had to make.

But whatever had forced Trace's hand, whatever had led to this drastic decision, there was no denying the pain it had brought. The deep wounds to the heart of the woman across the table from him. The hurt in her pale-blue gaze.

He sought that gaze. Inched his hand closer to hers. "But if it hurt you this badly, then maybe it wasn't the right thing."

The look in Siobhan's eyes was like a kick to his solar plexus. For the first time since he'd met her, her guard was down. Her whole face radiated a vulnerability that made him want to wrap her in his arms and hold her until her pain dissolved and all the bad memories faded away.

Pain and memories inflicted by people he knew. People he worked with. People he worshiped with. People he'd only known a short time but already considered family.

Siobhan had considered them family too. Pursuers had been her home.

What had happened? What had caused such a drastic rift between people he cared about?

"Yeah," she said finally. "I think . . . yeah, I think maybe I needed to hear that. Thank you." Her small hand found his, her delicate fingers interlaced with his rough, calloused ones, and he gave them a gentle squeeze.

"Sure."

Siobhan withdrew her hand, and with it went some of the vulnerability. He could almost see her guard inching back up as she fixed her attention on her latte. "I can practically see the question marks hovering over your head, Matt."

"What? I'm not—"

"Yes, you are. You're wondering what all went down. Why I was fired."

"Siobhan." He leaned down, hoping for another glimpse into those pain-filled eyes. "I—okay. Yes. I'm curious. About a lot of things. But I don't want to rush you or push you or force you to do or say anything you're not ready for."

"I'm *not* ready. Not really. But I—you need to know some of it. Now." She pulled in a breath and plunged ahead, her words tumbling out over the rapid picking pattern of the guitar onstage. "You need to know that this whole thing was about a guy. A relationship that I shouldn't have had with a guy I never, ever should've fallen for. We got caught, he spread a bunch of lies about me, and everyone believed him. That's why I lost my job. That's why all my friends disappeared. That's why"—her voice thick, she stood and gestured toward the guitarist—"that's why I can't even listen to these four stupid chord changes without wanting to throw something."

"Hey." He stood too. What should he do in this situation? Hug her? Leave her alone? Try to hold her hand again? In the end, he settled for shoving his hand into the pocket of his jeans. "I'm sorry, Siobhan. Truly, deeply sorry that they hurt you. I just . . . man, I wish there were words, but there aren't. There's nothing. Just . . . I'm sorry."

Siobhan wrapped her arms around her midsection and nodded, her gaze fixed on the floor. "And I'm sorry too."

Matt frowned. "You have nothing to apologi—"

"Yes. I do. Because what I'm about to tell you . . . might cost me my friendship with you too. I don't know."

The urge to touch her was nearly overwhelming. "I can't think of a single thing in the world that you could say to me that would make me not want to be your friend."

"Oh ho ho. That's what you think."

"Siobhan—"

"It was Trace."

Matt recoiled as if he'd been slapped. "What?"

"The relationship I never should've had. The guy I never should've fallen for. It was your friend. Your boss. Your mentor. Your stand-in dad. Matt, it was Trace."

Then she drained the last of her latte, chucked the mug into the plastic bin on top of the trash can, shoved open the door, and disappeared into the snowy night.

CHAPTER NINE

May 1876

"Mercy!" Annabelle Brennan turned toward Deborah, jaw slack, a late-spring breeze buffeting her bonnet. "Don't leave me in suspense, Deborah. What did you say?"

Deborah took a deep breath. "I said . . . yes." She was engaged. She was marrying Levi Martinson. Even though she'd had two days to process her life's dramatic new direction, the reality still hadn't quite sunk in.

Annabelle let out a quiet squeak. "Oh, my dearest, that's the most wonderful news I've heard all week." Mindful of the sleeping baby Thomas in her arms, she embraced Deborah, knocking her bonnet askew in the process. "Deborah! You're going to be a bride. A wife. Just as you've always wanted."

"Yes." Deborah adjusted her bonnet with one hand and rubbed her friend's back with the other. Oh, that she could fully share Annabelle's enthusiasm.

Annabelle pulled back, brow knit. "Then why am I the only one of the two of us who seems excited?"

Deborah paused, her hands knotted on her calico-covered lap, the Sunday afternoon silence broken only by the twitter of birds and the quiet burble of the creek. "Because it's not how I wanted it. Which sounds so very selfish, I know. And I should be grateful to be marrying at all, given my situation."

A gust of wind caught the corner of Annabelle's worn quilt, the quilt that had made the journey with her from Indiana, flapping over the corner of her friend's ever-present leather-bound diary.

Questions danced in Annabelle's dark-blue eyes. "But . . ."

"But is it so selfish to want to be loved? To be adored?" Frustration burst forth in a ripple of questions to rival the speed of the creek. "The way Elisabeth is? The way you are?" Deborah's gaze fell first on baby Thomas, then found Annabelle's husband, Jack, fishing downstream with the couple's adopted son, Oliver. As though to illustrate her point, Jack glanced over his shoulder, and his gaze landed on Annabelle, resulting in a grin and a familiar wave.

Longing crashed over Deborah, and she tore her eyes from the tender, intimate moment. "Oh, I don't expect you to understand."

Annabelle's hand, warm and soft, found Deborah's forearm. "And yet I do."

Deborah frowned. "You do?"

"When Jack asked for my hand, I thought—assumed, really—that he merely wanted a mother for Oliver. Indeed, I very nearly torched my chance with him when I delivered this ridiculous speech about how I'd rather be a spinster schoolteacher than marry someone who saw me only as the solution to a problem." A gust of wind blew a strand of dark-blond hair across Annabelle's face, and she brushed it away, her lips curved in a self-deprecating grin. "Mercy, how childish I was. How gracious was God to spare me from the life I'd have lived if Jack had walked away just then. Because he certainly could have. Had I been in his shoes, I doubtless would have."

"But from what you've told me, Jack kissed you the day he met you. And you felt the same for him practically as soon."

Annabelle carefully lowered her sleeping son to the quilt. "Oh, I thought I knew what love was back then. I thought it was head spinning and heart thumping and being so consumed with ardor that I couldn't even think."

Deborah chuckled. "That sounds very much like Isaiah and Elisabeth."

"And that's genuine, to be sure." Annabelle eased her hand from beneath Thomas's downy head. "But their love is still shiny and new. It doesn't bear the scuffs and scratches that a more mature love does. The dizziness, the addlepatedness . . . that changes as life happens. As God uses the two of you to mature each other, to spur each other on to good deeds." She gazed first at Jack, then trailed a fingertip over the rosy cheek of baby Thomas.

"I'm a different woman now than I was then, Deborah. And as much fun as the stars and the head spinning were, the life Jack and I have built together is even better. He's seen me at my best and at my worst. He held me up when grief for Emmaline seemed too great to bear, and I've done the same for him. We've raised Oliver together. We've made this precious little one. And each day, each moment, each new thing we get through together, whether good or bad, is another brick in the foundation of our lives. There's nothing magic about that. It's God's faithfulness and your own conscious choices. And that's the kind of life you can have with Levi."

Doubtless her friend was right. She and Levi, through the seriousness of the commitment they were about to make, would build a life together. It was only natural.

But would a marriage built purely on practicality ever blossom into any type of affection? Friendship? Dare she imagine . . . love?

"I also suspect that, in time, you and Levi will grow to love each other." Annabelle's expression was frank but compassionate. "But it will take time. Bear in mind that Jack's first wife had been gone for over a year before he met me. Time and God had begun to heal his heart in a way that Levi's heart hasn't had a chance to yet. His grief is still fresh."

Deborah nodded. Despite all the losses she'd endured, the death of a spouse was a pain she couldn't quite fathom.

Annabelle trailed a hand over her son's head. "Love might look a bit different for you and Levi than it did for Jack and me, but it'll be every bit as genuine. That, I'm certain of."

Footsteps crunched through the underbrush, one rhythm short and bouncy, the other slower and measured. Then Jack appeared, Oliver at his side, with a string of good-sized fish.

Annabelle tilted her face to her husband, the sun-dappled shade of the cottonwood falling across her delicate features. "Looks as though the two of you had a productive outing."

"We did, Mama. Look!" Oliver held up his line of fish.

Annabelle wrapped an arm around him, careful to avoid the slimy catch. "Mama is very proud."

"Papa is too" came Jack's Irish-tinged baritone, and he bent to kiss the top of Annabelle's head.

"Looks as though fish will be on the menu for supper, then." Annabelle started to rise, but Jack stopped her with a gentle hand on her shoulder.

"Take your time," he said with a grin. "Oliver and I found some wild strawberries and ate a fair bit more than our share."

As if to corroborate his father's story, Oliver let out a belch, impressive for one so small, then giggled. At a glance from his mother, he covered his mouth and mumbled an apology, but the mischievous gleam lingering in his eyes brought a smile to Deborah's lips.

"Besides"—Jack's gray eyes darted from Annabelle to Deborah and back again—"the two of you appear deep in important conversation."

"That we are." Annabelle's voice took on a flirtatious note. "And part of that conversation might even involve you."

Jack's dark brows disappeared beneath the shadow of his hat. "'Tis a good thing I'm headed back to the house, then." Giving an exaggerated shudder, he reached for Oliver's small hand and made his way back toward the Brennans' cabin, muttering under his breath about the intractable nature of womankind.

Annabelle gave a quiet laugh, then fixed her gaze on Deborah. "That man can be stubborn and pigheaded and drive me crazy a good bit of the time, make no mistake. But we made a commitment to the Lord to make our marriage work, and he's blessed our efforts with a deep and abiding love. The kind of love I'll pray finds you and Levi."

Deborah's throat thickened. What had she done to deserve such a wonderful friend?

"Thank you." Her gaze drifted to Oliver, bouncing along beside Jack, who'd slowed his pace to match his son's. "And . . . what of becoming a mother in the same instant one becomes a wife? The Lord didn't grant me the opportunity to watch Josiah and Mary Catherine and Nancy grow up. To help in their raising." Tears stung at the fuzzy memories of her younger siblings. "So I'm afraid I haven't the slightest idea how to care for Nora. How to be a mother to her."

"You forget I was the youngest in my family, Deborah." Annabelle smiled. "I had the same experience—or lack thereof—that you did. And both of us also share mothers who passed from this life too soon, and fathers who were consumed with grief. When I married Jack, one of my most persistent prayers was that the Lord would help me be a good mother to Oliver—and to Thomas—when I barely remembered the example of my own."

"And what was his answer?" Deborah thought of young Nora, all reddish-blond curls and chubby cheeks and impressionable innocence. How could God possibly trust Deborah—with all her tragedy and damage and scars—to train up this child in the way she should go?

"What Oliver needed most—and what Nora needs most—is love. Encouragement. A smiling face at the beginning of a day and a hug and kiss at the end of it. Gentle correction. Patient instruction. And trust me, Deborah—there will be days when patience and gentleness are nowhere to be found. But if there's a foundation of love, then those days will fade into the barest of memories."

Annabelle's hand found Deborah's and wrapped around her fingers. "Simply take one day at a time. Jack helped me a good deal at the beginning, reminding me of Oliver's likes and dislikes, teaching me the rituals and routines they'd developed. And from what I know of Levi, he won't hesitate to do the same for you. Don't be afraid to ask him for help. And don't be afraid to ask the Lord for help, either. I know I won't be. I'll be on my knees in prayer for you daily, my friend."

Her friend's wisdom caused the relentless beating of anxious wings in Deborah's belly to simmer down. Though she'd accepted Levi's proposal with a sense of determination, now there was a deep sense of hope. And yes, a hint of excitement too.

"Mercy, I certainly had a lot of advice to give." Annabelle's cheeks pinked. "I can only hope some small amount of it will be of use."

Deborah squeezed Annabelle's hand. "It helps more than you can possibly know. Thank you."

A stiff gust knocked her bonnet askew again, and she let go of Annabelle's hand to reach up and adjust it. At the touch of the fabric against her scalp, another worry surfaced. "If I could ask you one more question, Annabelle?"

"Of course."

"What if Levi thinks my scar is repulsive?" Deborah turned toward her friend. "What if he thinks *I'm* repulsive? What if seeing me sickens him?"

"Oh, my dear." Annabelle grasped Deborah's face in both her hands and looked her in the eyes. "Listen to me, Deborah. What should—what will—sicken Levi is what happened to you. Not the result."

"Thank you." Deborah pulled her friend into an embrace. Though Deborah's feelings toward the Almighty had been rather sour for the last decade, she had to grant that he had given her an enormous blessing indeed with a friend like Annabelle.

A friend Deborah felt she'd need to lean on more than ever in the weeks, months, and years ahead.

CHAPTER TEN

THE SYNCOPATED KNOCK on the doorframe of Matt's office brought a smile to his lips. There was only one person that knock could belong to, and sure enough, there stood Trace, backlit by the fluorescent light of the bustling church office hallway behind him.

"Hey, brother." Trace greeted him with a smile. "Your worship sets for next month look great. No issues. That new song looks especially good."

"Isn't it great?" Matt reached into the basket of snacks he kept beneath his desk and retrieved two bags of pretzels. After offering one silently to his mentor and receiving a nod of acceptance, he tossed the bag, which landed neatly in Trace's hand. "Those lyrics, man."

"Oh, no joke. They gave me goose bumps." Trace's words were punctuated by the pop of the pretzel bag as he tore it open. "I can't wait to see what God'll do with it."

"Yeah. Definitely." Matt's chair creaked beneath him as he leaned back, opened his own bag of pretzels, and studied Trace. Since his conversation with Siobhan the other night, he couldn't reconcile the two versions of Trace Jessup. The one he knew was aboveboard. The one Siobhan described was anything but.

He'd known Trace half his life. He barely knew Siobhan. And right now he wasn't sure what to think.

"You seem deep in thought, my man." Trace's voice broke the silence, and he popped another pretzel into his mouth.

Matt's stomach churned. "You might say that."

"You know you can ask me anything. Tell me anything. I've known you since your Mario Kart days."

Matt bought himself some time with another pretzel. *Lord, should I ask him? And should I ask him now?*

Not sensing a no, he took a deep breath and raised his eyes to meet Trace's. "I do have a question for you, if you've got a minute."

"Anything for my boy Matty B." Trace leaned over and shut Matt's office door, then settled back on the couch. "What's on your mind?"

Matt swallowed against the discomfort in his throat. "My friend Siobhan, she is the one who worked here. I asked her about it."

"Not surprised." Trace's mouth flexed in a ghosted smile. "Not too many women with that name running around Wichita."

The chair squeaked as Matt shifted his weight, choosing his words carefully. "She said the two of you . . . dated? Am I understanding that correctly? I mean, please know I'm not judging. Not at all. I'm just surprised. You've always held singleness in such high regard. Always said that was God's plan for you."

"It is." Trace squared his shoulders. "And the Lord used Siobhan to remind me of that."

So it was true. Siobhan and Trace. Together. They'd dated.

It was enough to make Matt's head spin.

"How so?"

Trace sighed. "I'm not proud of it, Matt. In fact, it's the period of my life I'm most ashamed of. My most grievous stumble in my walk with the Lord." A muscle in his jaw flexed. "God promises to not let us be tempted beyond what we can bear, and he provided several escape routes, but I chose not to take them. Siobhan and I had a relationship that was brief but sexual in nature."

Brief. Sexual. *Trace.* Trace Jessup. The man who preached purity from the moment Matt met him. The man who refused to be seen in public with a woman unless a third party was present. The man who, if meeting one-on-one with a woman for any reason, left the door to his office open. The man who constantly preached about the importance of being on guard against all forms of temptation.

He'd had a sexual relationship.

With *Siobhan.*

"And Siobhan knew where I stood. She knew how committed to singleness—to purity—I was. *Am*." Trace stood, twin spots of color standing out on stubbled cheeks. "But I'm telling you, that woman was relentless. Completely, utterly relentless. Those outfits, the way she'd always touch my arm when she was talking to me, that *hair*. She knew full well what kind of power a woman has over a man, and she wielded that power like a weapon. I couldn't resist her. No man could have."

Matt's eyes widened. Trace was always so careful. So controlled. So intentional. Matt had never seen him this wound up. Not when it wasn't planned as part of a sermon. And this wasn't planned. Nothing about this was planned.

"Thank God for Jesus." Trace's voice cracked. "Thank God for the cross. For forgiveness. Every day I'm grateful, Matt. Grateful to the Lord that even that sin was one Jesus's blood can cover. Grateful that God enabled me to make a clean break from Siobhan, that he guided us to let her go so she couldn't tempt anyone else."

Certainty landed, lead-like, in Matt's gut. "That's why you fired her."

"We had no choice, Matt." Trace spread his hands, but they trembled. Trembled. Trace's hands never shook. But the fluttering foil of the pretzel bag was proof. "Because yes, I was weak. Yes, I stumbled. But she was dangerous. She was a temptress. She'd have gone after every man on staff, and most of them are married. They have children. Families. And Siobhan would have destroyed it all."

"Now wait a minute." Matt rose from his chair, irritation sparking. "Siobhan isn't like that. At least not with me. The two of us are friends. She's never given any indication of wanting more than that." Why did that suddenly disappoint him? "And I don't appreciate you saying the kinds of things you're saying about her."

"And just how long have you known Siobhan, Matt?" Trace's gaze was piercing.

"Six weeks. Give or take."

"Six weeks." Trace shook his head with a slow, sad smile. "Then you don't know her at all. She starts off sweet and innocent. No hint of wanting anything more. Friendly. Professional. But that woman is smooth as butter, Matt. She'll make her move without you even knowing, and then you wake up and realize she's caught you in her web and it'll take everything you've got and then some to crawl your way out of it." Trace's forearm bulged as he squeezed the pretzel bag into a shiny ball of oblivion. "Learn from my mistakes. Please, Matt. I'm begging you. If you value your walk with Jesus, you'll stay far, far away from Siobhan."

Before Matt could say a word, Trace was gone, the office door shutting defiantly and the pretzel bag fluttering to the floor, pretzel crumbs and salt crystals spilling out all over the bland gray carpet.

CHAPTER ELEVEN

SIOBHAN TIGHTENED HER grip on the steering wheel as she and Matt headed to check another coffee shop off their list, this one in the city's Delano neighborhood. "Let me guess. He called me a temptress."

From the passenger seat, Matt offered a guilty smile. "I'm sorry."

"It's fine." She flipped on her turn signal. "Believe me, I've heard worse. To my face."

"From Trace?"

"And others. But mostly him."

"Really?" His eyes widened, then he shook his head. "Sorry. It's just hard for me to wrap my mind around it."

Irritation sparked at Matt's seeming incredulity. "Look, Matt. I know you look up to Trace. I know he's one of the most important people in your life, and I respect that, even though I don't respect him. And I don't want to burst your bubble, but Trace Jessup is not the guy you think he is."

"Yeah, I'm beginning to see why you'd say that."

Her irritation spent, she relented and glanced at her passenger. February sun highlighted his eyes. Brought out the green in their depths. "Okay. Back up. He might be that guy. I'll give you that. He was your father figure. The one who shared the gospel with you. I get it. He's super important to you, and all that's valid."

"Thank you." Matt's voice was barely above a whisper.

"But Trace is also someone else. He is someone else you've never seen and probably won't, because you're not a single woman who works for him and because he is that good at hiding that part of himself."

Matt nodded. "Yeah, I'm beginning to think he must be."

73

"I didn't realize what I was up against until it was too late." She pulled the car into a parking space, her tires crunching a pile of leftover slush. "And neither did any of the other girls."

The seat belt snapped as Matt unbuckled it, and the fabric strap swished against his jacket. "Wait—there were others?"

Siobhan sighed. Her hands fell to her lap. "He told you I was the only one, didn't he?"

"He said his stumble with you—that's what he called it—was his low point in his walk with the Lord, and he said he'd redoubled his efforts to stay pure." Matt opened the car door. "I mean, obviously I shouldn't believe that, either, but—"

Siobhan climbed from the car. "Trace Jessup and his famous purity charade is the worst-kept secret in the office, Matt." She slammed her car door shut. "All the other pastors know about it, but they won't say anything. Some of them, it's a relief, because they've got their own secrets, and they know if they keep Trace's, he'll keep theirs."

"Wait, what? Other pastors? Everyone knows?"

Oh, it was heartbreaking how innocent Matt was. How naive. Doubtless his faith would be next to crumble, and she'd be responsible.

But it wouldn't have been the first time she'd been blamed for someone's spiritual downfall. Probably wouldn't be the last.

"A couple of them didn't condone what he was doing," she offered by way of reassurance. "But they were too scared to speak up. Mostly they were afraid of losing their jobs. Pursuers pays well—as you're finding out—and it'll put you on the map as a pastor. Quite a few have gone on to plant their own successful churches. Couple book deals. You know the drill."

"Yeah."

Poor Matt. His wide-eyed gaze was on the brick sidewalk, wet with melting snow. His hands were stuffed deep in his pockets. The poor boy looked utterly gobsmacked.

"But the main reason they keep secrets is because Pursuers continues to win souls. That's their bottom line and always has been. And Trace has convinced them that regardless of what he's doing or who he's doing it with, the church as a whole is furthering the kingdom and reaching the lost and converting the sinners and all the things. His relationships give him the fuel to be Pastor Trace Jessup, and as long as the numbers look good, then the ends justify the means. It's all very Machiavellian."

Matt looked up from the sunny sidewalk with a tortured expression, one that twisted her heart. "Siobhan . . ."

"I know. I'm sorry." She reached out and rested her hand on the sleeve of his jacket. He glanced down at it but didn't jerk away. "I hate that I'm shattering all your illusions. Ruining your love for your new gig."

"It's not that." He pressed his lips together and looked her in the eyes. "It's . . ."

"What?"

"It's that . . . the picture Trace painted of you and the woman I see in front of me are so different. And the Trace you're telling me about is a stranger compared to the one I know."

She let her hand drop. "But you barely know me, and you've known Trace half your life. He's practically your father. I get it."

"I want to believe you, Siobhan. Truly. I do. I . . . I need to believe you. But I'm terrified of what will happen when I do. So I need . . ."

"You need proof. Sure. Trace is a crafty one, and that's probably exactly what he said about me." She glanced up. "Am I wrong?"

His uncomfortable expression was all the answer she needed.

"Okay. Hey. What about this?" A gust of chilly wind brushed blond hair in front of her face, and she brushed it back. "When he's first targeting a woman, he refills her coffee."

"Like, he takes the pot to her? Or he takes her mug to the kitchen with his?"

"Both." She shuddered. The memory of slimy chivalry, all those refilled mugs and clandestine brushes of fingertips . . . was why she only ever drank tea now. "And it's super quick. He doesn't linger. Doesn't chitchat. If you weren't looking for it, you'd never know. But when he's hot for someone, the coffee is his tell."

Matt nodded, his expression stony and determined. "Then that's what I'll watch for."

"It might not happen right away. Not unless he's already got a target." She glanced up. "Got any new staff members?"

"Other than me?"

Siobhan cracked a smile. "Pretty sure you're not his type, Matt."

"Point taken." He grinned. "Our worship assistant, Kayleigh, is pretty new. I think she started a couple months before I did."

Siobhan's gut clenched. "What's she look like?"

"Short. Brown hair."

"Oh, he likes brunettes. Especially if they curl their hair." She glanced over. "Does she?"

Matt frowned. "I think so, yeah. Never really looked at her that way." Then his frown switched to a gaze. A soft one. Tender.

Not predatory. Not like Trace.

Tender. Like he treasured her.

It warmed her heart. And it terrified her.

"But you're not brunette" was all he said. "And your hair's straight."

"Hair can be dyed," she replied. "And it turns out straight is easier than curls."

"I see." That odd gaze again. Doubtless Matt was trying to picture her with the chestnut curls she'd once had. Trying to suss out whether blond plaid-wearing Siobhan was the real one, or whether curly brunette Siobhan was who she really was.

She'd been trying to figure that out too. For the past three years.

"I'm sorry," he said again.

"Why do you keep apologizing?"

"Because the way my brain works, it requires evidence." Matt's hand slashed the February air in an emphatic gesture. "I mean, yeah, I'm a creative guy, but I'm also pretty analytical deep down. I like evidence. Facts. That's actually how I came to believe in Jesus. I read some apologetics. Realized it wasn't just a story. That Jesus as Messiah, as resurrected Savior, is in fact the only conclusion that makes any kind of sense."

"I get it." She rested her hand on the cool olive fabric of his coat. "Trace fooled me too, remember? I was once where you are. I only saw the good side of Trace Jessup. And he does have a good side—or at least a very effective facade. But I saw who he really is. And you will too. And I hate that you will, and I hate that I'm the cause of it."

"It doesn't sound like you're the cause of it, Siobhan." He placed his hand on top of hers. "If what you're telling me is true, then it sounds like he is."

He is. Trace is. Trace is the cause.

No one had ever said that to her before. Not the staff, not her supposed friends, not anyone. No one from Pursuers. She was the one to blame. Not him. He was essential, while she was expendable.

And she didn't realize how badly she'd needed to hear what Matt said until his lips formed the words.

He didn't entirely believe her. Not yet.

But he wanted to. He was open to hearing her side because he cared about her. He saw her pain, and his heart ached for it.

And that started a thawing, an intense warming, of her own.

He was a different kind of guy, this Matt Buchanan. He didn't just look at her. He made her feel seen. He was the kind of guy who if he kissed you, it would change you. Imprint your soul.

No. No, what was she *doing*? Thinking of kissing Matt? Thinking of kissing anyone? No. She couldn't. Kissing was bad. Kissing led to pain and disaster and all kinds of terrible things.

She slid her hand off his arm. Tore her gaze from his. Ignored the questions she could feel radiating from his eyes.

She couldn't kiss him because kissing led to destruction. And this . . . this precious friendship with this sweet, tender guy who wanted nothing more than the truth, even if it hurt him to hear it, was something she couldn't bear to lose.

Because for the first time since she'd left Pursuers, someone might be on her side. Someone wanted to believe her.

Someone made sure she wasn't alone.

And kissing? Kissing was a surefire way to end up alone.

Chapter Twelve

June 1876

"My dear sister." Elisabeth bent over the pile of floral fabric covering the kitchen table, her silver needle flying above a row of lace at the ruffled hem. "I do declare . . . your wedding dress . . . finished. There." With a satisfied sigh, she stood and whipped the dress off the table. It fluttered through the air, creating a slight breeze that ruffled the stray curls around Deborah's face.

Elisabeth turned to her, pink cheeked and hopeful. "What do you think?"

The dress was beautiful, of course, but Deborah had always thought so. A blue background the color of the Kansas sky, its pattern a neat array of white flowers, newly added lace at the collar and cuffs, it was one of the few surviving possessions of their mother's. A touch out of fashion, perhaps, and not strictly a wedding dress, but Deborah had always loved it.

"I'd love to see one of you girls wed in that frock," Papa had always said, a dreamy expression on his face. Naturally, Deborah had always thought it would be Elisabeth standing before the parson in Mama's dress, but Elisabeth was smitten with a new fabric that had just arrived at the general store. Deborah had been by her side to hear the delighted gasp, to hear the dizzyingly detailed description of how Elisabeth, ever the gifted seamstress, would do it up into a wedding dress the likes of which Jamesville had never seen. Still, she hesitated, given Papa's wishes, but with Deborah and Levi's hastily announced engagement, suddenly Deborah was the perfect choice to wear Mama's dress, and Elisabeth was free to create the gown of her dreams.

She'd burned the midnight oil for the past week doing just that, hunching over the table, pouring all her love for Isaiah and dreams of their future into the design of a fluffy, frilled, impractical creation that would require heavy alteration to be anything close to hardy enough for life on the Sedgwick County prairie.

Deborah had no such fantasies, neither for the wedding nor for the marriage that would follow. And so she was the one who'd wear their mother's dress. Fitting, in an odd sort of way.

"It's beautiful, Elisabeth. Your work always is."

"You really think so?" Elisabeth smoothed an imaginary wrinkle on the bodice. "Be honest."

"I do." The irony of the words did not escape her. "Truly. It's . . . perfect, Elisabeth. It's everything I could've ever dreamed of in a dress."

"Well, don't just stand there." Elisabeth whirled, dress in hand, dark eyes dancing. "Try it on."

"I'm certain it's fine. You're always precise with the measurements." Lord only knew how long Deborah had stood there while Elisabeth paced around her, measuring tape in hand, pins in her mouth, muttering to herself and marking the fabric with chalk. Mother had apparently been a couple inches shorter than Deborah and a fair bit rounder, if the alterations were any indication. Now Deborah wanted nothing more than to sink into a chair and rest for a few minutes before Levi came for his Sunday call.

Elisabeth blew a strand of curly dark hair out of her flushed face. "But your wedding is in only a week. If there are any alterations that need to be made, the sooner we start, the better."

"All right." Deborah slipped out of her damp, clinging day dress and pulled on the fresh, cool fabric of Mama's dress. The closest thing she'd had to a maternal embrace in a dozen years.

And now it was her wedding dress. She'd stand before the parson this Sunday and pledge her troth to Levi Martinson. An improbable event under improbable circumstances.

Would Mother have ever pictured Deborah marrying in such a manner?

Deborah clenched her jaw against a wave of tears. Oh, that the attack had never taken place. That Mama were here to watch her wed, to give advice, to help Elisabeth put the finishing touches on the dress. That her scalp was whole. That she was marrying for love and not necessity.

A quiet gasp from Elisabeth interrupted her reverie. "Oh, Bee-bee, you're even more beautiful than I imagined you'd be. Truly this dress was meant for you. It's sheer perfection."

Willing her tears away, Deborah stepped in front of the mirror. Her breath caught. The dress indeed fit her like a glove. Physically, anyway. But part of her still felt like a little girl playing dress-up for a pretend wedding, with a tree standing in as the parson and a handful of wild clover as her bouquet.

"Oh, look at you." Elisabeth slid next to her and wrapped her arm around Deborah's waist. "The blushing bride."

Deborah resisted the urge to roll her eyes. "That's from the heat." Her curls had escaped their chignon and turned to frizz around her glistening face. At least she hadn't needed to bother with her bonnet, since it was just the two of them in the kitchen. A small kindness on such a warm afternoon.

"Hullo?" a male voice called from outside. "Anyone home?"

Deborah gasped and glanced at the clock on the mantel. Was Levi early? No, he was right on time. Dress alterations had taken even longer than she thought.

"Oh, merciful heavens, it's Levi. You can't let him see you in the dress. Quick. Hide." Elisabeth scooped Deborah's day dress off the floor, shoved it into her arms, and pushed her into the small bedroom off the kitchen, shutting the door just as the front one creaked open.

Deborah slipped out of her wedding gown, accompanied by childish chatter and Levi's pleasant baritone through the closed wooden door. Elisabeth's voice soon joined the fray, chattering with Nora as though the two were long-lost friends. Elisabeth had always been so good with children. So natural around them. Not like Deborah.

Yet another way in which she felt ill-equipped for this version of life that was suddenly to be hers.

Her day dress in place, Deborah grabbed her bonnet from the hook on the wall and tied it in place, then sighed at her reflection in the bedroom mirror. Still hot and disheveled, though the bonnet covered her messy hair nicely. She needn't bother with pinching her cheeks, either, since the heat had flushed them plenty. Deborah smoothed her dress and squared her shoulders. This, it seemed, was as good as it got.

Still, her heart pounded as she exited the bedroom and fixed her gaze on Levi. "Good afternoon, Mr. Martinson. Nora."

Levi's lips curved. "We're to be man and wife in a week. Seems like it might be prudent to get used to calling me Levi."

Deborah fought back a smile. He had a point. "All right, then. Levi. Good afternoon."

He sought her gaze. "And may I call you Deborah?"

"You may."

"You could also call her Bee-bee." This from Elisabeth, sitting on the floor in most undignified fashion, playing pat-a-cake with Nora.

Deborah shot Elisabeth a glare, and Levi gave a curious grin. "Bee-bee?"

"Childhood nickname. The name 'Deborah' means 'bee.'" Ignoring her husband-to-be, she smoothed a wrinkle in her skirt.

"I see." Levi offered no further comment, much to Deborah's relief. "Shall we, Deborah?" He gestured toward the door.

Her name sounded so much different coming from him. Pleasantly so. "Yes please."

"Have fun, you two," Elisabeth called in a singsong voice. "Nora and her auntie Bess will have a grand old time, won't we?"

Auntie Bess? Clearly Elisabeth was far more prepared for Deborah's marriage than Deborah was.

Once they were out of the house, Levi shot her a sidelong glance. "I thought we might take a walk along the creek. It's shady there. Much cooler. Would that suit you?"

She offered a small smile. "That sounds lovely. Thank you, Levi."

"Of course."

They walked through the prairie grass in companionable silence broken only by the quiet muttering of chickens and the occasional moo of the milk cow, but Deborah's mind was anything but silent. Details and responsibilities and the overwhelming nature of taking on a man's household—a man's child—buzzed through her mind like the flies that circled in the pasture.

She turned toward him. "What time does Nora usually awaken in the mornings?"

"Pardon?"

"Your daughter. What time does she wake up for the day? I'll need to ensure I'm ready to give her breakfast when she rises."

"Oh." Levi's face, shaded by the brim of his hat, creased in thought. "I'm not sure how to answer that since I usually wake her and bring her with me when I'm choring. I'd imagine if allowed, she'd gladly sleep later than she does currently."

"What time?" Deborah pressed.

Levi seemed to snatch a figure from the air. "Maybe seven?"

"Seven." It was a start. "And when do you come in for lunch?"

"Usually don't," he replied. "At least, not now I don't. I try to bring something with me to the field to save time. Sometimes if I'm really absorbed in my work, I forget to eat entirely."

How had this man made it on his own for six months? "And what about supper? What do you enjoy eating? What does Nora enjoy?"

"Nora likes chicken. And strawberries. Bread. And as many sweets as she's allowed." A dimple creased Levi's cheek. "As for myself, I'll eat whatever's put in front of me. I'm not a choosy man." He turned to look at her. "And what about you, Deborah? What sort of food do you enjoy?"

She shrugged. "I've never put much thought into it. A body has to be fed, and around here, one feeds it what's available. Why?"

"Well, if we're getting to know one another, food seems to be a decent place to start."

Deborah frowned. "Oh, I wasn't—I'm not—I was merely asking so I'd know what's expected of me once we're wed. And as you just observed, food seemed a decent place to start."

Levi stopped in the shade of a cottonwood and doffed his hat. Damp strands of sandy hair clung to his forehead, and gentle blue eyes sought her gaze. "Deborah. I think it's best we clear the air."

She studied him. "I thought that's what I was doing."

"Perhaps, but . . . well, I just . . . this isn't—" He broke off, gaze on a patch of grass between his boots. "What I meant to say is this—I realize that our marriage arises from a situation of need. But I'm hopeful that eventually it can become more than mere arrangement."

A blue jay dove from the tree above them. "How do you mean?"

"Charity and I loved each other a great deal. And I'm well aware lightning might not strike twice. You and I may never fall in love. Love is . . . well, like it says in Proverbs, the love between a man and a woman is too great to understand. And I reckon if even King Solomon can't figure it out, then there's no hope for a man like me."

He grinned, and his amusement tugged at Deborah's lips as well.

"But whatever feelings develop—or don't develop—between the two of us, I want you to know that I know how to make a marriage work, and I'm committed to doing so with you. I want our home to be a place of peace and joy for Nora—and for you—and I'm willing to do what it takes to make that happen. The reasons for our union don't have to mean it isn't happy or joyful or fulfilling. I want the two of us to be companions, Deborah. Partners. Friends. And eventually . . . perhaps . . ." He broke off with a shake of his head. "Well, one day at a time, yes?"

Deborah blinked. That was the largest number of words she'd ever heard from Levi Martinson at once. No, at all. Combined. Multiplied many times over. But what wise words they were. What encouraging, hopeful words.

"That . . . seems sensible."

Levi bit his lower lip. "Apologies. I've rambled on quite more than I ever intended."

"You needn't apologize. I . . . appreciate what you've said." Because somehow in what he called rambling, she'd glimpsed a tender heart. A decent, caring, noble man. One she was suddenly grateful to be marrying. "In fact, I'm glad we had this discussion."

"You are?" He looked relieved. "Then . . . you're comfortable with this arrangement?"

Hope filled her heart. Curved her lips as she peered up at him. "I'm . . . a good deal more comfortable with it than I've ever been at any point since we made it."

Levi replaced his hat, his smile lighting the shaded portion of his face. "Good."

Deborah's shoulders loosened, and the bird in a nearby tree sang a song that resonated in her heart.

This marriage might not be what she'd dreamed of. But there was at least a chance God had a plan for it that surpassed those dreams.

CHAPTER THIRTEEN

SIOBHAN PUSHED HER empty dessert plate away and settled back with her mug of green tea amid the happy chaos of family. Family she'd never even met until three years ago when Mom reunited with Sloane, the daughter she'd abandoned on a city bus in Seattle. When Sloane married her financial-planner husband, Garrett, his family had not only brought her into the fold, but Mom too, along with Siobhan.

"That, my beautiful wife, was delicious as always." Across the table from Siobhan, Sloane's brother-in-law, Carter Douglas, leaned over and kissed the freckled cheek of his wife, Lauren, who smiled and wrapped her hand around his.

"Yeah, not bad, little sister." This from Garrett, two seats away from Lauren. He shoveled in the last of his blackberry cobbler with one hand while the other braced his daughter, sacked out on his shoulder, one small fist in her mouth. "Barely even missed the gluten." He grinned at his sister, who responded with an exasperated half glare.

"Yes indeed, that was mighty tasty, granddaughter." To Lauren's left sat her step-grandfather, Ephraim James. Despite the fact that Ephraim's skin was deep brown and Lauren's was pale, the two were as close as any grandfather and granddaughter. Ephraim and Rosie, Garrett and Lauren's grandmother, had been high school sweethearts in a time when the difference in their race had doomed their relationship. Both had gone on to marry others and live happy lives, but after the deaths of their respective spouses, the octogenarian lovebirds had reunited nearly two years ago. They'd wed in a quiet ceremony at the care facility where they both lived, much to the initial consternation—but eventual acceptance—of Ephraim's children and grandchildren back in Philadelphia.

Rosie sat next to Ephraim, trailing her fork through a leftover pile of cobbler crust. Her Alzheimer's had progressed to the point where she rarely contributed to conversation anymore, but she seemed content to observe, a small smile playing on her lips, her hand resting lightly atop Ephraim's. Despite her disease, she seemed happy. At peace.

"Guess that's our cue." To Siobhan's left, Sloane stood and collected plates.

Lauren rose to help, but Garrett got to his feet and motioned her back down. "What did Grandpa always say? World-class cook shouldn't have to do her own dishes."

"Point taken." Lauren sat back down and turned to Ephraim. "Carter and I can take you and Grandma home whenever you're ready."

"I think that's probably a wise idea, my dear." Ephraim rose slowly as Carter came around to help Rosie to her feet. The older woman regarded Carter with a blank yet pleasant smile.

"If someone wouldn't mind taking care of this for me . . ." Garrett eased his tiny daughter off his shoulder, but he didn't have to look far to find a pair of willing hands. To Siobhan's right, Mom was there, auburn hair tumbling over her shoulders, arms outstretched.

"Gimme," she said with an eager grin.

Smiling, Garrett handed over baby Domenica. "I figured you'd be the first volunteer."

Siobhan handed her plate to Sloane and watched the scene unfold. Mom kissing her granddaughter's fuzzy dark head. Carter and Lauren helping Rosie and Ephraim with their jackets. Garrett through the kitchen doorway, nudging the faucet with his wrist and squirting soap into the sink.

All these people were family now. *Her* family. It still blew Siobhan's mind sometimes.

Grabbing the empty coffee cups from where Rosie and Ephraim had been sitting, Siobhan followed Sloane into the kitchen and slid the cups into the dishwasher.

That stainless steel appliance was one of many modern touches to the old farmhouse, which had been built by a pioneer couple, Jack and Anna-belle Brennan. Through a series of diaries Annabelle had written through-out the late nineteenth century, Sloane had discovered her own ancestral connection to Jack and Annabelle, which had ultimately led to Sloane's reunion with her mother—their mother—and the half sisters' subsequent introduction.

Those diaries remained on permanent exhibit at the museum where Sloane worked, shedding light on a long-buried story and serving as tan-gible evidence of how God had orchestrated their family's events for well over a century. It still gave Siobhan goose bumps to think about it.

"Hey, how's that violin repair job coming?" Sloane replaced a jug of oat milk in the fridge, one Lauren's predictably healthy contributions to the meal.

"It's coming." Siobhan crouched to the cabinet where the plastic wrap was kept and grabbed the long rectangular box. "That thing's got some se-rious damage from an old injury."

"Like a car wreck?" Mom asked.

"That's what I wondered." Siobhan ripped off a section of plastic wrap and wrangled it onto the remnants of the cobbler. "That's what it's in for now, but this damage is older than that, and the repairs were well done but pretty rudimentary. I checked with Matt, but nobody in his family remembers anything that would've caused that kind of damage, so I'm not sure what happened to it. Ian thinks the repairs might've been made a hundred years ago. Maybe more."

Baby Domenica stirred, letting out a disgruntled squawk.

"Oh, what's the matter, little lady?" Mom bounced the tiny girl in her arms. "Is the kitchen getting a little noisy? Want to find somewhere quiet?"

"Yeah, it might be a little loud in here," Garrett agreed over the hiss of the faucet and the clatter of pans. "Sorry."

"Not a problem, Garrett." Mom draped a burp cloth over her shoulder. "We'll just go out on the sun porch."

Mom and Domenica headed out through the back door toward the porch, and Sloane turned to Siobhan. "Where's Matt's family from, do you know?"

"He moved here from Illinois, but he grew up around here. Not sure how long his family's been here, though," Siobhan replied. "Why?"

"Depending on where the violin was when it was damaged, there might've been someone there who could've fixed it. Even Wichita had a music store back in the pioneer days—Thomas Shaw Music Store opened in 1884. Older towns would've had repair shops and music stores even before that, so it's possible that whatever damaged the violin, the repair could've been done by a professional." Sloane reached for the carafe of coffee and dumped the dregs into her cup.

"Would there be any way to find out what happened to it?" Garrett asked.

"It'd sure help if we knew where the damage occurred," Sloane replied. "Otherwise it's a needle in a haystack. But if we can narrow it down, there might be records of the repair." She turned to Siobhan. "You said it was a diagonal crack across the back?"

"And one across the front too." Siobhan glanced out the window onto the screened porch, where Mom sat rocking baby Domenica on the swing, basking in the sunshine of an unseasonably warm February day. Some vitamin D and a conversation with her mom beckoned, so she turned back to Sloane and Garrett. "You guys good here?"

"Yeah, we got it." Sloane stuck another couple glasses into the dishwasher. "Keep me posted about what you learn from Matt. Even the tiniest detail might turn out to be a big deal."

"Yeah, definitely." Siobhan slipped out onto the porch, where Mom hummed a quiet tune to the no-longer-fussy Domenica, who lay content on Mom's shoulder, sucking a tiny fist.

Mom. A grandmother.

It was still crazy to think about.

"She calm down?" Siobhan asked.

"Yup. I think she just had a burp." Mom's long fingers rubbed the baby's tiny back. "But the sun isn't hurting anything. Sitting in the sun always used to calm you right down."

"Still does." Siobhan tossed a throw pillow off a nearby wicker chair and sat, the sunshine warm on her face.

"So what's the story with this violin?" Mom asked quietly.

"This guy brought it in a month or so ago."

"Matt? Is that his name?"

"Yeah." Siobhan avoided her mother's gaze. "It was damaged in a car wreck. He doesn't even really play it—it belonged to his grandma—but it's all he's got of hers, so he wanted me to fix it up. I didn't think it'd be worth anything. He said it was just a student model, but Ian found out it's actually really old. Maybe even a couple hundred years. I asked Sloane to do some digging. She said she would."

"I'll bet she wasn't too hard to convince." Mom's eyes took on the faraway look they always got when the conversation drifted to her firstborn. More so now that she'd become a grandmother. That she had a second chance with Sloane. A second chance to sit on a porch swing and snuggle a dark-haired baby girl.

Siobhan patted her mother's knee. "I'm glad she found you."

Mom's brown eyes shimmered with unshed tears. "Glad doesn't even begin to cover it, Siobhan. Leaving her on that bus was the worst mistake of my life—the worst in a long series of mistakes—but God wasn't finished writing our story. And I'm glad. So glad." Crimson lips found the top of Domenica's head, and Mom gave her granddaughter a gentle kiss.

It was suddenly easier than ever to picture a different dark-haired baby girl. To see Mom as a teenager. Clueless. Overwhelmed.

And terrifyingly easy to put herself in Mom's shoes. What if the relationship with Trace had resulted in a pregnancy? Thank God it hadn't. Even as an adult, Siobhan had no idea what she'd have done. And Mom had been just a teenager. How hopeless she must've felt. How helpless. How alone.

"Mom? Can I ask you something?"

"Of course." The words ruffled Domenica's dark hair.

"It's . . . about Sloane's father."

An arched brow. A warning glance. *Tread lightly.* "Okay . . ."

"How did you recover from that relationship?" Siobhan leaned forward, lacing her hands together and leaning her forearms on her knees. "Not the baby part. But the relationship part."

"You mean how did I get over him?"

"Yeah. I mean, he messed you up pretty bad, sounds like. But you moved on. You found love."

Mom gave a rueful smile. "Eventually."

"But how did you learn to trust again? How did you move on and find yourself able to love someone else?"

The porch swing creaked its gentle rhythm. "I won't lie to you, Siobhan. It took a long time. And it wasn't without a few more mistakes."

"Was Dad one of them?" she asked.

Mom frowned, as she always did when the subject of her past relationships and previous husband came up. As always, it looked like she was deciding how much she wanted to share.

Siobhan's biological father, Greg, hadn't been a total stranger—she'd spent three weeks with him in Seattle every summer as a kid—but the difference in geography meant she'd always been much closer to Todd, her stepdad, than to Greg. It was why she'd taken Todd's last name as her own.

Finally, Mom spoke. "Your dad was . . . well, at the time I thought I loved him, but looking back on it now, it was more of a desperation move. I wanted to prove to myself that Professor Danilo Dobroshtan wasn't my one true love. That I could attract someone good." A bitter chuckle. "Or at the very least, someone who wasn't already married."

"Enter Dad."

"Don't get me wrong, honey. Greg was a good man. Handsome, hard-working, a decent guy, but we had some irreconcilable differences. Money was tight back in Seattle, so when Boeing offered him a job here where the cost of living was cheaper, he took it. I thought that would fix things between us, but he was miserable. I thought it was the job, thought it was Kansas, but it turned out it wasn't those things. It was me."

"I'm sorry, Mom. That had to be really hard."

Mom waved a hand. "He tried to make it work—for your sake, if nothing else—but after a few months I knew it was over. He moved back to Seattle, and I stayed here. I was through with dating and men, and I was just going to focus on taking care of you and getting my real estate license."

Those early years were fuzzy but also held some of Siobhan's fondest memories. How Mom did it, she hadn't a clue, but Mom had somehow launched her real estate career while being such an amazing parent that most of the time Siobhan never felt like she was missing out by not having a dad. Mom was so warm, so caring, so full of love and life that, despite their financial struggles, Siobhan never lacked for anything. Nothing important, anyway. As glad and grateful as she was to have Todd join their family, those early years still filled her heart with warmth.

"But then when the time was right, God brought Todd into our lives." Mom's voice was rich with warmth and love.

"At Walmart of all places, right?"

"Yup. The cereal aisle." Mom's lips curved. "And Todd was wonderful. He knew I wasn't looking to get involved with anyone, so he was happy to be my friend. My confidant. My occasional handyman—and snake remover, of course. Remember that?"

Siobhan chuckled at the memory of that day in third grade. Of her mother, standing on the toilet lid, shrieking into her cell phone, utterly terrified of a garter snake that had found its way into their bathroom. Moments later Todd strode in to save the day.

"Todd was willing to wait until I was ready," Mom continued, "and when I was, there he stood. Arms open and heart full of love."

Siobhan smiled across at her mother. "I'm so glad you found him, Mom. You deserved love."

"And you do too." Mom's gaze was piercing but not unkind. "I know you've had it rough, Siobhan. I know your last relationship was hard on you. I know it ended badly."

"Like mother, like daughter, I'm afraid." How ironic that Siobhan would make the same exact mistake her mother had made. Falling for a man who simply saw her as a means to an end. A sexual outlet. Someone to be used, not loved.

"But my prayer for you is that you'll find someone like Todd. Someone who's patient with your damage and gentle with your heart and willing to wait until you're ready. Someone who loves you, baggage and all. And when you meet him, you'll know." Mom's eyes shone. "Because you'll feel so comfortable with him, beyond anything you ever could've hoped for. You'll feel safe. Protected. Cared for. Respected. And if you're anything like me, it'll take you a long time to see the wonderful man that's right in front of your face. But if he's anything like Todd, he'll wait for you until you do."

Patient. Protected. Cared for. Respected.

That sounded suspiciously like . . . Matt.

Perhaps her mother's prayer had already been answered.

The thought filled her with twin surges of hope and terror.

CHAPTER FOURTEEN

MATT'S PEN TAPPED his office desk, the absent-minded rhythm of his fidgeting an accompaniment to the worship music pumping in through his AirPods. *Impact Your Influence.* That was Trace's upcoming sermon series. And Matt was tasked with finding worship songs to go along with that.

The new one he was listening to was great, and the text was fabulous, but the range was a little wide. In the written key, he'd have a hard time with some of the higher notes, and if he lowered the key, then some of the other bits would be out of his range. In fact, most of the singers on the team, talented as they were, would struggle with this one. And if they did, then two thousand amateurs in the seats wouldn't have a chance. No, worship songs needed to be easily singable, and this one, great as it was, didn't check that box.

Reluctantly, he tapped his AirPod to advance to the next song.

Huh. This one was a possibility. The opening guitar riff was cool. Jed, their lead guitarist, would have a lot of fun with it. A quick scroll through the lyrics found a couple lines that would definitely work with the series. And the female vocals . . . Kayleigh would crush this. With that big, belty alto voice of hers, she'd be the perfect choice to lead this one.

He leaned toward his computer, his chair squeaking with the movement. When was she scheduled to sing next? First week of March. Perfect for the new series. He stood, pausing the track on his phone, and headed for the cluster of desks outside his office that included Kayleigh's. Hopefully, she'd like the song as much as he did.

She wasn't at her desk, though. Her trademark yellow cardigan was draped over the back of her chair, and her giant ceramic coffee mug was in the center. *Taste and See*, proclaimed flowy gold-foil letters.

"Hey, Matt." Trace strode through the office, giving him a brotherly pat on the shoulder. He waved at Becky, the worship department receptionist. Tapped the desk of Aaron, the worship intern, with his fingertips.

And then he passed Kayleigh's desk. He didn't break stride. Didn't even look down.

But he did pick up her coffee mug.

Matt froze, icy dread washing through him, along with the memory of Siobhan's words.

When he's first putting the moves on a woman, he refills her coffee.

Maybe it wasn't that. Maybe Trace wasn't up to anything. Maybe he was just trying to tidy up. Keep the office looking nice. Maybe Kayleigh had asked him to bring her mug to the kitchen so she could wash it.

But the ridiculousness, the naivete of those thoughts slammed him before he even finished them.

If you weren't looking for it, you'd never know. But when he's hot for someone, the coffee is his tell.

Trace disappeared down the hallway that led to the kitchen, mug in hand, and a second later, Kayleigh returned from another hallway. The details of her appearance hit Matt with near physical force.

Brown hair, softly curled around her shoulders.

Tight-fitting top, though one that at first glance would pass muster in the modesty department.

A skirt.

"Hey, Matt." She tossed him a wave and settled back down at her desk.

He returned the wave absently. Had he wanted to talk to her before? He couldn't remember. His mind was barely there. His stomach, however, was in knots.

Because if Trace was truly refilling Kayleigh's coffee, he'd be back any moment.

Less than a minute later, there he was, striding in from the kitchen, Kayleigh's mug steaming in his hand. Matt ducked back into his office and gave his AirPod a tap, changing it from Noise Cancellation to Transparency.

Transparency. There was a word. He almost laughed.

Through Matt's office window, Kayleigh dimpled her delight. "I was wondering where that went. Thought I was losing my mind."

"Oh, my apologies, Kayleigh." Trace gave a lopsided grin. "Didn't mean to scare you. I was just passing by, saw the sad sight of an empty coffee mug, and thought maybe you could use a refill." He set the mug on her desk.

"Oh." Kayleigh blinked at the mug, then beamed up at Trace. "Well, thank you kindly, Pastor. That's really sweet of you."

"Absolutely." He started back toward his office, patting Kayleigh's shoulder as he did so. Just a pat. Nothing unprofessional.

But the way his hand lingered on her shoulder, his fingertips grazing the neckline of her shirt?

That looked a whole lot less professional.

"Keep up the great work, Kales. You're a fantastic addition to the team."

"Thank you." Kayleigh settled back into her desk and reached for her coffee mug. If Matt hadn't been looking for it, he might've missed the sparkle in her eyes. The flush in her cheeks.

But he was looking, and it was unmistakable. The exact thing Siobhan had warned him about earlier this week had just happened right before his eyes.

That doe-eyed brunette with the curls and the skirt had once been his blond plaid-wearing Siobhan.

That freshly filled coffee mug had once belonged to her.

And that grateful smile, the one that made it plain as day she had no clue what Trace was up to, that was once Siobhan's too.

Matt shut the door of his office, his stomach plummeting. He felt helpless. Nauseous. The worship music playing in his earbuds was almost a parody now. God was still real, and Jesus was still there . . . but so was this.

His remaining illusions of Trace lay shattered around his feet, like the glass from the windshield in his truck after the wreck. His heart cracked like the back of his grandma's old violin.

Matt couldn't pretend anymore. Siobhan was right. Trace Jessup—his mentor, his friend, his boss—wasn't the man Matt had always believed him to be.

Okay, Lord. I know the truth.

Now what in the world am I supposed to do about it?

✦

Freshly showered and satisfyingly shaky after a vigorous bout with the punching bag, Siobhan pulled her coat out of her locker at the gym and reached into the pocket for her phone. A text from Sloane was waiting for her.

> Call me when you get this.
> I might have a lead on your violin.

Siobhan wasn't much for phone calls, even with Sloane, but this text contained the magic words. So on her way out of the gym, she tossed a cheerful wave to the desk attendant with one hand and dialed her half sister's number with the other.

"I got a hunch," Sloane said by way of greeting. "I started looking through some records the museum has from the Thomas Shaw Music Store in Wichita. It opened in 1884 and quickly became known as one of the best music shops in the West. And according to those records, there was a John Caldwell who brought a violin in for repair in May of 1885."

Siobhan slid into her car, warm and sunny despite the chilly winter day. "Let me guess. For a couple big diagonal cracks?"

"Not this time anyway. This repair ticket was for routine maintenance—a bow rehair, general polishing and inspection, that sort of thing. But Shaw noted in his records that the violin had large cracks on both the front and back that had previously been repaired."

"Sounds like Shaw wasn't the one who did the repair, then."

"If he was, I haven't found a record of it. My guess is whatever damage happened to this violin was before 1885. But here's the best part."

Siobhan started the car. "Oh?"

Sloane's voice switched from the phone to the car stereo. "According to Shaw, John Caldwell said the violin had been damaged in a frontier raid while the family was moving from their previous home in Ohio to Kansas."

Siobhan blinked. "A frontier raid? Do we know anything more?"

"Shaw's records didn't say. They were far more detailed about the violin and its condition in 1885 than anything prior to that."

Disappointment landed lead-like in her gut. "Oh."

"But in our case, that's still very good news," Sloane went on. "Because the odds of there being two violins with similar damage in the same area in the same time period are pretty small." Siobhan could hear Sloane's smile, and it mirrored her own.

"Likely not," she said.

"Well," Sloane said triumphantly, "then I think we may have found our violin."

CHAPTER FIFTEEN

June 1876

DEBORAH SELECTED A chicken drumstick from the sizzling, aromatic pan, then set it aside to cool on a cutting board while she arranged the rest of the piping-hot pieces on a platter. Levi hadn't said how Nora liked her chicken prepared—nor how he liked it, for that matter—but fried chicken had always been one of Papa's favorites. Perhaps her new family would enjoy it just as much.

The gold ring on the fourth finger of her left hand glinted in the late-afternoon sunlight, still shiny in its newness after yesterday's perfunctory wedding ceremony. And now she no longer lived with Papa. No longer made his fried chicken. Now she cooked for a man she barely knew, along with a little girl she was now tasked with raising. She reached for a knife and began cutting the drumstick into what she hoped would be bite-sized pieces.

It was a hefty amount to take in.

Voices cut the quiet outside, one deep and sporadic, the other high and issuing a steady stream of toddler chatter. Deborah replaced her cap, then placed the cut-up bites of chicken onto a plate and reached for a handful of freshly picked strawberries she'd found that afternoon. Levi had told her Nora liked strawberries, so perhaps this would be a first step toward winning the little girl over.

The door creaked open and in spilled Nora, cheeks flushed, curls disheveled from the afternoon wind, and her beloved doll clutched in her tiny hand. Levi stood behind her, dusting his worn Stetson.

Deborah greeted the pair with a polite smile. "Hello," she said to her new husband. Her new daughter.

"Oh. Hullo." Levi blinked, as though he hadn't expected to see her. She didn't blame him. Since last November, when he came in from choring, there hadn't been a woman standing at the stove. And before that, it had been Charity. No doubt Nora hadn't been out in the fields with him before, either. Perhaps she'd been playing at her mother's feet, only to shriek her delight and toddle toward him.

It was a hefty amount for all of them to take in.

Levi hung his hat on a hook and offered a smile. "Dinner smells delicious."

"Thank you." The warmth his compliment brought was genuine, the only pleasant warmth in the stifling kitchen. "Papa always said I made good fried chicken, so that seemed a good option to start with."

"Well, I'll never say no to a pan of fried chicken. Especially chicken that smells like that." He eyed the skillet appreciatively, then turned to his daughter. "Come on, Nora. Let's get you washed up."

While the pair prepared for dinner, Deborah put the finishing touches on the mashed potatoes—hers were never quite as good as Elisabeth's, but Levi had never tasted those—and some fresh peas she'd picked from the garden. Heart pounding, she rounded up the dishes and set them on the small table.

Here it was. Her first meal as a married woman. As a mother.

Lord, please let it go well.

Levi and Nora arrived at the table, and he helped her into her chair, then sat down and reached across for his daughter's small hand. "Shall we thank the Lord for this bounty?"

"Of course."

And then Levi reached out his other hand. To her. There it was. Right next to her plate. Palm up. Fingers open in invitation. He wanted her to take his hand. Her husband.

Heat creeping into her neck, Deborah slid her fingers into Levi's gentle grip. His hands were strong and rough from work but held within them a promise of care. The same promise he'd made to her yesterday. That was the first and only other time the two had joined hands, as a beaming Papa had recited the words of matrimony while Deborah had moved in a daze, her mother's dress billowing around her ankles in the summer breeze.

She was married now. She, of all women, had a husband.

Levi blessed the food, then released her hand. But rather than diving into his dinner, as she'd expected, he sat there studying her, an inscrutable expression on his face.

"Is . . . everything all right?" she asked.

"You're still wearing your . . ." Trailing off, he motioned toward his own head.

Heat crept into her cheeks, and her hand flew to the fabric covering. "Yes. I . . . I suppose I am."

"Must be awfully warm."

"Yes." Her vocabulary seemed to have shrunk to that single syllable.

"Deborah." The three syllables of her name were wrapped in compassion. "I know about . . ." He broke off and flicked a cautious glance toward Nora, who was devouring the small pile of strawberries on her plate. "What happened to you. Your father told me."

She nodded. She couldn't look at him. Not now. Not when the memories of that horrible day threatened to undo her.

"I know you bear a scar," he said. "And I know it's not something you like others to see. But we're man and wife now."

Tears stung her eyes. She couldn't. She couldn't let him see. Couldn't let anyone see. Though she'd grown her hair as best she could to cover it, the patch of bald, damaged skin atop her head was so ugly. So grotesque. He'd stare. Nora would stare. The poor little tyke would be terrified. She'd think her new mother a monster.

No, no, she couldn't let them see. Not now.

Maybe not ever.

"This is your home, Deborah." Levi's voice was quiet. Rich with compassion. "And I pray that someday you'll feel comfortable in it. If today isn't that day, then that's quite all right. I simply want you to know that when you are ready, you're more than welcome."

It was the look in his eyes. The tone in his voice. The compassion in the hand that reached out to hers, hovering uncertainly at first, then gently grasping her fingertips.

She wasn't ready to let him see her. All of her. Not yet.

Nor could she see herself being ready anytime soon.

But for the first time ever, her heart held hope that perhaps someday . . . she might be.

Chapter Sixteen

Matt's violin lay in pieces on Siobhan's workbench. Controlled pieces. Expertly broken-apart pieces. But pieces nonetheless. It was always intimidating yet exhilarating to have a stringed instrument disassembled and be tasked with putting it back together.

Especially one as old as this, with a history such as this. A survivor of an apparently brutal attack, if this was indeed John Caldwell's violin. The rudimentary glue had held the cracks together for well over a century, even with the new soundpost crack splitting pale, naked wood through the deep red-brown varnish.

Such damage would've destroyed many an instrument.

But not this one.

The door chimed, signaling a customer's arrival, and Ian's voice floated up from the back corner of the shop. "Could you get that, love? I'm up to my elbows in a very truculent string bass."

"Sure thing." Siobhan set down her tools, brushed her hands against her heavy apron, and rounded the corner to the public-facing part of the shop.

"Morning, ma'am," she said to the brunette wrangling a cello through the double glass doors. "What can I do for you?"

"Hi." The woman set down the heavy instrument with a thunk. "We just bought this cello for my son. We promised him if he stuck with it until high school, we'd buy him one, and he kept his end of the deal, so we kept ours."

"Good for him," Siobhan replied. "Where'd this instrument come from?"

"We bought it from a girl who graduated last year and isn't playing anymore. She said the cello was in good shape but that it might have some open seams and would probably also need a bow rehair. Her parents recommended your shop very highly."

Siobhan's heart warmed at the praise. "Thank you."

The woman turned then and brushed a chunk of windblown hair from her face, and . . . Wait. Was that . . .

No way.

But it was.

Jenisa Mills. Children's ministry assistant at Pursuers.

Her hair was shorter than it had been back then, with chunky honey-blond highlights Siobhan couldn't recall from before, but everything else was the same.

She couldn't have a son in high school yet, though, could she? Braeden had been in what, fifth grade when Siobhan left? Maybe sixth?

Wow. He very well could be in high school.

Jenisa hadn't recognized Siobhan yet. Or maybe she had but was pretending she didn't. Okay, that was cool. Siobhan would happily play along.

Despite the awkwardness clutching at her shoulders, she arranged her expression into one of pleasant yet bland professionalism and focused her attention on the cello. "Absolutely. Let's take a look."

The latches of the blue hard-shell case sprang open—a decent case. Not top of the line, but a good brand nonetheless, one that indicated the player took the protection of the instrument seriously. Within lay a luminous golden-hued cello and the slight musty smell characteristic of instruments that hadn't been played in a while.

Siobhan unfastened the Velcro strip around the cello's neck, lifted the instrument from the case, and turned it around to get a good look. Overall, the condition was excellent. No obvious cracks to repair, and everything seemed in working order. The edges bore a few dents and dings, but that was to be expected from an instrument that had survived life at a high school. Crouching lower, she gently tapped around the edges near the thin black strip of purfling, a surefire way to spot open seams. Sure enough, the normally hollow sound changed to a slight splat in one spot, the telltale mark of a seam that could use a fresh glue job. One opening on the front near the endpin, and another one on the instrument's left shoulder on the back side.

"Well, we do indeed have a couple open seams." Siobhan stood and pointed out the spots to Jenisa. "But it's a pretty easy repair. Just a little glue and twenty-four hours' drying time, and we'll be right as rain. I'll give it a more thorough once-over once I get it back in the shop, and I'll rehair the bow, but assuming I don't find anything else, we could have it back to you Thursday. Does that work?"

"Yeah, that sounds perfect." Then Jenisa's penciled brows inched together, and she leaned closer. "Wait. Siobhan?"

Siobhan sighed and pulled the instrument a bit closer, almost like a shield. "Hello, Jenisa."

"Wow." Jenisa flung herself toward Siobhan and engulfed her in a fragrant embrace, made all the more awkward by the cello between them. "It has been a *hot minute.*"

That was one way to put it.

Jenisa pulled back, hands still on Siobhan's shoulders, and gave her a once-over. "I barely even recognized you. That blond looks *amazing.*"

Siobhan smoothed her hair. "It was time for a change."

"How have you been?" Jenisa squealed, as though it had been only weeks since they'd seen each other, not three years. As though Jenisa hadn't been among those who'd cut Siobhan out of their lives, their silence a heavier and more effective condemnation than the harshest words ever could have been.

She maneuvered the cello back into the case. "I've been."

"You're working here now? How long have you—"

"Look." Siobhan tightened the neck strap and met Jenisa's brown eyes. "We don't have to do this."

Jenisa blinked. "Do what?"

"Pretend like we're long-lost friends who just bumped into each other at the grocery store. I'm not the person you knew anymore. And even if I was, you and everyone else at Pursuers froze me out. Acted like I was Hester Prynne wearing a giant red-letter A." Her jaw tightened, and she made a conscious effort to inject calm into her voice as she shut the cello case.

"You all made your choice. I'm more than happy to fix up your son's cello, but other than that I have nothing else to say to you."

"But I have something to say to you, Siobhan." Jenisa's tone was warm and soft. No anger. No malice. And perhaps even a little bit of regret?

Siobhan glanced up into a pleading gaze. "Okay."

Jenisa leaned in closer. "Are we alone?"

"It's just Ian in the back." Siobhan indicated her boss with a jerk of her head. "And he's elbows deep in a double bass. Plus, he's not one to eavesdrop."

Jenisa nodded, her lips tight. "I didn't see it then, okay?"

"Didn't see what?"

"Trace. For who and what he was. I defended the indefensible. All of us did. And I owe you an apology."

Siobhan blinked. An apology. From someone at Pursuers. That had always seemed slightly more likely than being able to build a stepladder to the moon, but only slightly.

"They pulled the wool over our eyes at that place." Jenisa's voice was quiet but intense. "I know that's not an excuse for what they—what we—did to you, but it's the God's honest truth. I didn't see it until I saw it, and then I couldn't unsee it."

Siobhan propped an elbow on the cello case. "You're not there anymore, I assume?"

Jenisa shook her head. "No. We left a little over a year ago. God led us to a church that wasn't toxic."

Siobhan chuckled. "Didn't know that was even a thing."

"It is, and it's so refreshing. It's been a place for us to be quiet and still and let God heal us. I'm happy to tell you more about it when—*if*—you're ready."

"I'll think about it." Siobhan paused, questions circling in her mind. "When did you figure it out?"

Jenisa leaned against the counter. "About Trace?"

"Yeah. What made you see the light?"

Jenisa sighed and bit her lip. Tears pooled along her lower lids. "He made a pass at me."

"At *you*? Wow. I thought he only went for single women." It shouldn't surprise her, though. Nothing about Trace Jessup should surprise her.

"Yeah, well." Jenisa fiddled with a colorful tassel on her designer purse. "The sad irony is, by the time Trace started in on me, I was in that category."

Siobhan's jaw dropped. "You and Philip split up?"

"Yeah. A couple months after you left."

"Wow. I'm so sorry to hear that."

Jenisa lifted a shoulder. "Thank you. We're blessed that it was amicable and that we're still good friends and co-parents."

"I'm glad for that." Jenisa. And Philip. Not together anymore.

"Me too. But . . ." Jenisa shook her head, as though to clear her mind of unpleasant memories. "As soon as Philip and I separated, Trace brought me a cup of coffee at my desk, said he was sorry to hear that Philip and I were having problems, and told me I could talk with him anytime about anything. I was so naive, so needy, so relieved to have someone—my pastor, no less—be so understanding about it, to make me feel seen and heard rather than judged because my marriage failed, that I believed him. And I did talk to him. A lot. Especially after hours. He said it'd be best to do that for privacy's sake."

"Because of his open-door policy." Her neck tightened. That eel.

"Oh yeah. Gotta keep that door open during the day so there's not even a hint of sexual immorality." Sarcasm dripped from Jenisa's words. "But at night . . ."

"No need for the open door. Because no one's around." She knew that closed door. Knew those after-hours conversations. Knew the feeling of that leather couch, the smell of his cologne . . .

"I truly didn't see what he was doing." Jenisa's voice shook. "I was vulnerable and hurting and messed up from my failing marriage. I needed a friend, and I thought with everything I had in me that that was what Trace was. But one night he gave me a hug. And his hands started wandering."

Siobhan shivered. She knew those hands. Knew exactly where they would've wandered.

"And then he tried to kiss me." Jenisa squeezed her eyes shut. "I fought back. Got away. Walked out the door that night and never went back. I submitted my resignation the next day. Became a substitute teacher at Braeden's school, and now I'm teaching sixth-grade social studies in Derby."

Siobhan's shoulders loosened. "I wish I'd had the courage to do what you did."

Jenisa sighed. "It wasn't easy. I know you know that. And that was when I realized that those rumors I'd heard about Trace, the whispers I'd heard that it wasn't your fault, that you weren't the hussy he made you out to be, that was when I realized how true it all was. He is a predator, and you and I—we're victims, Siobhan. Both of us. And probably others."

Victim?

That label had never felt right to her, and she'd refused to wear it. Because she'd loved him. Or at least, she'd thought she did.

Jenisa was a victim, sure.

But Siobhan?

She was no victim.

She was Hester Prynne.

"I'm so sorry, Siobhan. I'm sorry I didn't believe you. I'm sorry I jumped to conclusions. If it helps at all, no one believed me, either. I told one of the elders, and they said they'd look into it, but . . ."

"Nothing happened." Siobhan tipped a wry grin. "Yeah, I heard that line before too."

"That place is a ticking time bomb." Jenisa leaned in close. "I'm glad you got out. I'm glad I got out."

"Yeah." Siobhan exhaled under the weight that had simultaneously fallen on and lifted from her shoulders. "Thank you for telling me what happened to you. I know how difficult that must have been."

Jenisa peered at Siobhan, golden-brown eyes seeing more than Siobhan was comfortable with. "Have you talked to anyone about what happened? Seen a counselor or anything?"

"It's nobody's business but mine." The words were a little angrier than she wished they were.

"I get how hard it is. Believe me, I know." Jenisa rested a manicured hand on Siobhan's plaid sleeve. "But we have to bring it into the light, expose it for what it is, if we want any kind of justice. Any kind of healing. I can give you my therapist's card if you—"

"No." The refusal was crisp. Firm. "Thank you, but no. I'm not—I can't—no. Not right now." Matt was already flinging her past in her face enough. She didn't need to go digging around for more pain.

"Fair." Jenisa took her hand off Siobhan's arm, but her eyes radiated sympathy. "But at least talk to someone you trust. Even if it's not a mental health professional, it'll help you to share your story. At least it did for me. Think about it, okay?"

A car door shut in the parking lot, another customer heading in.

Siobhan squared her shoulders and reapplied her professional smile. "So like I said, Braeden's cello will be ready by Thursday."

Jenisa followed Siobhan's gaze and nodded. "Yeah. Thursday. That's perfect. I get off work around four."

"I'll make sure to have it ready. Just swing by and get it."

"Thank you," Jenisa said. "And . . . thank you."

"Sure. Thank *you*." Like Jenisa, Siobhan layered her expression of gratitude.

"You're welcome to come to church with me anytime, Siobhan." Jenisa's voice was quiet but urgent. "This place is different. I mean it."

Fat chance. "I'll think about it."

Jenisa's hand found Siobhan's and gave it a quick squeeze. "I'll see you Thursday, okay?"

"Yeah. Thursday."

Jenisa slipped out the door held open by a slender Asian woman with a violin case, and Siobhan moved the cello behind the counter.

Someone else believed her. Someone else *saw* her. Someone else knew the ugly truth because she'd experienced it for herself.

Was that good? Bad? Somewhere in the middle? She'd sort that out later. Right now it was business time.

Brushing her hair behind her ear, she smiled at her new customer. "Morning, ma'am. What can I do for you?"

Chapter Seventeen

July 1876

DEBORAH TOSSED A handful of flour onto the kitchen counter and reached for her rolling pin, one of her father's fiddle tunes hovering happily on her lips. It had been a productive day of cleaning, gardening, and mending, made all the more fruitful by the fact that Nora had gone with her father to Billy Stevens's place. The Stevens family had lost some fencing in a windstorm Thursday night, and Levi had gone to help with the repairs, while Nora had accompanied him to play with Billy and Dorcas's young daughter, May.

A welcome breeze from the window ruffled the thin patch of curls atop her scarred scalp as she gave the biscuit dough a final knead. Being alone in the house meant Deborah felt free to remove her cap, and she relished that freedom. Though she'd grown quite fond of Levi and Nora in the two months since her marriage, it was still nice to have a quiet day alone with her thoughts.

Nora had adjusted to her new situation smoothly, treating Deborah with affection and minding her as well as a child that age could be expected to. And as Annabelle Brennan had promised, Levi had been instrumental in helping Deborah and Nora get to know one another. He'd encouraged—though not pressed—his young daughter to call Deborah Mama, a title that warmed her heart every time it came through those sweet little lips.

And Levi. Though he was always a man of few words, she found them exchanging more and more as time passed. In the evenings especially, after Nora was in bed, the two of them would sit out on the porch. Sometimes they shared a companionable silence, him with a small repair task or a piece of whittling, and her with a bit of mending or a book. Sometimes they'd talk, the conversation unwinding like yarn on a spindle, slowly and smoothly. And just the other night, she'd said something that made him laugh. Levi's laugh was something to treasure. It shook his whole body, pinked his cheeks, and brightened his eyes. Something curious had happened in her heart as their mirthful eyes met. She wondered if the same thing had happened in his too.

She'd just folded over the scrap dough for another pass with the biscuit cutter when the door opened. With a gasp, she whirled around.

Levi. Standing in the doorway. One hand holding Nora's, the other holding a pie.

"Hullo." He doffed his hat and guided Nora inside, her tiny footsteps thumping on the wooden floor.

"Hi, Mama." The little girl stepped forward and flung her arms around Deborah's skirt.

Levi. And Nora.

What . . . what time was it? Were they truly supposed to be back this early?

All the blood drained from her face. Her neck. It coursed down to coil into an anxious knot in the pit of her stomach, one that had been present since the moment she married Levi.

Here it was. The moment she'd dreaded.

Levi, the man to whom she was tethered for the rest of her days, was seeing her scar.

Even if she stood before him without a stitch of clothing on—something that had yet to happen in this marriage from necessity—she couldn't feel more exposed.

Her heart clogged her throat. What would he think? What would he say?

And why did the whole world seem to hinge on the next words out of his mouth?

"Dorcas Stevens sent one of her famous rhubarb pies as a thank-you for sharing us for the day." He extended the pie to Deborah.

"Oh. That's . . . that's . . . How lovely of her." She took the pie with shaking hands, avoiding her husband's eyes. "You're—I wasn't expecting the two of you back so soon."

Levi hung his hat on the hook. "Many hands make light work."

"I see." Deborah swallowed hard against a suddenly parched mouth. She couldn't just stand here forever, staring awkwardly at Levi, holding the pie. She had to turn around and set it down.

A simple movement, but one which would leave no doubt in her husband's mind as to the severity and savagery of the scalping.

Well, then. Nothing to do now but get it over with.

She squared her shoulders and turned, setting the pie on the table.

Then Nora shrieked.

"Papa! What's wrong with Mama's *head*?"

Nora. She'd almost forgotten her young stepdaughter. When she turned back around, the little girl was clinging to her father's leg, her eyes the size of the pie pan he'd just brought in.

The sight brought a sting to Deborah's eyes and a knife to her heart. She couldn't blame Nora's natural curiosity. But in those big, terrified blue eyes was an echo of every openmouthed stare she'd received. Every cruel taunt. Every child who'd ever backed away in fright from her and Elisabeth.

It had helped some, having Elisabeth by her side to shoulder some of the load, to squeeze her hand in silent acknowledgment that she wasn't alone.

But Elisabeth wasn't here now. Now, it was just Deborah. Deborah and the two people whose opinions she valued far more than she ever could've dreamed.

Levi disentangled his daughter's grip from his pants and crouched to her level, turning her to face him. "That's called a scar, dear one."

Nora cast another wary glance in Deborah's direction. "What's a scar?"

Levi tilted his head and was silent for a moment. "Do you remember last spring when you fell and got an ouchie? Right here?" He lifted the little girl's blue-flowered dress and pointed to a spot on her knee.

Nora nodded.

"Well, the ouchie has healed, and it doesn't pain you anymore, but there's a little pink mark where it used to be. Do you see?"

Nora's hands found the hem of her skirt, and she hiked it up far more than was proper, examining the small joint with critical eyes. "Oh, there. I see it now."

"That's a scar. And that's what's on your mama's head."

"Oh." Nora glanced back toward Deborah, rosebud lips pursed in thought. "Then Mama must have had a very big ouchie."

A grin tugged at Deborah's lips despite everything. "Yes. It was a very big ouchie."

"But it means more than just a big ouchie, Nora." The softness in Levi's voice drew Nora's gaze, along with Deborah's. "It means your mama is a survivor. It means she went through something awful, but God was gracious enough to spare her and bring her into our lives. It means you're being raised by a very strong woman who serves an even stronger God."

What, if anything, Nora said in response, Deborah couldn't hear for the blood rushing into her ears. Never, not once, had she thought of her scar that way. She'd blamed the Lord for taking everything from her, for letting her be so seriously wounded, but in doing so she'd neglected the fact that he had spared her. That for whatever reason, though he'd taken Mama and Josiah and Mary Catherine and Nancy, he'd chosen to leave her and Elisabeth and Papa here on earth.

Levi and Nora were doubtless part of the reason why.

His eyes locked on hers then, and in their blue depths something flickered. It was subtle—so subtle she almost missed it—but clear enough that she didn't.

She'd seen it before. It was the same something that flickered in Isaiah's eyes every time he looked at Elisabeth.

Deborah's breath caught. Could it be? Even now? After he'd seen the thing she'd hidden from him, could it be that the dream of love wasn't dead?

"Papa?" Nora's voice seemed to come from a great distance. "Papa?"

Levi tore his gaze from Deborah's, and she could breathe again.

"Yes?" he answered his daughter.

"Can I go play now?"

He cleared his throat. "Of course. Unless . . . unless your mother needs help with something."

"No." Deborah's voice sounded odd. Rusty. "I'm fine here. She can play."

Nora ran toward the bedroom, strawberry-blond curls bouncing behind her, and Levi reached once again for his hat. "I'd, uh, I'd best get to choring."

He slipped out the door, leaving Deborah in the kitchen, biscuit dough clinging to her hands. Levi. The look in his eyes. She'd never seen that before. And she needed to look at him again. Soon. No, now. She needed to see if what she'd thought was there was actually there, or if her desperate imagination had merely dreamed it.

What would she do if it was the latter?

Oh, but what would she do if it was the former?

Calling quickly to Nora that she was heading for the garden, she brushed off her hands and headed out the door, leaving her bonnet tied to the peg beside it.

Her husband was already halfway to the barn, his long-legged, purposeful stride nearly impossible to keep up with in the best of times. She picked up her skirts and jogged after him.

"Levi."

"Yes?" He turned, mouth open at the speed at which she approached him. "Is everything all right? Did something happen?"

"Yes. No." Her breathing was fast, making words difficult to form, though whether that was from the speed at which she'd approached him or the reason, she couldn't decide. "Everything is fine."

Sandy brows pushed together in the shade of his Stetson. "Then what's the rush?"

Heat crept into her neck. Foolish girl, hurtling outside and scaring her husband half to death, just to ask a question that easily could have waited. But she was already outside, standing bonnetless in the blazing sun, and he had chores to attend to, and pretending she'd run out here for no reason would be even more foolish than stating the reason for which she'd come.

"Just now, in the kitchen, when you said . . . did you mean . . ." The rest of her question lodged in her throat, stuck fast like mud.

The corners of his mouth crept up ever so slightly. "Yes."

"So this . . . my scar . . . it doesn't . . ." Oh, words, words, how could they fail her at such an important moment?

That same something flickered in his eyes again, and her heart flipped. "Deborah."

The tenderness in his voice weakened her knees.

"I've wanted to say this for some time, but I feared you'd find it improper, given the, uh, circumstances of our marriage. But now I think it might be time."

"Say . . . what?" Did she utter the words out loud, or only in her heart? Had he heard them, or had they been a mere whisper?

He gently grasped her hand in his. "I've always found you beautiful, Deborah. Your scar doesn't change that. In fact, that testament of God's faithfulness, of his provision and sustenance through such a horrible event, to me it makes you even more beautiful."

Oh. *Oh.* Love flooded her heart. Nearly swept her feet out from under her. Now she understood the flushed cheeks and the shining eyes, because love for Levi had crowded out everything else. How could she think about anything else when such a beautiful man was looking at her in such a beautiful way, having said the very words her heart most needed to hear?

He looked like he was waiting for a response, and he deserved one, but what response could she give when she was too overwhelmed to speak? *Thank you* seemed so inadequate, but those two perfunctory words were the only two that came to mind.

"Levi, I . . ."

Could he read her mind? He must've seen the words she wanted to say before they even formed, because he'd taken a step closer to her. His eyes traveled over her face, her form, like she was a work of art. Then they locked on her mouth, but before he could move in closer, she'd already stretched up on tiptoe, braced her hands on his broad shoulders, and met his lips with her own.

The kiss was reverent. Gentle. Far more than the perfunctory peck at their wedding ceremony. The tender caress of his lips turned her limbs to liquid. It was the kind of kiss she'd always dreamed of receiving, the kind of kiss she'd wondered if it even existed, or if it did, if it could ever be bestowed on the likes of her. If a man could ever want to kiss her if he'd seen the jagged scar crisscrossing her scalp.

Yet here she was, bareheaded, with the kindest man she'd ever met gently cupping the back of her neck and wiping away twelve years of questions with the gentle movements of his lips on hers.

Yes, this kind of kiss existed.

Yes, it was for her.

Yes, even with her scar. In fact, this kiss was in part because of that scar.

For the first time in all of existence, she was grateful for the scar and to the God who, for unknown reasons, allowed her to receive it.

Because incredibly, improbably . . . Levi Martinson was one of those reasons.

CHAPTER EIGHTEEN

THE TRAFFIC LIGHT turned green, Matt pressed the gas pedal, and his newly repaired Tacoma roared to life. Maybe it would've been a better use of money to just let the insurance company total it out, but this was his truck. His baby. And man, it felt good to be driving it again.

A little odd too, truth be told. Because for the first time since he and Siobhan met, he was in the driver's seat.

She eyed him from the passenger seat with a wry smile. "Happy not to have some blond driving you around all the time anymore?"

"I'm just happy to be driving." He accelerated for a lane change. "Happier still that you're along for the ride."

He glanced her way to gauge her reaction, but he could hazard only a glance. Distracted driving, after all, was what had gotten him into the whole mess with the ankle and the truck and the broken violin. Not his own distracted driving, of course, but it had served as a needed wake-up call anyway.

"So now that you're free from the boot, where shall we celebrate?" she asked. "Pizza? Coffee?"

"Maybe after." He navigated the roundabout at the clock tower in the city's Delano neighborhood, a revitalized collection of shops and restaurants on the west banks of the Arkansas River.

"After what?"

"I dunno. Pool. Axe throwing. Bowling. Take your pick."

Siobhan chuckled, then stilled. "Oh, wait. You're serious."

"Of course I'm serious." He turned into a parking space. "Seems like all we do is sit around in some coffee shop or pizza parlor. Now that I finally ditched that silly walking boot, I need some action."

"So you want to throw axes to celebrate."

"Potentially." He grinned over at her. "What say you?"

She lifted one shoulder. "I'm up for anything that doesn't involve ugly rental shoes. But maybe take it easy on that ankle for a bit?"

She was right. He knew she was right. His ortho doc had said the same thing. But somehow, coming from Siobhan, he felt cared for rather than patronized.

With a sigh, he turned off the ignition. "Okay, if we have to stay on the sedate side, then how about a walk? It's not too bad for February." It truly wasn't. Sunny, mid-50s . . . Chicago wouldn't see this kind of weather until April.

Her cheek dimpled. "Sure, that sounds nice. Especially since I don't have to watch out for your crutches anymore."

"Hey," he replied around a chuckle.

Siobhan gave him a playful shove, and his heart thumped. It kept thumping as he climbed from the truck and locked the doors. It thumped more when he fell into step alongside her. No longer needing room for his crutches, he found himself walking closer to her than ever before. Close enough to catch a whiff of her fresh, clean scent. To see the faint smattering of freckles across the bridge of her nose. The—

Whoa. An uneven patch in the sidewalk snagged the toe of his shoe. He managed to right himself before he wiped out completely, but clearly he needed to focus unless he wanted to be right back in that walking boot.

Siobhan turned those blue eyes—now alarmed—on him. "You all right?"

He grinned. "Maybe you're right about keeping things sedate for a bit."

"I mean, if you really want to fling axes, the place is right here." She gestured to a hanging wooden sign two doors to their right.

"Nah. I'm good with whatever, as long as I'm with you." His thumping heartbeat changed to a roar of blood in his ears. "In fact, no matter what we're doing, when I'm with you, I just . . . don't want to be anywhere else. And when I'm not with you, I—"

"Matt. Stop." She held up a hand.

He stopped, both walking and talking. *Idiot.* Where had that mess of words come from? He and Siobhan were just friends. Okay, yeah, maybe there was a small chance he hadn't meant that in a more-than-friends way. But the certainty in his gut and her avoidance of his gaze signaled the crossing of a line.

A line Siobhan was clearly on the other side of.

She blew out a breath, her eyes on her boots. "Look. It's not that I don't . . . feel the same way about you, okay? That's not it at all."

Wait. He'd crossed the line, and she wanted to cross it with him?

She hadn't, though. She was still hanging back for some reason, and if it wasn't feelings, then what was it?

"Okay." His voice sounded rusty. "Then can I ask you what it is?"

"It's Trace." The words were barely audible.

Matt sought her gaze. "Look, whatever happened with him, it doesn't matter, okay? It doesn't bother me at all, and I—"

"No. Matt, I need to tell you more about what happened." She scuffed her shoe against the sidewalk, then looked up with pain-filled blue eyes. "I need you to let me talk. Because I don't know if I'll ever have this kind of courage again."

His brow furrowed, but he didn't talk. She must've interpreted his silent question, though, because she stepped forward, her gaze locked on his.

"It's not just Trace who looks bad in this story," she said. "I look bad too. Really bad. And I hate that I do, because it'll change your opinion of me, and I don't want it to—all kinds of don't want it to—because I like you. I really, really like you. But—"

"No. No but." Desperation clutched at his chest. "Because I like you too. A lot."

She smiled, slow and sad. "You like who you think I am. But I don't know if you'll like who I really am."

His gut churned. "Okay. Who are you really?"

Long lashes dropped, casting a shadow on her pale cheeks. "I've been asking myself that for a long time." She swallowed hard, then dug in the pocket of her jacket and pulled out her phone. After tapping through it for a few seconds, she held it out to Matt, and he cupped his hand around it to better see the picture on the screen.

It was a photo of a woman.

No. Not just any woman.

It was her.

Barely recognizable, though. Her face was coated with way more makeup than she usually wore, and her hair was brown. Brown and long and curled—none of which it was now. She wore a dress that, though not immodest in any way, was still formfitting.

She looked incredible.

But she didn't look like Siobhan.

"That's you?" He stared at the screen, then at Siobhan.

"*Was* me. At the height of my affair with Trace."

He handed her phone back. "It wasn't an affair."

"Yes it *was*." She jammed the phone back into her pocket. "Because I got to the point that I wanted it just as bad as he did."

Had she told him to stop talking? No reason to worry about that now. He couldn't form words if his life depended on it.

"I . . . never really dated before Trace." She started walking again, her steps slow, her gaze focused on some distant point. "I wasn't popular in school, my only friends were in the orchestra, and the guy I had a crush on all four years of high school friend-zoned me practically on day one. No one ever wanted me. No one pursued me. Everyone just thought I was that weird orch-dork in the UGGs, and I did nothing to dissuade them."

UGGs? Okay, that he could see.

"I loved music, but I didn't love the spotlight, so I majored in business. I took the worship assistant job at Pursuers thinking that'd let me be around music without having to be the center of attention, but one day I was in the zone in the office, and I must've been humming along while Keith—your predecessor—was jamming on his guitar, and he insisted that I start singing on the worship team. I agreed on condition that it was backup only. Not lead."

That he could definitely relate to. That had been his condition at first too.

"But Trace didn't notice me until I started playing violin. He said it was the missing piece to the team. He said it added something we hadn't had before. People in the congregation said the same thing. I'd never had that kind of praise before, Matt, and it was intoxicating. Trace always knew what to say. What to do. Looking back now, I can see there were red flags, but at the time I didn't, because Trace was so good at saying the exact things I needed to hear."

He stuffed his hands into his pockets. "Was that what drew you to him?"

"I thought we had this soul-deep connection. It was like he could read my mind." She broke off with a sigh and a shake of her head. "He made me keep it a secret for almost two months. At least, I think we kept it a secret. Knowing what I know now, it probably wasn't, but at the time I thought nobody knew. Until that one night when we got caught."

His stomach twisted.

"Tyler was the kids' pastor, and he was one of the few people on that staff with any kind of integrity. He didn't understand the protect-Trace-at-all-costs-because-people-are-being-saved mentality of Pursuers." Siobhan's words were bitter, her smile joyless. "He was—very quickly—'called' to a church in Oklahoma, but the damage was done. Rumors had started, and the congregation wanted answers."

A cool gust of wind blew a chunk of blond hair in front of her face, and she brushed it back, the shadows from the branches of a barren tree marring her porcelain complexion. "Trace assured me he could handle it and make the rumors go away. But then someone produced a photo of the two of us. Together. On the couch in his office."

The mental image made Matt shudder.

"Even spinmaster Trace couldn't make that go away, so he came clean. Made a full confession before the congregation. Tears and all. An Oscar-worthy performance." A corner of her mouth lifted in a wry smile. "But then he turned around and blamed the whole thing on me. Right there onstage in front of everyone."

Matt's heart sank. "No."

"Yep. I'd thrown myself at him. I was Potiphar's wife, and he was Joseph, except unlike Joseph he hadn't been strong enough to resist. I was too tempting, too aggressive, too seductive, and he was too weak."

The exact thing Trace had said to him in the office.

"Trace knew I'd dreamed of luthier school, and he made sure I got enough in my severance package to go to a one-year violin repair program in Minnesota. I think he assumed I'd stay up there, but my family's here. My home is here. Pursuers couldn't ruin that. But I didn't want to be . . . that person anymore. I didn't want to be the person who'd been too tempting, too seductive, too—"

"Siobhan." The name burst from his heart through his lips, louder than he intended, but his fury wouldn't allow for silence. "You're not too *anything*. He was manipulating you. Controlling you. Abusing you. It's not your fault."

She blinked in surprise, and he dragged a hand through his hair and pulled in a breath to steady himself. "Sorry. I know I should probably just keep listening. But there's not a word to describe how livid I am on your behalf. I'm so sorry for what he did to you. If he were here right now, I'd lay him out with a single punch. I'm not sure what I'm angrier for—the abuse or the lies."

Siobhan was quiet, her arms folded across her chest, her eyes on the laces of her boots. Was she angry with him? Had he crossed a line somehow? He didn't have the counseling training many pastors did. Had he done something wrong?

God, did I screw this up? I need some wisdom here. Please.

><

Angry. He was angry.

Made sense. She'd been angry for three years.

But he was angry with Trace. Angry at the betrayal. The fact that the man who'd changed his life for the better had changed her life for the worse.

He didn't know the truth, though. Didn't know whose fault it really was.

What would he say if he knew? What would he do?

She didn't want to lose him. She couldn't lose him. Terror tore through her. No. She couldn't lose Matt. He was starting to mean more to her than he ever should—than anyone should. Especially another pastor. Another pastor from Pursuers, for the love. She almost laughed. How stupid could one girl be?

But Matt was different. Wasn't he?

He wasn't Trace.

Or was he?

She thought she knew Trace. She thought she could trust him. But she couldn't.

Or was it herself she couldn't trust?

Maybe column A. Maybe column B. Maybe a previously undiscovered column C? Who knew anymore?

"Siobhan?"

Matt's gentle baritone cut through the storm of her thoughts. Her mouth went dry. She had to tell him.

She might lose him.

But lies had gotten her nowhere in the past. At least now she could hold her head high.

"Matt, you know how most lies have a grain of truth in them?" Her voice sounded like it was coming from a million miles away.

"Yes." She could practically feel the wariness in Matt's voice.

"This one does too." She pulled in a breath, and the words tumbled forth, as though they had been waiting for release. "My first kiss with Trace. The one that led to us having sex on the couch in his office. I initiated that kiss. He wasn't lying about that. So that kiss, and everything it led to . . . it was my fault."

"Oh, Siobhan." It was more sigh than sentence. But she didn't miss the disappointment.

There it was. The ugly reality. Matt was never going to want her now. He would never see her as anything but a harlot. A train wreck. Too far gone. All the things Trace ever said about her, all the things she fought against but somehow had come to accept as true, Matt believed them now. A shame. He was a really great guy. A *really* great guy.

How great a guy could he be, though, if he was going to side with Trace? But who cared? Because whose fault was it really?

Tears stung. It wasn't Trace who would cost her a chance with Matt.

It was her.

"Siobhan." Another sigh, this one shorter and angrier. "Look, I . . . I'm kind of at a loss here. Because you're blaming yourself for things he did to you. He targeted you, he made you trust him, and then he convinced you to let him do more. It doesn't matter who kissed who first when you were being manipulated and controlled. You're a survivor of abuse, Siobhan. Incredibly intimate abuse. And for that reason I'm hesitant to touch you, because I don't want anything to remind you of that. But every atom of my being, everything I have in me, is screaming at me to give you a hug. Would . . . that be all right with you?"

She jerked back. A hug. That was how it started with Trace. Just a hug.

But it wasn't just a hug—it was never just a hug—and now here was another pastor from the same church asking for the same thing.

But . . . Matt asked.

Trace never asked. He took.

Matt *asked*.

He was still asking. He stood at a distance, one arm at his side, the other absently rubbing the back of his neck. He wasn't reaching for her, but he wasn't leaving, either. Hazel eyes swirled with anguish and an ache for nothing more than to comfort her but also a willingness to hold back.

He wanted to hug her. Perhaps he even needed to hug her.

But he was willing to hold back if she said no.

She could say no to Matt, and it wouldn't change anything.

She could say no.

She could trust him.

And that made her want to say yes. A real yes. One she felt entirely free to give. Or not.

Matt was standing there, all earnest and supportive and rock solid and *I'm not going anywhere*, and she wanted—needed—to feel that. Feel the warmth of his arms around her. The sureness of his chest. His support. His strength.

The last man to embrace her was Trace Jessup, and she needed to wash that memory clean and start over fresh.

"Yes," she whispered.

The word was barely out of her mouth before his arms were around her, warm and solid and strong. He smelled clean. Like fresh-scented soap and laundry just out of the dryer. There was a protective fierceness in his hug too, as though if he just held her close enough, he could absorb all the pain out of her body and into his own. She melted into his arms, the breath leaving her lungs in a whoosh. His jacket was rough beneath her fingers. His stubble tickled her cheek.

He was truly *giving* her a hug. This embrace was a gift. He wasn't taking anything from her, and he didn't want anything more. There was no agenda. Nothing other than she was hurting and he cared about her and wanted her to feel better.

It was one of the most precious gifts she'd ever received.

After what felt like both an age and a breath, they parted, and Matt's eyes were wet.

"I'm so sorry, Siobhan." His hands left her shoulders with seeming reluctance. "I'm sorry for all you've been through and for all that people have said about you. But I want you to know something." His gaze turned fierce. "Nothing, absolutely nothing you just said changes how I feel about you. If anything, it makes me feel . . . more that way. Which I'm frankly terrified to tell you, because I don't want you to feel like I'm taking advantage of you."

She felt many things here at the moment, standing on the sidewalk, a cool breeze ruffling her hair, only a couple feet away from the man who'd just given her that delicious, soul-restoring hug. But taken advantage of was nowhere on the list.

"I want a relationship with you," he said. "But I don't want one until you're ready. And if that's never, then that's okay." A brief, nervous smile. "But I'm really, really hoping it's not never."

"It's not going to be never," she blurted. "It . . . it's not right now. But it's not going to be never."

He slumped with relief, a smile shining through, and it was so adorable she could've kissed him. Wanted to kiss him.

No. Not yet. She didn't trust herself yet.

"Good," he said.

"Thank you, Matt." She took his hand. Brushed her thumb over his knuckles.

He swallowed hard, his eyes still shining.

"For a thousand different things, thank you."

"Of course. And thank you," he replied. "I know it wasn't easy to share all that with anyone. I'm honored you chose to share it with me."

"You needed to know. I needed you to know." A small smile burst forth despite everything. "Gotta say, it wasn't as awful as I expected it to be."

He laughed. "Well, I'm glad for that."

It was the laugh that did it. That warm, rich chuckle, low in his chest. She wanted to feel his warmth again. Feel the solid wall of his chest against hers. She wanted physical proof, tangible proof, that he was warm and real and not going anywhere, and that he felt those things for her, and that he was willing to wait for as long as necessary.

"Can I . . . have another hug?" She felt silly for asking, but his arms were around her before she'd even finished the sentence.

"Always," he replied.

Always. Not a concept she was super familiar with. She wanted to cling to him. To tell him, *Hey, y'know what—let's throw caution to the wind and do this thing. Let's have a relationship and see where it goes.*

But she couldn't. Because *see where it goes* left open the possibility that it could go away. That she could destroy his life.

She'd already destroyed hers. No sense dragging him into the wreckage.

Not until she could be confident that she wouldn't make the same mistakes she made with Trace.

But she also never, ever wanted to let Matt go.

Chapter Nineteen

September 1876

"DID YOU FIND what you were looking for?"

Levi's question met Deborah as she stepped from the dimness of the Jamesville General Store onto the wooden sidewalk. One hand clutched a package of fabric, while the other kept a firm grasp on Nora's hand. The little girl had taken to roaming much farther than Deborah was comfortable with. It was one thing at home in familiar surroundings but another thing altogether here.

"I did indeed." Deborah placed her paper-wrapped packages in her husband's outstretched arm, then tucked her hand into the crook of his elbow. The prints she'd chosen would see both herself and Nora safely through another prairie winter, and another would do nicely for a dress for Elisabeth's upcoming nuptials. It cost a bit more than she would've liked, but Levi had headed her worries off at the pass on the way into town, telling her in no uncertain terms that she was to spend however much was necessary to properly outfit both herself and Nora.

She'd had to purchase greater lengths of fabric too, for the dresses she'd sew for herself. Levi didn't know that part yet, though. Deborah was waiting for the perfect moment to share her precious secret.

"Anything of interest at the post office?" Deborah asked above the sound of Nora smacking and sucking the sweet she'd received at the general store.

Levi flicked a glance her way. "As a matter of fact, I had a letter from my brother Nathaniel."

Deborah's brow furrowed slightly. Nathaniel ... which of Levi's brothers was that? Her husband was the seventh of eleven children, and though he'd recited the roll call of his six brothers and four sisters on more than one occasion, Deborah couldn't remember where Nathaniel fell in the order of Martinson siblings.

"Is he the oldest?" she asked.

"Second oldest."

"Ah. And how is he faring?"

A corner of Levi's mouth turned up. "Seems we'll be able to ask him that question in person soon enough. He wrote to tell me he's purchased the Jansen farm."

Deborah gave her husband's elbow a squeeze. "Oh, how wonderful. I'm glad to hear someone finally bought that place. And how lovely for it to be family." The Jansen farm, a formerly prosperous quarter section not far from their own, had fallen into disrepair in recent months following George Jansen's sudden passing. His widow, Aurora, had held on for a time, but the task had proven too great, so she'd opted to sell the land and return with their four children to her hometown in Indiana. Though Deborah would miss the vibrant Aurora, it was a comfort to know the land would be in good hands.

"Yes. Seems to have worked out well."

Levi's uncertain tone drew Deborah's gaze. "Are you not looking forward to having your brother nearby?"

"I am. It's just that I don't know Nathaniel well at all. He's fourteen years my senior and left home when I was about Nora's age." Levi tipped his hat to a passing matron. "He served in the army during the war, I know that. I believe he was a prisoner of the Rebs for a time, but I'm not certain how long. He hasn't had much stability in his life, but the letter says he's recently married and is looking to settle down."

Deborah's heart warmed. "Then I'm even more grateful the two of you will have a chance to get to know each other better. I can't imagine how I would've survived without Elisabeth."

"Yes. It's a good opportunity." He patted her fingertips. "And I, too, am grateful you've had your sister."

"Mama?" Nora tugged on Deborah's skirt, pointing toward a group of children playing near the livery. "May I?"

"Yes, you may." Deborah gave the girl a quick squeeze. "And thank you for asking this time."

Nora ran off, and Deborah watched her, a fond warmth blooming in her heart. "I'm so excited to see what happens with Nora and her brother or sister."

Oh. She stifled a gasp. That . . . wasn't quite the way she'd intended to share the news with Levi.

"Yes." Levi's tone was absent, his gaze fixed on the letter from Nathaniel. "I think she'll make an excellent big sister someday."

Deborah stopped, unable to hide her smile. "It's not . . . someday, Levi."

He lowered the letter slowly. A horse trotted by, its hooves clip-clopping in the dirt. "Are you saying . . ."

"I'm not completely certain yet. But certain enough." Heat crept into her cheeks. "Many of the indicators are there."

He rolled his lower lip between his teeth, his face unreadable as he tucked the letter back into his pocket. "I see."

She frowned up into his now-familiar face, shadowed by his hat. "Are you displeased?"

"No, Deborah. No. Not at all." His tone was urgent, the gentle hand on her upper arm reassuring. "I simply wasn't expecting . . . well, not this soon, at any rate."

She studied the wood-planked sidewalk between her shoes. Though they were now truly one flesh, it was still quite new. Tentative sometimes. An exploration of each other in body, mind, and soul. And they had only known each other a handful of times. For it to have already resulted in new life . . .

"Nor was I, to be honest," she said.

"But make no mistake, my lovely bride." Levi's blue eyes radiated warmth and welcome. "I am very, very pleased to be welcoming a new son or daughter into the world. *Very* pleased." He bent his head and brushed his lips against hers in a chaste but loving kiss.

Joy stung Deborah's eyes. Had she once thought she was settling for Levi Martinson because no other man would have her? Her hand slipped up to his shoulder. Every man in the world could want her, and she would only have eyes for him.

He pulled back, happiness bringing a shine to his eyes and creases to their corners. "I suppose our family will be expanding in all sorts of ways soon, then, yes?"

Deborah leaned into his embrace, her eyes on Nora, laughing and playing with the others. Oh, what a marvelous sister she'd make. And how wonderful for Nathaniel to be joining them soon. She tingled in anticipation of all the important moments they'd share and memories they'd make as a family.

A family.

She had a family.

Deborah's heart filled to bursting. Had she truly thought this plan second best? Had she made the decision to join her life with Levi's, to be his wife, to mother his child, because it was the lesser of two evils?

Oh, how foolish she'd been to doubt God's plan for her life.

Because everything was turning out far better than she ever could've asked or imagined.

CHAPTER TWENTY

"So THAT, MY friend, is how Avery Corrigan's shoe wound up on the roof of the church," Trace said to Matt amid the clink of forks and the quiet hum of conversation in the trendy downtown farm-to-table establishment where the two were eating breakfast.

Across the table, Matt forced a smile. Squeezed out a little laugh. "I never knew that story."

"Neither did I until about two years ago. Heard it when I got back in touch with a couple other Sawgrass youth group grads on Facebook. They were a couple years behind you, I think." Trace dove his fork into a massive bowl of egg whites and vegetables and everything else healthy. "Cade O'Reilly and MacKayla Jones. Did you know they're married now?"

"I didn't. Good for them."

Matt's smile faded as he studied Trace. For a moment—just a moment—it was almost like old times. Just sitting around, having breakfast and shooting the breeze with the man whose influence had saved Matt's life.

But now that knowledge came with an uncomfortable new truth: the man who'd saved Matt's life had also been the one who'd destroyed Siobhan's.

Matt had managed to steer clear of Trace at work, but this morning's breakfast had been, as Trace put it, corporate optional. Something important to discuss, he'd said. So, reluctantly, Matt had agreed.

His emotions had been a roller coaster from the moment he'd spotted Trace's black Jaguar on the street outside the restaurant. Bittersweet nostalgia one minute, a burning anger the next. Utter devastation the next minute, followed by desperate, grasping-at-straws hope that maybe it wasn't really as bad as Siobhan had said.

Maybe that conversation with her the other day hadn't actually happened.

Maybe it had all been a dream.

But the unmistakable scent of Siobhan's perfume still clung to Matt's coat, draped on the chair beside him. So their fierce, lingering hug—the memory of which had kept him tossing and turning the last two nights—really happened.

And if that hug had happened, then the rest of it had too.

But so had everything Trace had done for Matt in his younger years. And reconciling the two dramatically different sides of his mentor had been the other reason he hadn't slept much.

Weariness made him reach for his freshly refilled mug of coffee. Maybe he could keep Trace talking about their Sawgrass days. Painful though those memories were now, their conversation was safest kept planted in the past.

Please, God. Don't let him mention her. Because I have no idea what I'll do if he does.

Trace sipped his own coffee, then returned the mug to the wooden table. "All right, my brother. Down to business."

Matt cast a wary glance across the table. "What kind of business?"

"Accountability business. It's our first monthly accountability meeting."

Matt frowned. "Did I miss something in a staff meeting? Did we discuss this?"

"Nope." Trace dabbed his mouth with a napkin. "It's a brand-new thing the Executive Team came up with. It's on the agenda for the meeting tomorrow, but I figured you and I could get the ball rolling a day early."

Water splashed into Matt's glass, courtesy of the server. He thanked her, then turned back to Trace with a healthy dose of suspicion. "How's this going to work?"

Trace dug his fork in for another bite. "Basically, we as a pastoral staff are going to be intentional and proactive about holding one another accountable to living according to Jesus's standards. I'm going to emphasize accountability partnerships in a sermon series this summer, so this is a chance for us as pastors to model it for the congregation so they'll be more likely to do it themselves."

"You and I are accountability partners, then?" Matt reached for his coffee.

"Exactly."

"And we meet once a month to check in with each other? Ask the tough questions and make sure we're both on the straight and narrow?" He pondered his steaming cup of dark roast. Maybe this could be a good thing. Maybe this was God's way of providing Matt an opportunity to make sure Trace was keeping his personal life aboveboard. Maybe he could even ask point-blank if anything was going on with Kayleigh. Maybe it'd be a chance to—

"Well. Kind of." Trace's words knifed through Matt's hastily assembled plan. "I'm asking you questions. But you don't ask me."

"I'm sorry?" Matt straightened, his coffee halfway to his lips. "How's that a partnership if I can't ask you the same kinds of things you ask me?"

Trace tilted his head to the side. "I'll level with you, Matty. As much as I love you, and as much as I'm willing to be an open book with you, I'm your boss. We're not equal partners here. I'll be accountable to another of the senior pastors. He'll ask me the same sorts of questions I'm about to ask you."

I'll bet you this entire breakfast it's your yes-man, Jerry. The uncharitable thought set Matt even more on edge than he already was.

"Then why didn't you pair me with someone who's not my boss?" he asked.

"I figured you'd probably be more comfortable with me, given that you barely know everyone else." Trace leaned closer, his gaze earnest. "Matt, I promise the questions I've told Jerry to ask me are tailored to me and my sin patterns, my areas of weakness. They're much, much tougher than anything I'll ever ask you. After all, like it says in James three, we who teach the Word will be judged more strictly."

The hypocrisy was dripping as much as the syrup Matt had slathered over his stack of pancakes. Pancakes that seemed fluffy and delicious a moment ago. Now they just tasted like cotton balls.

"All right, Trace. Ask away. I've got nothing to hide." *Unlike you.* He barely kept the bitter words in.

Trace's face lit like a neon sign. "Good. Glad you're on board."

Did Matt really have a choice?

"How's your walk with the Lord, Matt?"

Awkwardness clawed at his gut. "Good as ever."

"Fantastic," Trace replied. "Can you elaborate?"

"Well, I'm in the Word first thing every morning." Matt floundered for answers that were both honest and worded in such a way to get Trace to back off. "Like you always said back at Sawgrass, pray before you pick up your phone. I feel like I pray throughout the day too, not just in the morning. I try to keep God in mind with everything I do. Not sure how successful I am at it, but I try."

Trace's smile slid across his face. "Great, Matt. That's wonderful to hear. I'm proud of you."

Matt's heart gave a jolt. *I'm proud of you.* Those words got him every time. Even this time. Despite everything. He hated that.

"What about your online life?" Trace pressed. "Would you say you spend more time with Jesus or with your Facebook friends?"

Matt shrugged. "Honestly, it depends on the day. I try not to be on there too much, but some days I fall down the rabbit hole."

"Same's true for all of us, I suspect." Trace offered a sympathetic smile. "But this might be a growth area for you. What would you think about setting a goal to spend ten minutes less on social media each day, and replace it with ten more minutes in the Bible?"

"Sure. I can do that." Seemed easy enough, anyway.

"What about, y'know, the rest of the World Wide Web?" Trace's voice was low but intense. "You looking at anything you shouldn't be?"

"No, sir." Matt straightened in his chair. "Haven't since I got saved."

"Excellent. Keep it up." Their server slid the check onto the table, and Trace picked it up and gave it a look.

Matt reached for his phone. "What's my share, Captain? I'll Venmo you."

Trace waved a hand. "No, no, put that away. I got it."

"You sure?"

"Absolutely." He slid a credit card from his wallet and tucked it beneath the check.

"So is that it for the accountability?" Matt asked.

"Just one more question." Trace hesitated a moment, then leveled Matt with that steely gaze. "How's your offline social life?"

Matt shrugged. "Fine."

"You making friends?"

His pancake-filled stomach grew unsettled. "Yes. I'm settling in quite well."

"Anyone more than that to you?"

He set his fork down with more force than he intended. "Respectfully, Trace, if you want to ask me about Siobhan, just come out and ask."

"All right." Trace straightened in his chair, his gaze devoid of all humor. "What's going on with you and Siobhan?"

"We're friends." Never mind how her embrace shot electricity through his whole body. Never mind how having her in his arms, molding his body to hers, brought a deep clarity that this was right and good and exactly as it should be. That in her arms was the only place he ever wanted to be.

Technically, given that Siobhan had told him she wasn't ready to be more than friends, he was still giving an honest answer.

But Trace's tilted head indicated he wasn't buying it. "Just friends?"

"Yes." The answer was firm. "Just friends." *Until she's ready for more.*

Trace leaned back and laced his arms behind his head. "I'm in a little bit of an awkward spot, Matt. I mean, I'm not going to tell you who to be friends with, but it does make things a bit uncomfortable, you having her in your life. That woman nearly tore our church apart. It was by God's grace alone that we survived."

The simmer of irritation turned to a boil, spitting and splashing and hissing on the burner. It wasn't her fault. But because of Trace's lies and manipulation, she believed it was. And that was the worst part of all.

Matt's jaw tightened. His fist clenched on his lap. "It was by God's grace alone that she survived too."

"What? I can't believe you're falling for this." Trace's voice reached a timbre Matt had never heard before. "Siobhan Walsh is a liar, and she—"

"Whoa." Matt held up both hands. "Stop right there. You're my boss, and I get that, but I won't have you speak about my friend that way. I believe her."

Trace eyed Matt with nothing short of sympathy. "Oh, Matty. She got to you. Gotta admit she's good. The woman is an expert."

Was Trace so deep in his own delusion that he genuinely believed his version was correct?

Trace must've sensed Matt's hesitation, because he leaned closer, eyes pleading. "C'mon, Matty. It's me. You've known me over half your life. In fact, who's been part of your life—consistently—longer than I have, hmm? Who let you sleep in his guest room when you didn't have anywhere else to call home? Who's been there for you time and again when no one else was?"

Matt dragged a hand through his hair. "That's all true, Trace, and I appreciate it more than you know. I'm grateful for all you've done. Nothing's ever gonna change that."

Relief softened Trace's features. "Good."

"But I'm really not comfortable being between you and Siobhan. Whatever happened is in the past. It's forgiven by the blood of Jesus, and I'm just trying to move forward and settle into my new job and be the best follower and representative of Christ that I can possibly be."

"Then you need to leave Siobhan in the dust." Trace jabbed the table with a forefinger. "Trust me, Matty—she'll only hold you back."

Matt drew back. "I'm sorry—did I miss something in my contract that dictates who I'm allowed to be friends with?"

"Not at all. But who you're friends with is an excellent indicator of how trustworthy you are. How invested you are in the mission of Jesus. And in turn, what level of responsibility you'll carry at Pursuers."

Matt scooted his chair back from the table. "Are you threatening me? Threatening my job?"

"No, Matt. By no means." Trace scrawled his name across the credit card slip. "But Jesus is moving in our church. He's moving mightily. Week after week people are coming to him left and right. And either you're going to be on board with what we're doing—and how we're doing it—or you're going to find yourself run over. And spending time with Siobhan? That's an excellent way to get run over."

CHAPTER TWENTY-ONE

October 1876

"THOSE BISCUITS LOOK divine."

Deborah turned away from the batch of biscuits she'd just pulled from the stove and beamed at the praise of her sister-in-law, Nathaniel's wife. Maggie was right. They did look divine.

"Thank you kindly. And they'll be even better with some of that delicious blackberry jam you brought."

Maggie waved a hand, wisps of red hair dancing around her face. "Oh, it's nothing, Deborah. I'll teach you to make it." Hazel eyes turned conspiratorial. "That is, if you'll teach me the secret of those biscuits."

Deborah smiled. "I'd like that."

So this was what it was like to have a sister-in-law. Maggie Martinson was pleasant, with pink cheeks, a kind smile, and a penchant for witty observations that had already made Deborah laugh more than once. Here on the frontier, connections were vital, and Deborah was grateful to have made one with Nathaniel's wife, particularly since Maggie had some experience delivering babies. Although Deborah was planning to have the doc assist her in bringing her son or daughter into the world, babies came on their own timetable, and there was only one Dr. Maxwell. Having Maggie nearby eased Deborah's mind on that front.

Like she and Levi, Maggie and Nathaniel had married mostly out of necessity when Maggie's first husband, John, had been thrown from a spooked horse. Maggie, a young widow with two children, and Nathaniel, the town's lone bachelor, had married two years ago, and now the family had come here to Sedgwick County. Though Deborah hadn't seen

Maggie and Nathaniel interact much yet, the glow in Maggie's eyes told Deborah that she and her husband had bonded just like Deborah and Levi had.

The door creaked open, and here came the men now, dusting off their hats and laughing at a shared joke. The brothers, practically strangers before Nathaniel's arrival two weeks prior, seemed to have gotten well acquainted. Though Levi was a couple inches taller than Nathaniel, the brothers shared similar facial features. The same straight, longish nose, the same angular face, the same lanky build. But where Levi's hair was sandy and his eyes a pale blue, Nathaniel's hair was deep brown, almost black, and his eyes a piercing sapphire. He bore an odd scar on his wrist, and he parsed his words even more than his brother did.

Levi hung his hat on the hook beside the door and crossed the small kitchen to kiss Deborah's cheek. "Everything looks and smells wonderful."

Deborah stirred the pot of beans on the stove. "Thank you."

Levi leaned in, low and close to her ear. "And the food does too."

Deborah gasped and turned toward the mischievous grin of her husband. "Levi!"

Chuckling, he went off toward the small sitting room, where Nora played with Maggie's two children, nine-year-old Benjamin and six-year-old Kathleen.

Within moments everyone was gathered around the table. There wasn't much elbow room, but food was plentiful and the company in good spirits. Deborah glanced into the freckled faces of her niece and nephew and at her stepdaughter's red-blond curls, and her heart filled to near bursting. None of these people were her blood, yet all of them were her family. It was as though God had indeed restored the years the locusts had eaten.

As Levi bowed his head and blessed the food, adding special thanks for bringing Nathaniel and Maggie and their family safely to Sedgwick County, Deborah caressed his calloused fingertips and marveled at God's provision in her life. At the blessings he'd poured out on her, finally and at last.

When the prayer finished, Deborah speared a chicken drumstick with her fork and cut it into bite-sized pieces with her knife. "Here, Nora."

A breeze from the open window rushed in to cool her forehead, but then the breeze did much more—it ripped the knit cap from her head and tossed it toward the wall behind her.

"Oh. Pardon me." Deborah stood, the chair scraping against the floorboard, and bent to retrieve her cap.

That was when she heard the gasp.

"Kathleen," came Maggie's sharp voice. "Manners."

"I'm sorry, Mrs. Martinson." The chastened child fastened her gaze on her lap.

"As am I." Maggie's pale skin flushed pink. "Clearly my etiquette lessons need some work."

Deborah replaced the cap, her own cheeks warm. "Don't think a thing in the world of it. It's an old injury. An attack by Sioux warriors when I was very young." It was the standard explanation she gave to horrified strangers, but since marrying Levi, the explanation was much less embarrassing and awkward. No longer did she shy away from her disfigurement. It wasn't something she sought to put on display, of course, but Levi's love and care had softened her heart and boosted her confidence.

She glanced from one curious pair of eyes to the other. "If you have questions, you may ask."

Benjamin's eyes were wide with curiosity. "How old were you?"

"I was seven." Deborah reached for the dish of Maggie's blackberry jam. "Not much younger than you are now."

"Does it still hurt?" Kathleen's voice was small and timid.

Deborah slathered jam on her biscuit. "I get headaches from time to time." Her tone belied the excruciating pain she sometimes found herself in. Mercifully, she hadn't had a headache since marrying Levi, but she'd have one soon enough. They always seemed to worsen in cold weather. Dread knotted her stomach at the thought, but she ordered it away. Things were fine now. All was well. "Other than that, no."

Maggie's face paled. "Did that happen here?"

"Not here in Sedgwick County, no. It happened while we were traveling here, a little to our north." She hastened to reassure her new sister-in-law. "Besides, it was twelve years ago. The Natives who lived in the area then are mostly gone now, and the ones who remain mostly keep to themselves. We've never had a problem at all. It's very safe."

"Good." Maggie reached for another biscuit. Beside her, Nathaniel's face had paled. His gaze was fastened firmly on his plate.

"Do you remember the attack?" Benjamin again.

The crisp spring morning, where nothing in the world seemed wrong. The running footsteps. The terrified screams. Then the tug of her hair, the flash of the knife . . .

"Yes." She cut off her memories with a single syllable, ordering them back into the box where she kept them. That was in the past. It was over.

And yet it wasn't. She'd suffer the effects of that attack for the rest of her days.

Levi shot her a brief, concerned glance. "All right, let's switch the conversation to something else. We all have scars and wounds. All of us. Some of those are more obvious than others. But it's important to remember that everyone who bears a scar is a survivor, a victor over the thing that hurt them."

Maggie nodded in his direction. "Well said, Levi."

"Thank you." The two simple syllables couldn't begin to convey Deborah's gratitude, but Levi's gentle smile told her he'd received the deeper meaning.

Deborah smiled brightly at the group—her family—and hefted the bowl of mashed potatoes. "Would anyone like some more?"

Benjamin's small face brightened. "I would, ma'am."

"Aunt Deborah will do just fine." She passed him the bowl. As she did, her gaze slid to Nathaniel. He looked no better despite the change in conversation topic. His hands shook. His effort to avoid making eye contact was obvious.

Had he suffered something similar? Levi had said Nathaniel had been a prisoner of war. Or did her wounds simply make him squeamish?

Either reaction was understandable. And in the past his obvious discomfort at being around her might have been bothersome. But on this night, safe and secure in Levi's love, the arrow that would have once pierced her heart now bounced off its surface and clattered harmlessly to the floor. Levi had modeled for his family how she was to be treated. He'd gone over and above to reassure her that he found her beautiful, and as a result her love for him grew deeper every day. It must've taken time for him to get used to her disfigurement, no doubt, but thanks to his devotion, for the very first time, she wasn't letting it define her. He had given her the strength, the confidence, to handle whatever reaction came from others.

Levi had grown accustomed to her injury. She was certain that, in time, his brother would too.

CHAPTER TWENTY-TWO

"SIOBHAN?"

Ian's form in the doorway appeared nearly indistinguishable through Siobhan's magnifying headset. "What's up, Ian?"

"There's someone here to see you." Blurry Ian motioned toward the doorway. "Dark hair, has a baby, says she's your sister."

Smiling, Siobhan removed her headset. "Sure, send her on back."

A moment later, Sloane appeared. Brown eyes glimmered behind her glasses, a smile danced around her lips, and a sleeping Domenica lay nestled in a flowered sling.

Siobhan rose from her workbench, gave Sloane a gentle hug, and caressed Domenica's fuzzy dark head. "You look excited."

"This little lady slept through the night last night," Sloane enthused. "It's amazing what a few hours of uninterrupted sleep will do for a person."

"Good for you, my dear." Siobhan laid a gentle kiss on her niece's forehead. "Keep it up, okay? Your mama needs sleep."

"Sleep isn't the only reason I'm excited." Sloane's gaze fell on the violin, which lay disassembled on the workbench. She gave a quiet gasp. "Wait, is that *the* violin?"

"It is. It's seen better days, but I promise I'm getting there." She glanced up at Sloane. "Okay, you've basically turned into a human heart-eyes emoji. I'm guessing this means the violin and your excitement are connected?"

"Indeed they are. I did some digging on John Caldwell. It turns out the attack was quite brutal."

Siobhan blinked. "Oh?"

"Yes. Apparently John and his family were part of a wagon train heading west, and the party was attacked by Sioux warriors. John was off hunting at the time with most of the rest of the men, so they all survived. But his wife and kids were attacked. The wife and three of the children died, but two daughters survived. Everyone was scalped."

"Gahhh." Siobhan's hand flew to her mouth. "Scalped? And they *survived*?"

"It was rare, but it did happen. I knew of one other scalping survivor—a guy named Robert McGee—who was attacked in the 1860s. He made a career out of public appearances and for a while was believed to be the only person who ever survived a scalping."

Siobhan's skin crawled. "Can we stop talking about scalps?"

"Only one more mention of the word—promise—but it'll be worth it." Sloane pulled her phone from her pocket. "I tracked down an obituary for one of the daughters." She tapped the screen a couple times, then held it out for Siobhan.

Siobhan took the phone and read the obituary aloud. "'Deborah Caldwell Martinson, widow of Levi Martinson, departed this life Thursday last at the home of her son Bartholomew in Harper County, Kansas, where she had resided since her husband's death in 1914. Deborah was born in Miami County, Ohio, in 1857, but moved to Kansas with her family as a young girl. She married Levi Martinson in 1876, and to this union were born five children, one of whom preceded her to heaven. Mrs. Martinson is known for surviving a vicious tomahawk attack when only a child but recovered and served the Lord as a faithful Christian until he called her home and granted her a new body free of disease and blemish.'"

At the list of survivors and funeral information, Siobhan stopped reading and returned the phone to Sloane. "That's pretty impressive. Do we know any more than that?"

Sloane tapped the screen. "Sometimes this site has some information. I had planned to do some more research during Little Miss's four-o'clock feeding, but since she slept right through it, I didn't get the chance."

"You're probably not sad about that," Siobhan replied, then frowned. "Wait, you actually might be."

Sloane looked up and grinned. "Normally, yes, but sleep conquers all right now."

Turning back to her phone, she tapped the screen, then gasped. "Oh look, there's Deborah's gravesite."

Siobhan craned her neck to better examine the photo of a simple gray headstone engraved with the woman's name and dates. But . . . wait . . . did that say . . .

"If Deborah died in Harper County, then why's she buried here?"

"*Here*?" Sloane drew closer.

"Sedgwick County. Jamesville, actually. Isn't that up by the farmhouse?"

"*What*? Give me that." Sloane grabbed her phone back, then clicked through to Levi's page on the same site. "Levi died eight years before Deborah did. When he passed away, they were living in Jamesville. His obituary said they'd been there a number of years."

"Wow." Siobhan took in the tiny text. "Wonder if they knew Mom's family back in the day."

Sloane's dark eyes widened. "Okay, clearly one night of sleep isn't enough to make up for the last three months, because that literally did not occur to me until just now." She gasped again. "I wonder if Annabelle mentioned Deborah in any of her diaries."

Siobhan grinned. "You mean you don't have those things memorized?"

Sloane gave a good-natured roll of her eyes and tucked her phone into a pocket in the diaper bag. "Shockingly, no. And I haven't read them in a while. If Deborah was mentioned, I don't think she was a major player, but I also wasn't really looking for that specific information."

Siobhan smiled. "Looks like you've got some new research to occupy your non-baby hours."

Sloane wiggled her eyebrows. "There's almost nothing I love more than research."

⤞⤝

November 1876

Fiddled strains of "Amazing Grace" underpinned the chaos in the kitchen as Deborah pulled the turkey from the oven. Levi had hunted it just that morning—a divine provision on this special day. To her left, Papa's new wife, Abigail, helped Nora peel carrots, while to her right, Elisabeth mashed potatoes, her cheeks flushed with the warmth of the stove.

Deborah wasn't used to having this many helpers in the kitchen. This many bodies in her home. But on this, her first Thanksgiving Day as a married woman, there was ample room in her heart for all of them.

Papa had always insisted on a proper Thanksgiving celebration since President Lincoln's declaration of the holiday back in '63, and that very first celebration back home in Ohio would've stuck in her mind even if it hadn't been for the circumstances surrounding it. Mama, whole and healthy and alive, her belly large with the presence of baby Nancy. Mary Catherine and Josiah, both blond, blue-eyed cherubs, to her right, while she and Elisabeth sat on Mama's left. And Papa at the head of the table, brimming with excitement for their new life in Sedgwick County.

"Just think, girls," Mama had said, Papa's enthusiasm reflected in her warm brown eyes. "Next Thanksgiving Day, we'll be at our new home."

"With one more mouth to feed," Papa had added, the twang of his out-of-tune fiddle punctuating the words as he turned the tuning pegs. But the joy in his voice belied his severity—he was looking forward to meeting the new little one as much as any of them were.

That day, as Papa lifted his bow to play and they raised their voices in song, it seemed nothing could ever go wrong. That God would protect and preserve them, that a year from then they'd be settled in a house just like that one, in a new part of the country, helping spread the gospel to the Kansas frontier.

But God hadn't.

The next Thanksgiving had passed with no feasting and little fanfare. Elisabeth and Deborah were still largely bedridden from their wounds, and Papa had been so busy caring for both them and his fledgling congregation that the holiday had scarcely been mentioned. The cabin was cold. Quiet. Nothing at all like she'd pictured it.

Little by little, though, they'd crawled back to life, and their family had expanded to be even larger than it had at first. Her little house would be cozy—dare she say even crowded—but it didn't bother Deborah a bit. For the first time since that too-good-to-last Thanksgiving Day of 1863, it would be more than just Papa, Elisabeth, and Deborah at the table.

A sharp gasp to her left drew Deborah's attention. Elisabeth's hand had flown to her cap-covered head.

Deborah put an arm around Elisabeth. "Another of your headaches?" Elisabeth's had always been more frequent and more severe than Deborah's.

"I'll be fine." But the weak smile, the pale complexion, didn't match her confident words.

Deborah pulled a chair from the table. "Sit. Rest. I'll bring you some water."

Elisabeth waved a hand. "Dr. Maxwell says it's nothing to worry about."

Deborah pulled up short. "You've been to Dr. Maxwell for these? Recently? Are they getting worse?"

"Just a precaution, Bee." Elisabeth's normally quiet voice raised in volume, the closest her sister ever got to expressing irritation. "I wanted to make certain all was well before the wedding."

"Elisabeth."

Her eyes flashed. "All right. I've been having them a bit more frequently than I used to. No worse, just more frequent. Dr. Maxwell believes it's stress from the upcoming nuptials, as well as the weather. I've always had worse headaches as the weather turns colder, and so have you."

The anxious knot in Deborah's chest loosened a fraction. Dr. Stephen Maxwell had shepherded this little prairie community through a wide variety of ailments, dating back to even before Deborah and her family had arrived in the county. His steady, reassuring demeanor and expert touch had calmed many an anxious settler, including Deborah herself several times.

"Are you eating enough?" Deborah eyed her sister with concern. "You know how you get when your mind is occupied with other things."

"Yes." Elisabeth returned her potato masher to the bowl. "Especially after today."

"All right." Deborah conceded the argument with a grin. "If you're eating enough, and if Dr. Maxwell's not worried, then I suppose neither am I."

"All he said was that he'd like me to rest more, but I told him that could wait until after the wedding." Her smile cleared away the remnants of their argument. "We had a good laugh over that."

If the good doctor was laughing, then he truly wasn't concerned, but Deborah still whispered a prayer for Elisabeth as she handed the butter to Nora to put at the center of the table.

Cool air burst in at her back, and she turned. Nathaniel and Maggie had arrived, followed shortly by Levi, who greeted her with a peck on the cheek, his lips refreshingly cold against her overwarm skin. Levi scooped up Nora and kissed the top of her head.

A flurry of introductions followed when Papa came in from the parlor, violin in hand.

"Nathaniel, this is my sister, Elisabeth, and her husband-to-be, Isaiah." Deborah indicated the pair. "This is Levi's older brother, Nathaniel, and his wife, Maggie."

Elisabeth stepped forward with a gracious smile. "It's lovely to meet you both, especially since I've heard so many good things from Deborah and Levi, and it's wonderful that you've been able to move closer to family."

"Yes. Family." Nathaniel's voice sounded stiff, and an odd, indecipherable expression had taken up permanent residence. He stepped back, avoiding eye contact with everyone, Elisabeth in particular. His eyes had gone a deep, stony blue, and his jaw seemed carved out of limestone. It was the same odd reaction he'd given Deborah last month when they'd first met.

Perhaps Nathaniel was uncomfortable around groups? Or people he didn't know well? She'd ask Levi about it later.

"Oh, what a lovely fiddle, Pastor Caldwell," Maggie enthused. "I've seen you play it at Sunday meetings, but I've never had a chance to view it up close. Isn't it lovely, Nathaniel?"

Nathaniel eyed Papa's fiddle as though it were a coiled rattlesnake. Were musical instruments something else that bothered her new brother-in-law? "Quite."

"Thank you kindly." Smiling, Papa tightened the small screw on the bottom of the bow. "It's been with me a long time, and we've been through quite a lot together."

"I think everything's ready, Papa," Elisabeth called from the kitchen.

"And it smells absolutely delightful, my dear," Papa replied. "But before we eat, shall we sing a blessing?"

The tightly packed assembly nodded, and Papa lifted the violin to his chin.

Praise God from Whom all blessings flow;
Praise Him all creatures here below;

A rustling at Deborah's back drew her attention as she sang. A deep masculine voice murmured an apology, though no one else seemed to notice.

Praise Him above ye heavenly host;
Praise Father, Son, and Holy Ghost.

The song still rang in the close air as the door opened and Nathaniel slipped from the cabin without a backward glance.

Chapter Twenty-Three

THE AXE LEFT Matt's hand, arced through the twelve feet between the line and the board, and thwacked into the target. Not quite a bull's-eye, but given where some of his previous throws had landed, he'd take it.

"Nice shot." Siobhan congratulated him with a raise of her glass.

"Thanks." It was a nice shot. But was it nice enough? That was the existential question. Truth be told, he didn't mind too much if Siobhan won. His ankle was healed enough for them to finally do something more adventurous than sitting around in coffee shops or strolling past the axe-throwing place. They weren't really keeping score, either. At least, not on the outside.

But on the inside, Matt's competitive urge was indeed keeping score. And he had this thing in the bag—unless her last shot was better than his.

Siobhan raised the axe above her head—the two-handed grip she'd been using all evening and which had served her rather well—then blew out a breath and let the axe fly.

It wasn't quite a bull's-eye, either. But it was a couple inches closer to the center than his.

Crap. She'd beaten him.

"Yes!" She pumped a fist in victory as she strode toward the target to retrieve her axe, and he tossed her a wry grin.

"Thought you said we weren't keeping score."

"Maybe *we* weren't." She yanked the axe from the board and turned around with a triumphant smile. "But *I* was."

"I was too." He reached for his Dr Pepper.

Siobhan set her axe aside and slid into the seat across from him. "Shall we not keep score next round too?"

"Sounds like a plan." He sipped from his glass, then set it back down on the wooden table. "Hey, changing the subject. You free Friday night?"

A coy expression flashed from beneath her long lashes. "Might be. Feel like letting me kick your butt at axe throwing again?"

"Hey," he protested with a chuckle, indicating his ankle. "I'm out of shape."

The contention was partially true, at any rate. He'd been able to maintain his upper-body workouts while rehabbing his ankle. And there was at least a small chance he was flexing his bicep as he put his drink on the table. Another small chance she was noticing, if the direction of her gaze and the curve of her lips were any indication.

His heart soared even as his mind gave that heart a swift kick. *Friends, Matt. Just friends just friends just friends.* She wasn't ready for anything beyond . . . whatever this was. And there wasn't much reason to push the envelope. Not when they were both enjoying it this much.

"Excuses, excuses." The ice in her glass clinked as she polished off the last of her drink. "What's Friday?"

"Couple buddies of mine and I are putting on a night of worship."

Her right eyebrow shot up. "Night of worship?"

His heart sank at her defensiveness. "Yeah. But it's not at church. We're playing at Frontier Coffee. Figured that might be more comfortable for you?"

"Maybe." Her lower lip slid between her teeth. "It's with Pursuers people, though, right?"

"Nope. It's mostly guys from Westlawn Community. I met their worship pastor at a conference last summer, and we jammed until super late one night. We always joked that if we were ever in the same town, we'd have to do a worship night together, and here we are."

"I see." She studied her empty glass as though it contained a secret formula for turning Diet Coke into plutonium instead of some melting ice cubes and watered-down club soda. "Nobody from Pursuers, then."

"Nope. That's why I decided to invite you to this." His heart hammered in his throat, and he lowered his voice. "There's no chance Trace will be there."

She flashed a guarded glance. "None whatsoever?"

"Nope. He'll be in Florida on a leadership retreat."

"I appreciate you thinking of that." Her voice was barely above a whisper.

"Sure. I know anything to do with Pursuers—other than me, thankfully—is a nonstarter for you. Which I get. Believe me." He punctuated his contention with emphatic hand gestures. "I won't ask you to do that."

"But you're asking me to do this."

"I'm inviting you to do it." *And really hoping you'll say yes.*

"You know I don't do church. Or anything that even smells like church." Her voice had taken on an icy quality. "I told you that the day we met. And just because you and I are . . ." Her right hand gestured back and forth between the two of them.

"We're . . ." He was simultaneously hopeful and terrified about how she'd finish that sentence.

"Friends," she finally said, in a tone that meant anything but, "doesn't mean that's changed."

His heart sank further. "Yeah. I . . . I get it."

Her hand landed atop his, cool and slightly damp from her glass, and her eyes pled with him to understand. "When church is at its best, there's absolutely nothing in the world like it. But when it's bad, it puts you through the meat grinder. And I can't go through that again."

He nodded, heart aching. "I can't fathom how badly they hurt you. But this . . . this isn't that. It's not those people. It's not even the same music. The Westlawn guys mostly picked the songs, but I double-checked the set list to make sure none of them are things you'd have done at Pursuers."

Siobhan studied him, her expression unreadable. "You want me to come that badly?"

"Well, yeah," he admitted. "Because you've never heard me play. And that's a huge part of who I am, and it's something I really want to share with you. So it would mean the world to me if you'd come."

She tilted her head, and a nervous chuckle escaped him.

"Guess my plan to play it cool kinda backfired, didn't it?" he said.

A slight smile lightened the moment. "It's okay. You're cute when you beg."

"I'm not begging *yet*." But he would if he had to.

"Okay." Siobhan nodded, glass in hand. "How about I tell you I'll think about it. No begging required."

"Phew." Matt pantomimed wiping his forehead but was surprised to see a sheen of actual sweat on the back of his hand when he pulled it away. "I'll remember this kindness, Siobhan. Truly."

"See that you do." She tossed back the ice, crunched it between her teeth, then set down the glass with a thunk. "All right, Buchanan. I'm in a butt-kicking mood again." She retrieved her axe and strode toward the starting line.

He had his work cut out for him, all right. And not just with the axes.

His heart ached at how far from God she was. He knew he might never get her in the door of a church, but if he could just bring her back in touch with authentic believers, with a community that didn't bring up painful memories, with folks who'd love her just the way she was, then maybe she'd let God heal her heart. That was the pastor in him.

The man in him? The man whose feelings for her were far beyond what they should be? He wanted to get her in that door too. Because if he couldn't share music with her, if he couldn't share faith with her, then there was a line beyond which the friendship couldn't responsibly go. A line his irresponsible heart was already past. And the further it got, the more shattered his heart would be when things reached a potentially devastating end.

The pastor and the man were both worried for Siobhan, for entirely different reasons.

And God help him, he wasn't sure which version of himself was more worried.

>✦<

The next afternoon, Siobhan set down her file and blew the dust off the small football-shaped piece of spruce she'd been working on for the past two hours. This was the trickiest part of repairing a post crack—fitting the patch precisely to the instrument.

She wedged the patch into the spot she'd planed from the back of Matt's violin and filled in with chalk so she'd know when she'd achieved a precise fit. "Come on," she said softly. "Work this time."

Still not a precise fit. "Crap." More planing necessary.

"Everything all right over there?" Ian's clipped tone cut through the rasp of sandpaper from the opposite side of the workshop.

"Yes. No. I don't know." The strands of hair that had escaped her ponytail puffed up with her sigh. "It's this patch for the post crack."

"Patches are always the most painstaking part." Ian paused in his sanding. "Would you like some help?"

"Honestly, no."

"I see." Ian regarded her over the rims of his reading glasses. "Then would you prefer to continue struggling on your own for several hours? Or would you like someone with a bit more experience to come alongside you and give you some tips?"

Siobhan cracked a smile, her shoulders lowering a fraction. "Well, when you put it like that . . ."

Ian made his way to Siobhan's workbench, his shadow falling across the surface littered with wood shavings and tools. "You're making progress, even though it may not feel like it."

Siobhan leaned back in her chair, rolling her shoulders to relieve some of the tension the work had caused. "Wouldn't be so sure about that."

Ian examined her handiwork, the tiny patch rotating back and forth in his weathered fingertips. "A little more on the left. See how the chalk isn't quite picking up there?" Ian picked up the file and gave it a few smooth, practiced strokes, then fit the patch back in and pulled it out. "See? Looks just about ready."

Siobhan eyed the smooth wooden surface, now evenly coated with chalk dust and ready for glue. "How did you *do* that? I've been working on this sucker for hours."

"You've not been doing this long, love." He gave her shoulder a fatherly pat. "It's all right to ask for a hand on occasion. Some things—many things—require a master's touch."

"Master's touch, huh?" That was a bit uncharacteristically braggy for Ian, who was one of the humblest people she'd ever met. Though if anyone had room to brag, it was him. Decades of experience and a top-notch pedigree meant people had come from miles around—in multiple states—for him to service their stringed instruments. He could charge three times what he did, he could demand whatever concessions he wanted from his customers, and people would jump to accommodate him. But he didn't. His prices were more than reasonable, his service unmatched.

"I mean of course, our heavenly Master." Ian chuckled. "What? You thought I meant myself?"

Siobhan leaned back in her chair. "You've certainly got the credentials for it."

"Bah." Ian waved a hand and started back toward his workbench. "What I've got is a lot of hard-won experience and the God-given wisdom to know when to stop trying so hard and let him take over. Some things only he can heal."

"What happens when he's the one who caused them in the first place?"

Ian's bushy gray brows arched, no doubt echoing Siobhan's own surprise. She'd told him bits and pieces of her Pursuers story over the years, and he'd always been a patient, nonjudgmental listening ear who'd prayed for her, even when she thought it wouldn't do any good.

But never had her tightly lidded trauma burst out like this. Had she actually said the words out loud? Was that really the root of her bitterness? She'd been angry with Trace for ages. Angrier still with herself for falling for his act.

But not until this moment had she admitted being angry with God.

"I thought I was serving God," she said in answer to the question Ian hadn't asked. "I thought I was doing what he wanted. And I made mistakes. A lot of them. But Trace—and then everyone—" She broke off, the pain bursting from her in a growl of frustration. "I feel like God set me up to fall and then laughed at me when I did. He's supposed to be an ever-present help in time of trouble. He's supposed to be a God of grace and forgiveness and second chances. But ever since that time, ever since I left Pursuers, it feels like he's left me too."

That was it. The crux of her pain. And when she finally peeled back the layers of anger, the hurt was nearly unbearable. Her eyes stung. She wanted to double over and howl with anguish.

She'd missed Trace—or at least, she'd missed the way he'd manipulated her into feeling loved and wanted.

She'd missed her friends, her community, her place to belong at Pursuers.

But most of all, she missed God. She missed feeling his love. Sensing his presence. Knowing that she was filling a purpose for his kingdom.

"I feel like he's forgotten me," she choked out. "Or worse, abandoned me. Or—even worse—decided I'm his enemy. I mean, maybe I was never really a Christian at all. Maybe I was only duping myself into believing I was his daughter."

Ian studied her as she palmed the tears from her face. She didn't like crying at all, ever, let alone in front of someone else. Someone she admired.

But Ian's expression was one of kindness, not judgment.

"When's the last time you opened your Bible, Siobhan?" he asked. "I know church isn't a place you feel safe right now, and that's understandable. But when's the last time you sought out sound biblical teaching? Watched a service online from someplace other than your old church? When's the last time you've even prayed?"

He was right. The leather-bound Bible she kept on her nightstand was covered in a thin layer of dust. She couldn't remember the last time she'd opened the Bible app on her phone. And praying? Ha. She didn't pray anymore. It seemed like another lifetime since the last time she did.

Siobhan didn't verbalize the answers. She didn't have to. Ian could see the truth thudding into her soul. Written all over her face.

"Perhaps, then, God isn't the one who left."

Perhaps he wasn't. Perhaps he was right there waiting, arms open, for her to stop wishing for the pig slop and start on the long journey home.

And perhaps that worship night of Matt's was the perfect start to that journey.

Chapter Twenty-Four

MATT LEANED BACK in his office chair—leather, cushy, only the barest of squeaks—and breathed deep of the pine-scented candle he'd purchased to cover up the smell of microwave popcorn. Regular popcorn never bothered him, but the fake-buttery-cheesy scent of the microwave stuff always triggered his gag reflex.

Siobhan kept telling him they needed to try this gourmet popcorn place she knew about on the west side. "You've never had popcorn until you've had this popcorn," she'd said often. Despite his general apathy toward the snack, he eagerly anticipated going to check it out with Siobhan. Probably a whole lot more than he should.

Matt clicked open his Spotify playlist for the upcoming worship night, then grabbed his guitar from its stand and joined in midway through the first verse of the opening song. The guitar resonated against his midsection. The strings were cool beneath his fingers, providing pleasant resistance for the pick.

This practice session was less about learning the music—he had that down—and more about being in the right headspace. He was comfortable enough leading at Pursuers now that his nerves had moved from center stage to somewhere close to the wings.

But this wasn't Pursuers. This was out in the world.

And this was a thing Siobhan might actually come to.

Would she? It terrified him how much he hoped she would. But what if being back in a worship-music mindset was too painful for her? What if, instead of drawing her closer to God, it had the opposite effect, flinging her back onto the path she'd fought so hard to climb? What if—

A knock sounded on his door. "Matt?"

He turned. "Hey, Kayleigh."

"There's a call for you. Line four. I told the guy you were practicing, but he said to tell you that all the practicing in the world wouldn't mean you weren't a hack. His words. Not mine." She gave an apologetic wince.

A grin eased across Matt's face, and he set the guitar back on its stand. Only one person on the planet would have said that to him. A blast from his not-too-distant past and probably the most welcome voice he could imagine on the other end of the line. "Thanks, Kayleigh."

She backed away, still looking confused. "You're welcome."

Matt leaned toward his computer and paused the playlist, then picked up his office phone and pressed the button. "Rhys Powell. Took you long enough to call and check on me."

"Took you long enough to answer one of my calls," the worship pastor retorted. "I've been trying your cell all afternoon."

Sure enough, a glance at his watch revealed a couple missed calls from Rhys. Must've forgotten to turn off Do Not Disturb after his morning planning meeting with the worship staff. "Fair point."

"How's the new gig going?"

Matt could picture Rhys in his office, one Converse-clad shoe propped on his desk, a can of honey mustard pretzels at his right hand and a mug of Coke at his left.

"It's going." Matt settled back into the chair and spent the next few minutes hitting the high points for Rhys, the man whom he'd first approached years ago about playing rhythm guitar on the worship team at church, only to find himself leading a team within a month. Rhys's patient explanations and unwavering encouragement had given Matt the confidence not only to survive in his new role but thrive. And look where he was now.

"Night of worship and you haven't even been there three months yet," Rhys commented around a mouthful of pretzels. "That's ambitious."

"You'd know," Matt retorted with a chuckle.

The wry laugh from Rhys confirmed his thoughts had gone the same direction.

"You've told me all the nuts and bolts, but that's not what I really wanted to know." Rhys's voice took on an earnest quality. "I want to know how you're doing."

"I'm okay." It was more reflex than actual reply.

"Just okay?"

"Night of worship might have me just a little bit stressed."

"Yeah? How so?"

Matt shifted in the chair, his eyes fixed on the small photo of him and the worship team at Sawgrass Christian in Illinois, taken at his going-away party. "It's just . . . okay, this thing's supposed to be kinda laid-back and chill, right? Except laid-back and chill is the opposite of how I'm feeling." He chuckled. "You'd think the bright lights and HD cameras and everything here would scare me."

"They don't?" Rhys asked, then crunched another mouthful of pretzels.

"Not anymore. But this does." Matt reached for a pen and bounced it on the desk.

"You guys doing a super-stripped acoustic kinda thing?"

"Yup. Coffeehouse style."

"Yeah, those are always intimidating." Rhys swallowed, and his voice cleared. "I mean, don't get me wrong—I love those more than just about anything, but when you don't have a full band and tech crew, it's almost like you're up there without your pants on."

Matt laughed at the mental image. Rhys Powell always did have quite the way with words. "I don't mind the acoustic stuff so much. I'm feeling the weight of my calling, I think."

"How so?"

"Like, my literal job is to help people meet with God. It's my job to take people out of their harried, super-busy lives, where maybe they ran late for church because one of their kids couldn't find their shoes or the dog got sick on the rug right before they were supposed to leave, or maybe they have to leave right after to have dinner with their dysfunctional in-laws or whatever. That hour and twenty minutes they're in our building, though, that's our chance to reach them. Might be the only chance we get."

He sighed, anxiety squeezing out of his heart like a toothpaste tube someone had clenched in a fist. "And at a service, there's communion, there's the sermon, there's lots of ways to reach people. But at something like this, there's just the music. That's it. That's their one shot. And some of the people who might come to this would never darken the door of a church. Maybe they got hurt by the church—bad—and they've fallen away from God, and they'd rather get a root canal than go back in that building, but they might come to a coffee shop to listen to some fool strum his guitar for a bit. But if I can't do something, if I can't say something to make them let their guard down and see Jesus for who he really is, then what have I accomplished?"

He broke off, gulping pine-scented air and reeling at the onslaught of words that had just spewed out of him. No wonder he'd had trouble getting in the right headspace.

Rhys was silent for a moment. "Sounds an awful lot like there might be a specific someone you're trying to reach. Am I close?"

"Too close, my friend." Matt was too. He was way too close to Siobhan, if thoughts of her were hijacking him like this. If he cared more about her response to his music than he did any of the other precious souls who'd be likely to find their way in on Friday night.

But desperation for Siobhan to see God for who he really was, not who the enemy was making him out to be, clutched at him to the point of pain. If he could just do something, say something, play something. If he could just—

"You know God doesn't need you." Rhys's gravelly voice broke into Matt's anxious litany.

"I'm sorry?"

"The book of Luke says that if we stay silent, then even the stones will cry out God's praise. He doesn't need you to reach people, Matt. He doesn't need you to perform for him. It's not about you at all, and I know you know that. It's about Jesus and what he did on the cross and what he continues to do every minute of every day. Sometimes he chooses to reach someone through us and our music, and sometimes he doesn't." Rhys cleared his throat. "Your job isn't to think about the audience at all. It's to shut everything out—close your eyes if you have to, that's what I do—and just sing to Jesus. Remember who he is and how he changed you from who you used to be. For me, that alone would get me to play until my fingers bleed and sing until my voice gives out."

Rhys's words smacked Matt in the back of the head with all the subtlety of a two-by-four. Of course. It wasn't about him. Wasn't about Siobhan, either, or anyone else who might find their way into Frontier Coffee on Friday night.

It was about Jesus. Nothing more, nothing less.

"Wow. All those hours in seminary are paying off," Matt said with a wry grin. "You're starting to sound like a real preacher."

"For the cash that degree is costing me, it better," Rhys replied.

Matt leaned back in the chair. "Things going okay? That church plant still in the works?"

"Full steam ahead."

"And they still want you in the pulpit?"

"Haven't wised up yet," Rhys said around a laugh.

When they ended the call a few moments later, Matt returned to his playlist—and his guitar—with a far lighter heart. It wasn't about the chords or the lyrics or anything else. Of course he wanted them to be as excellent as he could make them. God deserved nothing less. But even more important than having his fingers in the right place and his mind on the correct verse was having his heart where it needed to be.

He wasn't sure how much time passed or how many songs he worshiped through, but his throat felt raw when he finally opened his eyes and returned the guitar to its stand. Peace flooded his soul.

Then Trace strode through the office with a coffee mug in hand, and he placed it on Kayleigh's desk. Matt couldn't hear her reply, though with the dazzling smile that lit her face, he didn't need to.

In response, Trace leaned in and wrapped an arm around Kayleigh's shoulders. The standard evangelical side-hug . . . but it lasted a little too long. His cheek grazed the top of her head a little too closely. And her head rested on his shoulder just a little too much.

He had to confront Trace privately. Soon. For Siobhan's sake. For Kayleigh's. And for the sake of all the women in their office.

Had he been worried about Friday night? He had no need. Siobhan probably wouldn't show at all. Not that he blamed her.

But on the off chance she did, his prayer was that she wouldn't see him. Wouldn't even know he was on the stage.

He prayed that all she'd see was Jesus.

Chapter Twenty-Five

Siobhan rang the doorbell of the old farmhouse, and a moment later her half sister's blurred image appeared through the frosted glass.

The door creaked open, and Sloane appeared in full, her hair a riot of dark-brown curls, her eyes shadowed by purplish rings, and a pajama-clad baby draped over her left shoulder.

"Thanks so much for coming all this way." She stepped aside so Siobhan could enter.

"Not a problem at all." Siobhan hung her purse on a hook inside the entryway. "I always love an excuse to see the two of you. And the house, of course." She greeted her sister with a brief, gentle embrace, then kissed her niece's sweet-smelling cheek.

It still blew her mind that this old farmhouse up on Jamesville Road, the stately white one she'd admired every time she came out this way, had belonged to her family. Even more mind-blowing was the fact that she'd never have known that if not for the historian half sister she'd never even knew existed.

"Come on, little lady." Sloane softly patted Domenica's back. "I know you've got a burp in there somewhere, and as much as I love you, I don't want you to spit up all over Annabelle's diaries."

Siobhan chuckled as they made their way into the living room. The soaring stone fireplace, original to the home, now boasted a fleecy white stars-and-planets-themed infant swing off to the right. The gray suede couch was littered with a nursing pillow and an assortment of burp cloths. The hardwood floors—refinished in the 1940s, Sloane had said, and given a good polishing three years ago—now contained colorful baby toys.

And sure enough, there on an end table sat a brown leather book. The diary of Annabelle Collins Brennan, a Sedgwick County pioneer whose husband, Jack, had built the farmhouse and whose writings had provided clues to Sloane's own identity.

Just then a decidedly unladylike burp—surprisingly loud for such a tiny human—emanated from Domenica.

"There it is. That's what we've been waiting for." Sloane removed the burp cloth from her shoulder, stained with a tiny bit of spit-up, and dabbed her baby's lips. "There you go."

"Wow, I heard that one from all the way in there." Garrett came in from the kitchen, an impressed grin stretching his lips wide, two lidded cups in hand.

"Earl Grey?" He held out a mug to Siobhan.

"Yes please, and thank you." She took the mug from her brother-in-law, who then turned and set Sloane's mug on a table far from the diary.

Sloane kissed her husband's cheek. "I've taught you well."

Garrett gave her a quick embrace, then held out his hands, blue eyes radiant with love. "Ready to come hang out with Daddy for a bit, Domenica?"

Domenica responded with a loud squeal and a wide grin as Sloane handed her over. Garrett swooped the little girl skyward, then tossed her a couple inches in the air and caught her. Domenica's high-pitched giggles blended with Garrett's deep chuckle.

"Just because she spit up once doesn't mean she won't do it again," Sloane warned.

"I'll take my chances." Garrett gave the delighted Domenica a couple more tosses, then snuggled her close, smothering her cheek with kisses as he retreated upstairs.

Sloane picked up the diary on her way to the couch, then tossed the nursing pillow aside and sat down. "Pull up a patch of chaos," she said, adding the burp cloth from her shoulder to a basket on the other side of the fireplace.

Siobhan waved a hand and reached for her mug. "Your place is far neater than mine, and I don't have a baby to blame it on."

Sloane took a long, grateful sip of tea, then set the mug aside and picked up the diary. "Okay, so I found a few mentions of Deborah in this one."

She opened the fragile, yellowed pages to a spot marked by a bookmark from a local indie bookstore. "It looks like the two were friends."

"Have you read the passage yet?" Siobhan asked.

"Skimmed some of it." Sloane scooted closer on the couch. "But then Domenica got fussy, and I didn't have time to read most of it. Anyway, here's where it starts."

※

December 1876

"Ouch."

Deborah peeked around the table where Elisabeth was perched, the smart black tips of her shoes peeking out of the voluminous folds of floral fabric, to Annabelle Brennan, who was sucking the tip of her index finger.

"Are you all right?" Deborah asked.

Annabelle pulled her fingertip out of her mouth and eyed it critically. "Just a bit of a pinprick."

"Goes with the territory, I suppose." Deborah returned her attention to where she was pinning fabric at the front. Elisabeth had finished her dress a month or so prior, but predictably she'd lost enough weight over the last couple weeks that it needed to be taken in. Dark circles ringed her brown eyes too, but beyond the signs of exhaustion shone a deep, radiant joy, the kind that came only from the eager anticipation of marrying the love of one's life.

Deborah slid a pin into the waistline of Elisabeth's dress. Had she once envied her sister and Isaiah? What they had was certainly special, all sunshine and roses and exuberance. But what she and Levi had, though decidedly quieter, was no less deep or meaningful. And the babe within her womb proved that their marriage had progressed far beyond a mere business arrangement.

But had Elisabeth's hands always been that pale? Had the slender fingers always shaken?

Deborah peered up at her sister with a critical eye. "Elisabeth? Are you all right?"

"Of course." She flashed a smile. "Why?"

"You're looking pale."

"I'm just a bit tired, is all."

"For weeks before Jack and I wed, I was too excited to sleep," Annabelle piped up from where she was crouched on the floor, eyeing the lace on Elisabeth's hem.

"But your hands are shaking." Deborah straightened and took in the hollows beneath her sister's cheekbones. "Elisabeth, when is the last time you had something to eat?"

Elisabeth waved a hand. "I'm marrying the love of my life in five days. It's been so hectic preparing that I've scarcely had time."

"*Elisabeth*." Deborah narrowed her eyes. "When?"

"Yesterday, perhaps? The day before?"

Deborah met Annabelle's blue gaze, and Annabelle handed off the hem of Elisabeth's dress to Deborah. "Hold this. I'll go find something."

"There's some fresh bread from this morning," Deborah said. "And butter in the crock."

"There isn't time, Annabelle," Elisabeth protested. "As soon as we finish with the measurements, we have to start sewing. Deborah's dress might need altering as well. That babe is growing faster than anticipated, and I—"

"*No*, Elisabeth." Deborah hastily jammed pins into the hem of the dress. "You need to stop and breathe and have something to eat. You can take ten minutes to care for yourself."

"At least have some milk," Annabelle urged.

"I'll have plenty of time after the wedding," Elisabeth argued.

"But Isaiah loves you, wedding or no," Annabelle pointed out from the kitchen. "He'd rather have you whole and healthy than for you to have run yourself into the ground preparing for a ceremony that'll be over in a flash."

Elisabeth sighed. "All right. I'll eat something. Promise. Just as soon as I finish . . ."

She trailed off, and Deborah glanced up in alarm. "Elisabeth?"

What little color remained in Elisabeth's face had drained, and she slumped.

With a shriek, Deborah lunged forward but grasped only the hem of the dress. A pin jammed into her palm, the pain sharp, and the small cabin filled with the sound of tearing fabric. A cry from Annabelle. The shattering of a plate.

The sick thud of flesh on the wooden kitchen table.

"Oh no, Elisabeth. No, no, no, no." Deborah discarded the scrap of fabric that had once been her sister's train and ran around the table to where Elisabeth lay.

"Oh mercy!" Annabelle tossed the bread aside and knelt among the remnants of the plate. "Elisabeth?"

No response.

"Oh God, not her head. Please not her head. Please, please, not her head." But Deborah's frantic whispered prayer went unanswered. Crimson bloomed beneath Elisabeth's brilliant white cap. Onto the wooden floor. Too much. Far, far too much.

"It must be her scalp." Annabelle yanked a towel off the kitchen counter and pressed it to the wound. "Here. Hold this."

Deborah replaced her friend's hand with her own.

"Good." Annabelle hurried to stand. "Keep pressure on it. I'll fetch Uncle Stephen. He can stitch the wound closed, but we have to stop the bleeding."

"Hurry, Annabelle."

But her friend was already out the door, in a frantic race against the flood issuing from Elisabeth's scalp. It had already soaked through, painting the flour sack towel a brilliant red and dampening Deborah's fingertips.

So much blood. So very much.

Deborah grabbed for the first absorbent thing she could find. The wad of floral fabric that had once been her sister's wedding dress. She added it to the pile in her hand, pressed down, and prayed.

CHAPTER TWENTY-SIX

A STIFF DECEMBER wind buffeted the cabin, seeping through the cracks in the chinking, and Deborah leaned forward to readjust the blankets on Elisabeth's bed. A needless gesture, perhaps, since Elisabeth was still flushed with fever, but she tucked the blankets beneath her sister's chin nonetheless. Dim lamplight flickered across the quilt and cast shadows over Elisabeth's face. She stirred but didn't wake up.

Deborah retreated to the rocker at the foot of the bed and stifled a yawn. The clock on the wall displayed a shockingly late hour, but for the past three days, time had been measured in twice-daily visits from Dr. Maxwell, in the appearance of meals brought in by caring neighbors, and in the length and direction of the shadows as sunlight—and now moonlight—streamed through the window. She and Papa and Isaiah had taken turns keeping watch at Elisabeth's bedside.

One thing was certain, though no one had yet been brave enough to speak it aloud: Elisabeth's wedding to Isaiah—planned a mere two days from now—would not take place as scheduled.

The question now was, would it ever?

As Deborah had feared, the paper-thin, hideously scarred flesh that just barely covered Elisabeth's skull had burst apart when she'd fainted and hit her head on the kitchen table. Though Annabelle had returned with her uncle in short order, and though the good doctor had applied every ounce of his considerable skill and experience, the dreaded infection had set in. Now, Dr. Maxwell had said during his evening visit, Elisabeth was in the Lord's hands.

Papa, stationed at Elisabeth's bedside, leaned forward, his face lined and craggy in the flickering lamplight. "This brings back so many memories of when you girls were small. When this first happened."

Deborah stilled in the chair, afraid a creak would snap her father out of his trance. Too scared to even breathe. Because Papa never talked about that dreadful day.

"You were so little to have suffered so much. Both of you." He glanced toward Deborah, eyes swimming with tears. "Hour after hour, when we didn't know whether the Lord would take you home or let you stay, I wondered why he spared me."

Deborah closed her eyes against the onslaught of memories. It had been calm that night as the band of settlers made camp on the trail. It being a Sunday, there was no travel that day. The men, having spied a buffalo, had gone off in hopes of bringing fresh meat for dinner. Mama heated water over the fire, preparing to do some washing. She and Elisabeth stayed in the shade of a tree, while the youngest children rested in the wagon.

Then came the thunder of hoofbeats and the chilling war whoops. The general buzz of discomfort in the camp. Discomfort shifting to outright terror as warriors descended. Then the pressure of a hand on her throat, the searing pain in her head . . .

"I wasn't there." Papa's voice rasped a brokenness Deborah had never heard. "I was trying to provide for you, but in so doing I failed to protect you. I failed as a father."

"No you didn't, Papa." Deborah rose from the chair to kneel beside her father. "You've been there for us every day since. You've been here to care for Elisabeth and me. We weren't orphans. We had you." She squeezed her father's calloused hand. Ran a finger over the rough, indented tips of fingers that danced across the fiddle strings. "We still have you."

"I know, and I'm grateful for that." Eyes close to overflowing, Papa returned Deborah's squeeze. "But everything in me would have traded places with the two of you that day. I would do anything to have taken your pain. I'd do anything to be in this bed right now instead of Elisabeth." A tear dove down his cheek and dropped onto the bedclothes as he turned back toward Elisabeth.

"You know what it's like to take on others' pain, Lord." His voice broke.

"So you must understand how much I wish this could be me right now." He gripped Elisabeth's hand and bowed his head. "Let it be me, Lord. Let it be me. Make it be me."

﹥﹤

Deborah jerked awake sometime later to a half-whispered moan from the bed. She'd fallen asleep there in a kneeling position, her cheek pressed into her hand. Her knees ached as she raised herself to stand.

But the sight that greeted her was almost too much to hope for.

Elisabeth was awake. Her eyes were open.

"Elisabeth." Hot tears flooded Deborah's eyes. "Hello."

"Hello." The voice was barely recognizable, rusty from disuse.

Deborah moved quickly to fetch a dipper of water. Reaching beneath her sister's neck, she raised Elisabeth up just enough to take in a few sips of water past her parched lips.

"Thank you." A frown flickered across Elisabeth's pale forehead. "What . . ."

"You fainted," Deborah explained. "Your wound broke open. Dr. Maxwell stitched it closed, but you've had an infection."

Elisabeth gasped. "Isaiah. My wedding. When is it? What day is it? Where's Isaiah?" She tried to sit up.

"No, Elisabeth. No. Lie back down."

"But—"

"Isaiah has barely left your side. We sent him home earlier so he could get some sleep. He'll be back in the morning."

This seemed to placate Elisabeth enough for Deborah to ease her back down toward the pillows.

"When is the wedding?" she asked softly. "I haven't missed it, have I?"

"The wedding is whenever you get better." *If you get better.* Deborah ordered the doubt into silence.

Elisabeth's eyes slid closed. "I need to see him."

"We'll send for him as soon as it's light." Deborah replaced the blankets. "I'm certain he's as eager to see you as you are to see him."

"He needs to know . . . I forgave him."

"Forgave him for what?" Brow furrowed, Deborah placed her hand across Elisabeth's forehead. Still burning up.

"For this."

Deborah fished in the basin of water for the cloth and wrung it out. "Lizzie, that's crazy talk. Isaiah didn't do this. This was a Sioux."

"Told you . . . wasn't . . . a Sioux."

Elisabeth's eyes opened. Focused but glassy. She was still feverish. "The man who did this, he had blue eyes. A scar on his right wrist. It was—"

"Shhhhh." Deborah sponged her sister's forehead. "Don't try to talk. Save your strength. We'll send for Isaiah in the morning."

"Forgive."

"You don't need to forgive Isaiah."

"Not . . . Isaiah." Her eyes opened again. "Nathaniel."

"Nathaniel? Levi's brother?" How high was Elisabeth's fever? It had to be higher than she thought.

"I forgave him." Elisabeth's voice sounded stronger than it had all morning. "Please. Forgive. You forgive. You need to. Jesus would . . . Jesus did. Forgive . . ."

Alarm churned in Deborah's gut. Elisabeth was clearly delirious. Getting worse.

They needed Dr. Maxwell again.

No. Not Dr. Maxwell. He couldn't help.

Only God could provide what they needed now.

Because right now what they needed was a miracle.

✦

"So Elisabeth fainted, fell off the table, hit her head, and . . ." Siobhan shuddered. "I'm almost afraid to ask, but did she recover?"

"I was just checking on that." Sloane turned another page, then looked up, the light in her brown eyes noticeably dimmed. "The diary says Elisabeth died at daybreak two days later. On what would have been her wedding day."

Angry tears jabbed the backs of Siobhan's eyes. "That sucks. I mean, she'd been through that horrible thing, she'd recovered, she'd found the man of her dreams, and then right when everything was finally going her way and her future was bright, she dies? Why does God *do* stuff like that?"

"I don't know." Sloane's words slipped out on a sigh. "I wish I did. But I also know you're not the first person to ask the question. Annabelle asked it after Jack died. He'd worked for years to build them a home, and practically the second they moved in, he fell off the roof and broke his neck."

"Seriously? That's rough."

"That's pioneer life, though. Life in general, honestly." Sloane turned another few pages in the diary and skimmed the faded script. "Annabelle seems to be the person Deborah leaned on most after Elisabeth died. She mentions repeatedly that Elisabeth, on her deathbed, urged Deborah to forgive the man who'd scalped her."

Siobhan gave a bitter bark of laughter. "Yeah, good luck with that."

Sloane, though, seemed lost in the faded, fragile pages. "According to the diary, Deborah says Elisabeth always maintained her attacker was a white man dressed as a Sioux."

"Wait, what? Was that a thing?"

"Wasn't common, especially around here, but it did happen." Sloane flipped a couple pages in the diary. "Sounds like Elisabeth was quite feverish, and she was very young when the attack took place, so who knows how much of what she was saying was grounded in reality. But it wasn't unheard of for white men to disguise themselves as Indigenous people and commit horrible acts of violence, which they then blamed on the innocent. Stirring up trouble between Indigenous tribes and white settlers was usually the goal. And the result."

Siobhan's stomach turned. "That's horrifying. And Deborah was supposed to forgive that? I know I couldn't. Not in a million years."

Sloane tilted her head and fixed Siobhan with one of those unnerving, soul-penetrating looks.

Siobhan frowned. "What?"

"Well—and believe me, I'm not trying to toot my own horn here—but I eventually forgave our mother."

Siobhan blinked, jarred once more at the reminder that the loving woman who'd raised her—the one who'd made Rice Krispies Treats on the regular, who was a constant presence at class parties and those ill-fated ballet lessons, who stopped at nothing to celebrate the little moments, even when it was just the two of them and they were living in a low-rent apartment, whose love Siobhan never once questioned—was the same woman who'd given birth to Sloane and then abandoned her on a bus in Seattle.

"I'm impressed." Siobhan shifted on the sofa. "Because that's a lot to forgive."

"It was. Is, I should say." Sloane reached for her tea. "Because forgiveness is quite the process. It definitely doesn't happen all at once. But my therapist finally helped me see that by holding on to all the bitterness and anger, I was hurting myself way more than I was hurting Kimberly."

The truth pierced Siobhan like a narrow knife that wiggled around. Avoiding Sloane's too-perceptive gaze, she picked at a loose cuticle. "And do you feel better having forgiven Mom?"

"Yes. Without question." Sloane's voice was confident. Firm. "But when Domenica was born, I was surprised that I had to deal with it all over again. Now that I had a baby myself, I understood more thoroughly what Kimberly went through. And that made me even less able to understand how she was able to leave me on that bus. Because I love my daughter with the fire of a thousand—no, a million—suns. Leaving her somewhere, just walking away, never knowing if she was safe or cared for or loved—I can't even fathom doing that. So the fact that Kimberly was able to do that with me . . ."

"I'm sorry." Siobhan laid a hand on her half sister's shoulder. "That is a lot to work through."

"It was. Is."

Siobhan tucked one leg underneath her and turned toward Sloane. "How did you even start? Like, how did you get to the point where you even wanted to try to forgive Mom? Because it doesn't sound like Deborah wants to forgive her attackers, and I don't blame her." *I don't want to forgive Trace, either.*

Sloane tilted her head and was silent for a moment before answering. "For me it started when I realized how much God forgave me. That we're all equally in need of Christ's forgiveness. Anyone who breaks part of the law has broken the whole thing, according to the Bible. We're all equally lost and all in need of Jesus. And compared to the debt we owed him, even the worst thing someone does to us pales in comparison. Which, I mean, that's kind of a lot to wrap your head around too."

"Sounds like the church guilted you into forgiving Mom."

"I don't know that I'd put it like that," Sloane replied. "Because even after I learned how important it was to forgive her, I still didn't want to. I ended up asking God to help me want to." A wry smile. "No, first thing I had to ask him was that he'd help me *want* to want to forgive her. But he answered that prayer. And then I actually wanted to. And then he helped me forgive her. Lots of counseling, some hard conversations, and a lot of prayer, but God changed my heart. It wasn't easy—sometimes it still isn't. But just take it one step at a time. That's all God asks for us to do. Just take the next step he shows us."

"Right." The next step. Siobhan wasn't ready to forgive Trace yet. She wasn't even ready to go back to church yet.

But maybe God wasn't asking her to do something huge like that. Maybe he was just asking her to start with something small. Something small that still felt large, but with crystal clarity she knew the next step God wanted her to take.

If she was going to take that step, though, she'd better hurry.

She stood, stomach knotted yet underpinned with a strange sense of peace. "Sorry to cut this short, but I have to run."

Sloane set the diary aside. "Yeah? Where to?"

"To take the next step."

CHAPTER TWENTY-SEVEN

IT WAS SEVEN minutes past the scheduled start time for the night of worship when Siobhan ordered herself through the wooden doors of Frontier Coffee. For almost fifteen minutes, she'd paced the sidewalk outside, gravel and salt from a late-season storm crunching beneath her boots and her breath puffing up around her face.

What was she doing here? A night of worship? She was through with that sort of thing. Forever. Or so she thought.

But Matt—and maybe even God—had pulled her soul toward this place.

Could she truly trust either of them?

Guess there's only one way to find out.

By the time she stepped from the frigid outdoors to the warm, cozy indoors, the lights were dimmed and the place was full, but she was able to snag a spot at a table in the far back corner. A quick scan of the crowd revealed no familiar faces, though even if there had been, likely no one would've recognized her. Her shoulders loosened a fraction.

She slid her coat off and draped it over the back of the tall wrought iron chair, then perched awkwardly, half on the edge of the seat, every cell in her body screaming with self-consciousness. This wasn't who she was anymore. She admired all these people who'd never been wounded, all these poor naive saps who had no idea how badly the church could sting.

It was amid this backdrop of bitterness that she watched Matt walk onto the small stage, along with two other guys she didn't recognize. One took a guitar from a stand, while the other sat down on a cajon—the rectangular wooden drum popular in acoustic sets—and gave it a few experimental taps with his fingertips.

"How y'all doing tonight?" Matt asked the crowd of fifty or so, who responded with tentative applause and a couple semi-enthusiastic whoops.

He was nervous. She could tell by the pink flush creeping up from his collar. By the way his knee bounced up and down as he sat on the stool. It made her feel special—privileged, even—to know the man onstage in a way few here did.

But then his gaze found hers, and the incandescent smile he gave her chased away every lingering bit of late-winter chill. That smile was worth all the hours of agony of this decision, and all the discomfort sitting here brought. She was here for him. As a friend. And the smile told her he knew how difficult it was for her and how much it meant for him to see her there.

"All right, guys, here's what's up." The dark-haired man next to Matt spoke up. "My name's Eli, this here's Matt, and over there is Connor."

The guy on the cajon gave a friendly wave.

"We're just some pals who've wanted to get together and worship," Eli continued. "We've been talking about it for years and we finally made it happen."

"Helps that we finally got this knucklehead to move to Kansas so we could all be in the same state," Connor put in.

The audience chuckled appreciatively.

"So we're gonna do just what Eli said." Matt leaned forward to adjust his mic. "Worship. You don't have to sing. You don't even have to pay attention. That's fine with us, because what we're doing up here tonight isn't about us. It's all about Jesus. That's who deserves our worship. You're welcome to stand, stay seated, kneel, keep scrolling your phone and drinking your coffee, whatever. Just know that Jesus loves you, and we love him, and we're going to sing to him tonight."

More applause, particularly from the front row.

Eli strummed a couple chords and then they were off, launching into a riff Siobhan hadn't heard before. For this song, anyway, Matt had remained true to his word. This wasn't anything she'd ever done at Pursuers. And since she didn't know the song, she felt no pressure to sing along.

The audience certainly seemed to know it, though. The front two rows in particular got into it, clapping and raising their arms and swaying with the up-tempo beat.

And Matt. His right hand flew across the strings so fast, it was almost a blur. His fingers found the chords expertly—he'd clearly put in the necessary practice time.

But one look at his face told her performing was the furthest thing from his mind. His eyes were closed, he moved with the beat, but his face—his face was so radiant it practically shone in the soft stage lights of the coffeehouse.

She'd seen a lot of people get up on stage and play songs about Jesus. But this was one of the few times she could call it worship. His expression was one of eager bliss. Pure adoration. The look of a child who'd drawn a picture or made up a story and approached a parent with that creation, knowing the parent would respond with eager praise and unabashed, unconditional love.

She had never, not once, seen this at Pursuers. It was all about image there. False lashes and hair spray and making sure everything was ready for those ever-present HD cameras. Performance and perfection and pressure. Pressure that, like a boa constrictor, had slowly squeezed the life out of worship.

Tonight was what worship was supposed to be. Not perfect necessarily, but authentic. Real. Matt was just being himself. A great guy who had some musical talent but who first and foremost loved Jesus.

Maybe . . . maybe not every church was like Pursuers. Maybe not everyone who claimed to follow Christ was like Trace Jessup.

No, there was no maybe about it. Matt was living proof.

He wasn't the only one. She tore her gaze from him to see the same worshipful adoration on Eli's warm brown face and Connor's pale, freckled complexion. They were real, all three of them, in a way that nobody at Pursuers was when she was there.

Perhaps not even herself.

And if there were still real, authentic Christians out there, then maybe God was still out there too.

And if that were true, then maybe Ian was right. Maybe God hadn't moved.

Maybe Siobhan had.

From the stage, the praise chorus melded seamlessly into a classic hymn. One she hadn't heard in decades. Pursuers didn't do hymns.

But Matt apparently did.

The centuries-old song swelled in her heart and floated unguarded past her lips, so softly she barely knew she was singing. But her lips moved. Her hands, clenched in fists in the pockets of her vest, loosed. Started to lift heavenward.

Worship was happening in her soul. Real worship. Authentic worship.

For the first time in a very long time.

Maybe ever.

Her cheeks were wet. How long had she been crying?

Too long for comfort.

Nowhere near enough for healing.

But healing was happening. Right here, right now. She couldn't explain it, couldn't control it, couldn't do anything about it except stand and sing and weep and lift her hands. It was as though God was wrapping his arms around her, body and soul. The blood of Jesus was washing all her wounds, all her hurt places. She had work to do still. But this—falling into the embrace of the one who had never left her—was undeniably a good beginning.

After years of wandering, years of hungering for pig slop, she'd finally admitted that she needed her father. Just like the prodigal son, she'd taken those first exhausted, dusty, defeated, humiliated steps home.

><

Matt's arms trembled as he set his guitar back into its case on the little table just off the tiny stage. His fingers were sore, his shirt was damp with sweat, and he had the beginnings of a monstrous headache. Physically, he was spent. But spiritually, he was fuller than he'd ever been. How the night went from a musical or technical standpoint, he'd never know. Didn't care, either. All he knew, all he cared about, was that he'd spent the last two hours in the presence of God, soaking in his love and sharing it with those around him.

Including Siobhan. She came. She actually came. As soon as he took the stage, he spotted her sitting at a tall table in the back. Not that he was looking for her. Okay. Fine. He was looking. But even if he hadn't been, she'd be fairly easy to spot, with that pale-blond hair and uncertain half smile.

He refused to let her be a distraction, though. As he had since his conversation with Rhys on Tuesday, he prayed for focus, and God answered that prayer with a resounding yes. By the bridge of the first song, Matt had all but forgotten Siobhan was even there.

Couldn't forget now, though, because the crowd had thinned out, and she was walking toward him. Her purposeful steps made him more nervous than anything had all night. Now that it was over, now that he'd poured himself out onstage, he was dying to know what she'd thought. Did she love it? Hate it? Did it bring back bad memories for her? Did it cement her decision to have nothing to do with church?

It had done something to her, that was for sure. Her face was blotchy, and her blue eyes were bright and rimmed with red. The sight made his heart—and his legs—lurch toward her with an indescribable yearning ache.

But beyond her tears shone something else, something that became more obvious the closer she came to him. Siobhan looked . . . lighter. Healthier. Her face shone with a joy she couldn't hide if she tried.

"Hey." Her voice was husky. She stood a mere foot away from him, close enough for him to reach out and touch, and God have mercy, did he want to. But given the situation, given where they were and that it was a church thing, a worship thing, he didn't want to do anything that would bring back any more bad memories.

"Hey, you made it." He shoved his hands into his pockets, fists clenched.

"I did." She did the same, hands in the pockets of her vest. "Wasn't sure I would, to be real truthful, but . . . I did."

What was even happening? Their conversation was surface-y. Inane even. But so much shimmered beneath that surface. She looked like the same Siobhan, yet not. She wasn't the same Siobhan at all. Something had happened tonight. Something big.

"Well." He swallowed hard. "I'm really glad you did. Thank you. Y'know, for coming."

"Thank *you*, Matt. You sounded amazing." Her gaze flitted to the floor. "I mean, don't take this the wrong way, but most of the time I wasn't watching you."

Fair enough. He hadn't been watching her, either.

"I was for a little while, but you just looked so happy and at peace and in love with Jesus that after a couple minutes, you swept me right up with you."

"And?" Matt could barely breathe.

"And I met with God. Prayed. Sang. Worshiped. For the first time since I don't even remember when."

Her hands were out of her pockets now, fluttering around like nervous birds. Her fingers were so graceful and delicate he couldn't stop staring at them. Couldn't stop staring at her. She looked so . . . so different. Like the Siobhan she'd always been, but more alive. Like the part of her that had been missing had come back. Even though he'd never seen her look quite like this, she looked more herself than ever.

More beautiful than ever too.

"I'm not okay yet, Matt," she said. "I know it's going to take more than one night of worship to make me okay. But for the first time in a long time, I think . . . no, I *know* I will be."

His heart surged with so much emotion he wasn't sure how such a small part of him could contain it all. "That's wonderful, Siobhan. I'm really glad you shared that with me."

"Thank you. And thank God," she added with a nervous chuckle and a glance skyward. "But thank you. For playing tonight. For worshiping. And for inviting me to come."

"Sure." There was so much more he wanted to say, but further speech proved impossible, thanks to the surge of emotion in his heart.

He couldn't kid himself any longer. Whatever distance he was supposed to keep between himself and Siobhan, whatever reasons that distance was supposed to exist—right now none of them came to mind—had been obliterated. He was more than just closer than he should be.

He was in love with Siobhan.

That was a problem, wasn't it? Wait, was it?

It used to be, back when she was keeping God at arm's length and wanting nothing to do with church. But now he could share this part of himself with her. She'd taken a giant step forward, at any rate. The distance that had once been between them, taken up by the elephant in the room that was church, seemed much smaller now.

The physical distance was much smaller too, as she'd stepped toward him. Her gaze had left his eyes and landed on his lips. Hers were soft. Pink. Slightly shiny with the remnants of some kind of gloss. And inching closer. Her arm twined around his neck, and what little oxygen he had left in his lungs deserted him. Every nerve was alight, and he trembled with anticipation. He'd thought about kissing her, sure. Would even have admitted to wanting it.

But he had no idea how badly he'd wanted it—needed it, even—until right now, when the kiss was imminent.

And then imminent became actual, and his knees almost gave out. His bones turned to water, his body to liquid, as he melted into her. She was so soft and sweet and raw and vulnerable and the gentle pressure of her lips against his upended his universe.

Behind closed lids, his eyes stung. God was good. He was so, so good. Because he brought Siobhan back to himself and then brought Siobhan to Matt like this.

Had his heart been full onstage?

That was nothing compared to how full it was right now.

Chapter Twenty-Eight

February 1877

THE RUFFLED RED-FLORAL fabric of Elisabeth's go-to-meeting dress was soft beneath Deborah's fingertips, and she blinked back yet another wave of stinging tears. An endless parade of tears in the past two months. How had the well not yet run dry?

It was too soon to go through Elisabeth's things. Deborah felt like a carrion bird picking at a carcass. But her practical side had won out. Elisabeth no longer had any use for her earthly possessions, and knowing her generous spirit, she'd want her things to be put to good use by those who had need.

It helped—at least marginally—that Deborah wouldn't be wearing the clothes herself. Even before the coming babe had altered her shape beyond her wildest imaginings, Elisabeth's shorter stature and daintier figure meant the two had never been able to share clothes. But this soft crimson fabric dotted with creamy flowers could be reimagined into a frock for Nora perhaps. Or a blanket for the baby. And the scraps, perhaps they could be pieced into a quilt for Papa.

Papa. The creak of the rocking chair from the sitting room was the only indication of his presence in the house. He'd said very little since that cold, raw Christmas Eve when they'd buried Elisabeth. The church had given him an indefinite bereavement leave, so he'd spent most of his days in that old rocker. Sometimes reading his Bible, sometimes murmuring prayers, but mostly just staring into the fire. Even his new bride, Abigail, hadn't been able to pierce the fog of his grief.

But the creaking stopped. A moment later footsteps on the floorboards pierced the quiet, and then Papa appeared in the doorway.

Deborah's heart lurched at the sight of him. Red-rimmed eyes peered from a face grown ashy and gray, with deeper wrinkles than she remembered. He appeared to have aged a decade since Elisabeth's death.

He clutched his old fiddle, still in its case, and held it out toward Deborah. "Take this home with you, would you please?" His voice was gravelly.

Deborah blinked. "Are you sure? It's your—"

"It reminds me of too much. I don't even want to look at it anymore, much less play it." Each word was heavy and sounded as though it came with great effort. He set the violin on the bed, then turned and walked out of the bedroom. A moment later the rhythmic creak of the rocker started up again.

Her throat thick, Deborah caressed the rough black surface of the case, then undid the metal latches. Weak winter sunlight hit the fiddle's golden wood and further hollowed out the ache of loss.

She'd spent nearly two months mourning Elisabeth's loss, but she'd lost Papa too. Even in the days following the raid, he hadn't been like this. He'd been filled with energy and purpose, flitting from her bed to Elisabeth's and back again, washing wounds, changing bandages, delivering sips of water, and taking them on grueling trips to Kansas City to meet with surgeons.

Likely he'd been too busy to grieve. He'd never had an opportunity to pause. But now, with Deborah married and the church placing him on leave, he had nothing but time. Perhaps this mourning was not only for Elisabeth, but for Mama. For Josiah and Mary Catherine and Nancy.

Perhaps that was why the violin lay silent. Why he didn't even want to see it.

Deborah removed the instrument from the case and ran a finger over the scar on the top, the lingering reminder of the crack it had suffered when it fell from the wagon on the day life shattered for them all. She and the fiddle had much in common—scarred survivors of a horror that had now claimed nearly everyone in the family.

She brushed her fingers over the cool metal strings, careful not to make a sound. Not that she was capable of much in the way of fiddle playing anyway. Papa had tried to teach her years ago, but his musical talent didn't seem to have been passed down, because neither she nor Elisabeth had ever taken to the instrument. Of course, her wandering attention during his brief attempts at lessons hadn't helped the cause.

Maybe she'd ask Papa to try again someday. Though she doubted he'd have any better luck this time around, maybe it would help to restore the man she knew and loved.

She turned to lay the fiddle back into the case, but . . . what was that? Setting the instrument on the coverlet, she peered into the case. Yes, that was a piece of paper peeking out from the lining. A gentle tug pulled it free.

It was a letter, dated shortly after Thanksgiving.

A letter from—*oh*. Deborah gasped at Elisabeth's familiar, nearly perfect penmanship.

Heart pounding, Deborah scanned the single page.

To my dearest Papa and Bee-bee—

I know not why the Lord has compelled me to write this letter to you, nor why he is so insistent that I do it now, but he has, and so I shall. I'm not certain whether you are ever even meant to see this, but God has made it clear that it is time to reveal my secret—at least on paper—and trust him to do with this missive what he will in his time.

Since the attack, I've known the man who scalped me was a white man. Papa, I know you told me to keep silent about this, that you believe I was suffering from delusions related to my trauma. But I know what I remember. He was wearing war paint and Sioux dress, but his skin was pale and freckled. He bore a crooked scar on his wrist. And I shall never forget the intensity of those blue eyes for as long as I walk this earth.

Never in my wildest dreams did I expect to see those blue eyes again. But I have. They reside in the countenance of one Nathaniel Martinson.

Deborah jumped up and clasped her hand to her mouth. No. Not—not Nathaniel. No. It *couldn't* have been Nathaniel. Levi's brother and her sister's attacker could not have been the same man. Could *not* have been.

But Nathaniel did bear that same distinctive scar. And his intense blue eyes were certainly unique.

Elisabeth hadn't been feverish. She hadn't been suffering delusions during her final illness.

She'd recalled clearly.

The man who'd scalped Elisabeth was Deborah's own brother-in-law.

It took several moments for Deborah to gather her courage and bend to retrieve the letter. It fluttered like a cottonwood leaf in her shaking hand as she read on.

When I first saw him, I didn't think it possible. Surely he couldn't have been the only man with those piercing eyes. That crooked scar. But his odd reaction to meeting me, the way he refused to look at me—or you, Bee-bee—slowly convinced me. And the way he left during Thanksgiving made me absolutely certain.

The day following, I went to see him.

I told him I remembered him. I knew what he had done. Papa, Bee-bee—I know neither of you will approve of what I did, but I needed to see him. I needed to look into those eyes not as a victim of his cruelty, but as one who—by God's grace—survived. One who thrived.

He confessed immediately, with rivers of tears, how he and a few others had attacked our party to make it appear as though the Sioux had done it. Their aim was to stir up trouble between the white man and the red. Immediately upon his act, he felt sick at what he had done. He ran away from the group that afternoon and eventually joined up with the army. He didn't speak much of his life between then and now, but I sense a period of aimless wandering and self-loathing.

He told me he'd thought we all died. He never imagined someone could survive such an attack, let alone both of us. That was why he acted as though he'd seen a ghost, because in his mind, he had. He was the one who invaded our wagon. He was the one who tossed the violin aside. He remembered it, and when he saw Papa's violin, when he saw the two of us, he knew.

Papa, Bee-bee, as I stood there talking with him, the most curious thing happened. I forgave him. It was entirely a work of the Lord to stand there looking into those blue eyes that have haunted me for so long and tell him I held no ill will against him. And that was one of the most beautiful and incredible moments of my life so far. I wish I could describe in words the peace that flowed through me as I laid down the burden I've carried for so long.

My prayer is that the two of you will be able to experience this same peace. This same miracle—and I do not use the word lightly— of forgiving Nathaniel. Know that I pray that God will do the same incredible work in your hearts and minds that he has done in mine.

Love always,
Elisabeth

No. It couldn't be. It simply was not possible. The raid was behind them, the perpetrators strangers. Faceless Sioux warriors who'd gone on to parts unknown, never to resurface.

But Elisabeth wouldn't invent this. What could she possibly gain by pinning such a hideous crime on an innocent man? And Nathaniel's lack of innocence would certainly explain why he couldn't look at her and would barely talk to her. Why he acted so strangely around her.

He wasn't repulsed by her scar in the way others had been.

He was repulsed because of his own guilt.

It couldn't be, but it was. It was him. The man who did this to her, to Elisabeth, to them, the one who, the moment of her passing, became a murderer . . . he was part of Deborah's family.

It was one thing when her attackers were strangers. When she had no expectation of ever seeing them again, not even the barest imaginings that she'd come face-to-face with them.

But now one of them had been in her home. She shared his last name.

It was too much. It was all too much.

Deborah tossed the letter toward the violin case, choking back sobs so as not to alarm Papa. Had he seen the letter? Did he know? Should she tell him?

And Levi. How could she even look at him now? Look at Nora? At— dear God in heaven—her unborn child? What if those intense blue eyes were passed on to the innocent babe in her womb? How could she go on knowing the same blood that coursed through the man who'd spilled her sister's blood lived in her husband? In her child? In the baby who had yet to make his appearance known?

And Elisabeth wanted her to *forgive*?

No. Absolutely not. Never.

Far be it from her to deny Elisabeth anything... but forgiving Nathaniel?

That was simply too much to ask.

Chapter Twenty-Nine

Siobhan rubbed a final coat of polish onto the top of a viola, the melody of Bach's B-minor partita floating through the air of the shop. Sacred or secular, *Soli Deo Gloria*—to God alone be the glory—was Bach's inscription on nearly every composition. And for the first time in a long time, a similar desire to glorify God floated up within Siobhan's heart. As she polished, she hummed her own countermelody to the partita—an affront to the composer, perhaps, but God had put a song in her heart, and if he was the only one who could hear her? She doubted he'd complain too much.

The bells at the door jangled, a jarring percussive element to the unaccompanied violin piece, and she smiled as she gave the viola another pass.

"Welcome in," she said. "What can I do for—"

The rest of the question died in her throat, unuttered, and slid back down, along with the rest of her improvised Bach. Because the man standing before her held no instrument, nor was he the customer who was due to pick up the viola.

It was Trace Jessup.

"Hello, Siobhan." His voice was as smooth as the polish, his smile every bit as oily.

She froze, the cloth in her hand, her stomach roiling at the violation of her inner sanctum. The tearing off of her cover. The tornadic destruction of the illusion of safety she'd built around herself.

He'd found her. Somehow, someway, he'd found her.

"I . . . wasn't expecting to see you again." She willed the quaver from her voice. "In fact, I was hoping to never see you again. I took several steps to make sure of it."

"And yet there aren't too many women in Wichita named Siobhan." He trailed a fingertip over the glass surface of the front counter. "Especially women who'd attend a night of worship put on by my new worship pastor, who I happen to know thinks quite highly of you."

Her stomach clenched. The night of worship—that sacred, holy moment where she'd finally surrendered and started her walk home toward God, where she and Matt had discovered new common ground, where they'd *kissed*—oh, how did Trace know? How *much* did he know?

"You weren't even there," she blurted. "Matt said you were at some retreat in Florida."

"That I was." The fingertip trailed the edge of the glass. Her skin crawled at the memory of his touch. "But social media is a powerful thing."

"Someone tagged me? But I—"

"Relax, Siobhan." His voice gave her goose bumps. Not the good kind. "A couple of my congregants took a selfie. Matt just happened to be in the background talking to you."

Nausea surged. Was it before the kiss? After? *During*? What if Trace had seen the kiss? His knowledge of the moment would taint it beyond repair, like someone pouring battery acid over a perfect slice of New York cheesecake.

"I almost didn't recognize you." Trace's gaze raked over her hair. "Never would've thought it, but blond suits you."

She yanked her hair back from his predatory stare, corralling it behind her shoulders. "What do you want, Trace? Why are you here?"

He smiled with his lips but not his eyes. "I want you to stay away from Matt."

"I don't think that's anything you have the right to tell me."

"Ah. But he is my worship pastor. My employee. My subordinate." *As you once were.* He didn't have to say the words. They came through loud and clear.

"But what's more, he's a bright star," Trace continued. "Frankly, he's one of the most talented worship leaders I've ever seen. And I won't let him become ensnared by the same trap that almost befell me."

Siobhan's eyebrows shot to her hairline. "You're the one who trapped me, Trace. You put a target on my back from the moment I walked into that office. You were relentless. You were predatory. You—"

"Oh, come off it, Siobhan." Trace slapped the counter for emphasis. "I heard a lot of sounds from you while we were together, but not a single one sounded like a complaint. If you'd said no, I'd have respected that. I'd have backed off. You know that. I don't need to force myself on anyone." His eyes warmed, that puppy-dog look she'd found so difficult to resist in another lifetime. "You can spin it all you want, sweetheart, but you were into me too."

Her stomach roiled for a different reason. Because he wasn't wrong. She hadn't said no.

But now, for the first time, she was beginning to see the difference between not-a-no and an enthusiastic, qualm-free yes, especially when that yes was in response to someone who wasn't manipulating her. Wasn't using her.

"Besides, I'm not the one who started it." Trace's eyes glittered with the same intensity she remembered from three years ago. "I tried to stay pure. I fasted. I prayed. I did all the things. Everything I did for you, I only meant as a friend. I never intended for it to turn into what it became. Not until you kissed me."

"Wait, what?" Her world tilted on its axis. "But you brought me coffee."

"As a friend."

"You listened to me. You invited me into your office. All those texts, all those late-night conversations—"

"I'm sorry to burst your bubble. But I truly wanted nothing more than friendship." His mouth flexed. "Okay, eventually I wanted more. I can't deny that. But it was a mistake. One I've apologized for and paid for and repented of."

You haven't apologized to me. That was what she would have said, had words been something she was capable of.

"I'm not blameless, Siobhan. I'll admit that. But neither are you. That first kiss was your idea. And no amount of mental gymnastics on either of our parts will ever change that."

He was right. She'd initiated that kiss. But his eyes had fixated on her lips. His relentless pursuit, his hungry glances, his flirtatious comments, his accidentally-on-purpose touches had worn her down until she had no resistance left. Trace's strategic, slow-burn plan had seeped into her mind, into her heart, into her body, as invisible and insidious as a computer virus. Even if there'd been a way out, she was so under his spell she wouldn't have seen it. He was her boss. Her pastor. He needed her to help him reach the lost. That was what he'd always told her. He'd made her feel indispensable. A vital part of his valiant mission.

And it had all been a lie.

Hadn't it?

"I was too weak. Too lonely. Not in the Word enough." Trace paced back and forth, dragging a hand through his dark hair like he always did when he was stressed. "And you were too beautiful, Siobhan. Too much for me to resist. Now, Matt's a stronger man than I am, I'll grant that. But he's not infallible. I'm not sure any man is."

He stopped then, his gaze fixed on her. "You're gorgeous, Siobhan. Even when you try not to be, you still are. You're impossible to resist. So I'm asking you—begging you, pleading with you—if you care about Matt at all, please stay away from him. Please don't be a distraction to him. Please don't do to him what you did to me."

Before she could respond, he was gone, and she was left staring at the viola on her workbench. The open bottle of polish. The abandoned polishing cloth.

It had only been a few minutes since she last held these objects. It might as well have been a year.

Was it really only Friday that her faith struggled up from the rubble under which Trace and Pursuers had buried it? She'd felt so clean then. So pure. So forgiven and free.

But here was her past, rushing in to remind her of all she'd once been.

And now her freedom felt like an illusion. A mirage. A mere emotional response to Matt's music.

Would she ever truly escape the shackles of Trace Jessup?

Ian's ancient Buick rumbled into the parking lot, and a moment later the bells jangled to announce his presence. He jerked a thumb at Trace's departing Jaguar.

"Who was that, love?"

She sighed. "That is the reason my life is—and will always be—a dumpster fire."

And then she laid down the tools of her trade, brushed past her boss, and walked into the chilly rain.

><

The last car in the church parking lot—save one—pulled out, its tires gripping the gravel left over from the last ice storm. It was one of the sound guys—Siobhan pulled her hood over her face to avoid recognition, but she needn't have bothered. He was fixated on his phone the whole time, barely even looking up to get into the car.

Finally she exhaled, her breath puffing up around her face in the refrigerator of a car. She climbed out. No use putting it off anymore. The big silver Tacoma, the only vehicle left in the lot, indicated that Matt was alone, as she knew he would be after worship rehearsal.

Her shoulders hunched against nerves and cold, she steeled herself and walked through the huge wood-and-glass doors of Pursuers Church for the first time in over three years.

The smell was the same. Stale coffee, leftover doughnuts, and a whiff of the ever-present fog machine. But the foyer had been redesigned since she was last here. Not surprising, as Pursuers was constantly remodeling, renovating, and rebranding, all in the name of reaching people for Jesus, and the fundraising was every bit as constant. No stone unturned, no wall unpainted, and no piece of technology even the slightest bit outdated. That seemed to be the ticket in twenty-first-century American evangelicalism.

The worship center was different too. All black—better for the church's online congregation, she knew—with new sound panels on the walls.

And their shiny new worship pastor on the stage, popping his earbuds into a case he held in his left hand.

Matt looked up at her entrance, and his face lit beneath the dimmed stage lights. "Siobhan. Hey." Stuffing the earbuds into the pocket of his jeans, he came down the stairs, his cheeks creased and eyes alight. "Pretty sure you're the last person I expected to walk through that door."

He wrapped her in his arms, his stubble scratchy yet soft against her cheek, his scent fresh and clean despite the long day. How did he manage to work so hard and still smell so good? She rested her chin on his shoulder for just a moment, eyes closed, breathing him in. His hands were on her back, warm and strong and protective. If they could just stay like this forever, if she could forget about everything and put it all away and just—

He pulled back, his face still shining with affection, and she had to look away. That joy was about to disappear.

Because she was about to break his heart.

Best to do it now, though, before they got in any deeper.

"Siobhan?" His smile slipped at the edges. "What's wrong?"

She looked around, suddenly cold. Why did Pursuers always have the air conditioner set to Deep Freeze?

"Are we . . . no one else is here, are they?"

"Nope. Rick was the only other one left, and he took off a few minutes ago."

"Okay." Her hands shook. Her voice shook. Everything shook. "Okay."

Matt's hands lay warm and heavy on her shoulders. "Breathe, Siobhan."

She tried, but the air wouldn't come. Her lungs wouldn't work. All she felt was the shaking.

"Come on." Matt's voice sounded five hundred miles away. "You can do this. Breathe with me. In."

She did. It was shaky, but she did.

"Breathe out."

Air whooshed from her lungs. Ragged, but it was there.

"Breathe in."

Her eyes stung. This man, this wonderful, beautiful man who'd done nothing wrong, who wanted only to care for her—

That was exactly why she had to forge ahead.

"Breathe out."

Air came out. Calmer this time. More resolute. No matter how she felt about it, this was the right thing.

"Better?" His eyes were rich with concern, and a wavy lock of hair had fallen over his forehead. She resisted the urge to brush it back.

"Yes." *No.*

"It's a big step for you, coming here." He brushed his hair back and looked around the worship center, as though trying to see it through her eyes. "But I'm glad you did. I mean, I never expected you to walk in here again, and the fact that you did, it's huge, and I'm just so—"

"I needed to do this here." Her voice was so cold that she didn't recognize it as her own.

His brow creased. "Do what here?"

She fiddled with the sleeve of her jacket. "Matt, I—we—this needs to end."

"What needs to end?" He sounded confused.

"Us."

"What? Why?"

There was the hurt she expected. Snapping her head up, she gestured around her. "Look at all this. This is your dream job. This is where God wants you. I knew that before, but after worship night, after watching you do your thing, seeing how amazing you are at it, I don't want to stand in the way of that."

He stepped back. "But you're not. If anything, I'm closer to God than I was before I met you. I'm better at this job because of you. You inspire me."

The same line. Not word for word, but the same general sentiment, spoken in this same building. A different man, but not different enough.

"And that's exactly why this needs to end. Because right now, maybe I inspire you. But before long, I'm going to distract you. I'll tempt you. I'll derail you."

"Where's this coming from?" Eyes that had radiated love before now darkened with confusion and pain. "Is this . . . is Trace behind this?"

She pressed her lips together.

"You're not a distraction, Siobhan. You're not derailing my mission—you're part of it. God brought you into my life when I wasn't looking for anyone or planning for anyone or . . . or anything." He grasped her upper arms. "I never expected to find anyone I wanted to be in a relationship with. To think about a future with. But I did. I found you."

She avoided his gaze. "You only think you want those things with me."

"You think I don't know what I feel?" Desperation shredded his voice. "You think I don't know what it's like to want to be with someone?"

"You really want to be sloppy seconds to your boss?" she snapped. "Your mentor? You want to be with someone who had sex with your boss on a couch you can see from your office window? You? A person whose literal job is bringing people closer to God? That's who you want to be with? Really, Matt?"

He was silent.

Too silent.

He didn't need to say a word, though. The raw pain on his face was evidence enough. Finally she'd gotten through to him. Finally he saw her as she really was, not as he wished her to be.

"Is that really how you see yourself, Siobhan?" His voice was thick.

"It doesn't matter." She stepped back with a sad smile. "Because now that's how you see me."

"I never said that."

She wrapped her hand around the keys in her pocket. "You didn't have to."

Then for the second time in three years, she turned her back on everything and walked out of Pursuers Church.

CHAPTER THIRTY

February 1877

THE POTATO SKIN spiraled beneath Deborah's knife, its tough brown exterior pooling before her. Normally she made a game out of it, trying to see how cleanly she could peel the tuber, but today there was no pride in the accomplishment. No satisfaction.

Only the white-hot anger that had gripped her from the moment she'd read Elisabeth's letter.

At first she hadn't thought Levi and Nathaniel looked alike, but the better she got to know the brothers, the more similarities she saw. Levi's coloring was softer—light-brown hair and gentle blue eyes, whereas Nathaniel's hair neared ebony and his blue eyes pierced—but they boasted the same cheekbones. The same chin. The same high forehead.

Her husband resembled her sister's murderer. And because of that she could barely look at him. Hadn't spoken to him in three days. Levi had tentatively tried to broach the subject a time or two, but she'd shut him down, and so he'd stayed away. Rightly so. What could he possibly say to her? What could she say to him?

The family she'd married into had played a part in destroying her own.

The door creaked open, and a chilly gust of wind hit her back. Her shoulders stiffened, and the movement caused her to nick a finger in her haste. Biting back a decidedly unladylike word, Deborah dropped the knife and stuck the tip of her finger in her mouth.

"Hullo, love." Boots stomped and fabric rustled.

She pulled her finger from her mouth and inspected the wound in the split second before blood rushed to the surface. Nothing serious, thankfully. Just a small round circle of flesh missing from the tip of the finger that bore Levi's ring.

Her scalp wound—her situation—in miniature.

"Good day?" Her husband's voice pierced the fog.

"Mm." She wrapped her bleeding finger in a towel.

"Where's Nora?"

"With the Brennans." Levi would doubtless be disappointed, as he always looked forward to his daughter's enthusiastic greetings. But Annabelle had offered, and Deborah desperately needed a few hours free from childish chatter.

Not to mention a pair of blue eyes shockingly similar to those of the man who'd murdered her sister.

"Good." Levi's reply was crisp enough that she finally looked at him. "Because you and I need to have a conversation that I don't think is appropriate for young ears."

She cautiously peeked beneath the towel. The bleeding had slowed but not yet stopped. She rewrapped her finger. "We've nothing to discuss, Levi."

"Respectfully, I disagree." The tone he used with her was pleasant enough but firm, holding no room for argument. "Because I'd like to discuss just how long you intend to punish me for a crime I had nothing to do with."

He wanted a conversation? All right. He'd have one.

"Your brother handed me a life sentence of suffering," she spat. "He tore my sister's scalp from her skull. The men he was with did the same to me. They killed my mother. My siblings. And ultimately Elisabeth too. I believe I've earned the right to be angry."

"I'll not disagree with you on that." Levi flung his arms out wide. "You think I'm not angry as well?"

"Doubtless you are, and I'm sorry for that. But given all that's happened lately, I don't believe I'll stop being angry anytime soon. If ever."

Blue eyes flashed. "Nor do I."

Deborah flung the towel aside. "Your brother and his cohorts ruined my life, and you're angry with *me*?"

"No!" The word was short and sharp, like a dog's bark, and she jumped despite herself.

Levi pulled in a breath, and when he spoke again, his voice was quieter but still intense. "Deborah, I'm not angry with you at all. Hurt by your recent silence, yes. But my anger is reserved for my brother." He lifted his hands and tentatively rested them on her upper arms. "You're bone of my bone, flesh of my flesh. Do you not think that if someone hurts you, they do the same to me?"

The baby stirred within her, as though to emphasize Levi's point.

"I can't possibly imagine what you've been through," he continued. "What you're going through. Frankly, I've never felt so helpless. So frustrated. Because what happened to you is so big, so massive, that anything I say or do to try to alleviate your suffering feels like flicking droplets of water on a wildfire." He sought her gaze and held it. "But I'll keep flicking those droplets because I love you, and if it helps even a fraction, then I'll give those droplets everything I have."

With a weary sigh, Deborah leaned her forehead on her husband's shoulder. He always did know just what to say. What to do. The anger bled from her as she absorbed his warmth, his strength, the scents of cold and woodsmoke.

"But may I ask one thing of my wife?" He lifted her chin with his fingertips. His thumb feathered over her flesh. His expression was without pretense, his eyes pleading, with a slight sheen of tears.

Throat thick, she nodded.

"Please, I beg of you, stop punishing me. Nathaniel is more than a decade my senior. He left home when I was younger than Nora. I had no knowledge of his life until just a few months ago."

"I know."

"Then please don't allow Nathaniel's crimes to cause any more damage. I'll not let him destroy our marriage, Deborah. I simply won't. I'll fight for it, even if it means I have to fight you."

She stepped closer, her belly a circle between herself and Levi. "I don't want us to fight each other. Not really."

"I'm glad for that." He sounded relieved.

"But never in my life did I ever think I'd come face-to-face with the man who attacked Elisabeth." Deborah stepped back to the counter, memories swirling, and picked up the abandoned potato, smooth and cool beneath her fingers. "And in my wildest dreams, I never thought I'd have someone in my family who's capable of such savagery."

"*All* men are capable of such savagery," Levi pointed out. "The Bible makes that clear. Only by surrendering to Jesus can we be free."

She wanted to argue. She wanted to say that there was no way Levi could do something so heinous, or Papa, or Nora, or herself, but Levi was right. There was no arguing with Scripture.

"But by the same token, if we surrender to Jesus, then he can transform us. He can change the leper's spots. He can melt the heart of stone. And I've seen it." Levi's voice shimmered with urgency. "Whatever my brother was, he is no longer. I'm quite confident of that."

"You've only known him three months," she replied. "How do you know his transformation is genuine? Have you . . . spoken with him? About the attack?"

"He doesn't remember much, Deborah. It was traumatic for him too."

She gave a derisive snort. "You expect me to feel sorry for him?"

"Of course not," he replied. "But what I would ask—not expect, but ask—of you is that you listen. Especially since you're the one who broached the subject. If you're not ready to talk about this now, then we can wait until you are."

Was she ready?

No.

Would she ever be?

Likely not.

But she was curious. Desperately so.

"I would like to hear what he said to you. I think."

"Are you certain?" He wrapped an arm around her, warm and tight, as though willing her his strength. "If it's too much, we can stop at any time and revisit it later."

Deborah nodded. "Yes. I would like to know what justification he could possibly have. What excuse he's come up with that makes this all right."

"None" came the quick reply. "Nathaniel makes no excuse. Offers no defense. And he does not expect you to forgive him."

"Good." The word burst from the depths of her in a bark of bitterness. "Because forgiveness is the last thing he deserves."

"It's the last thing any of us deserves, yet the Bible commands us to extend it as freely as it has been extended to us."

She whirled on her husband. "You believe you have the right to lecture me about forgiveness? You, who can't fathom what I've been through?"

"Elisabeth could," he pointed out quietly. "And she forgave him. Nathaniel said as much."

Deborah slammed the knife down. "I know she did. She wrote me a letter urging me to do the same thing. And of course she could forgive. Elisabeth was the perfect one. The sweet one, the one everyone adored, the one whose scars somehow made her more beautiful. She was sweetness and light and perfection personified. Of course she could forgive Nathaniel the moment she laid eyes on him. But I'm not her."

Levi studied her, his expression cautious but wise. "Are you jealous of Elisabeth, love?"

Jealous. She tried the word on in her mind. "She was so beautiful, so delicate, so graceful. No matter what happened to her, she didn't let it faze her. Her headaches were worse than mine, but she hardly ever complained. She never snapped. She was the opposite of me in nearly every way. And I . . . I envy her ability to forgive."

"It sounds like you want to forgive him, then."

"What I want is to be free." Tears pooled in her eyes. "Yet another reason to be jealous of Elisabeth, because she's free now. She's whole and healed and perfect and in heaven with Jesus, where everything makes sense and nothing is broken and all is as it should be. She's with Mother and Josiah and Mary Catherine and Nancy, and she's free of all her pain and suffering. And I'm still here."

Levi stiffened, and she hastened to reassure him. "It's not that I don't want to be here. I do. Because I love you and Nora and this little one. I want to be here to see them grow up. To grow old with you. I want those things."

"But you want to be free too." Levi caressed her upper arm.

Something broke within her at his words, and a tear spilled down her cheek. "Yes. Yes. More than anything."

"I understand that feeling." He pulled her closer. "Not for the same reasons you do, but I do understand."

"What do I do, then? How do I forgive Nathaniel? How do I even get to the point where I'm capable of it? Where it's a choice I can make?"

Levi sighed, his breath whooshing past her ear. "That's not something I can tell you how to do. If it was, I'd do it in a heartbeat. But what I will do is pray for you. For God to shower you with wisdom and abundant clarity and a soft heart. Both for you and for Nathaniel."

His name and hers, mentioned in the same breath by the man who loved them both. Who was caught in the middle of a horrible situation through no fault of his own. And who would grab them both by the arms and drag them to the throne of God, kicking and screaming if necessary, because of that love. The man who'd fight her to save their marriage. Who'd fight to ensure her faithfulness to God.

"Levi?" The question was soft, tremulous, and his lips found her temple. "Yes?"

"Thank you for loving me."

"Of course." His kisses trailed down her cheek, and his grip on her waist tightened. "And I always will."

CHAPTER THIRTY-ONE

MATT SAT ALONE onstage in the worship center the next morning, trying to focus on the words of the worship song. On the simple four-chord pattern. Usually it put him into a meditative state. Removed his focus from the seen and set it on the unseen.

Usually.

But not today.

Today, all he could think about was Siobhan.

It had been such a pleasant surprise, her coming in after worship rehearsal. But his pleasant surprise had quickly turned to concern at the look on her face. Shock when she broke it off with him.

Heartbreak when she walked out the door.

"Forgive me, Lord. I just can't right now." Frustrated, he pulled the guitar from over his head.

"I doubt he'll need to forgive anything I just heard." Trace's voice came from the back corner of the auditorium. "That sounded great to me."

Matt's shoulders tensed, and the leaden grief in the center of his chest melted into a glowing ball of anger. This was the person to blame for it all. This man was the reason the woman Matt loved had walked away.

He turned, his breathing fast and shallow with his frantic efforts to maintain composure. He couldn't say what he wanted. Do what he wanted. Not here. Not in God's house.

"What'd you say to her?" he managed.

Trace stepped into the spotlight and blinked. "To who? Siobhan?"

I never want to hear that name cross your lips ever again. You don't deserve to utter such a beautiful word.

He hadn't spoken the words aloud, but he didn't need to. The slight quirk of Trace's smile was all the confirmation Matt needed.

"I merely reminded her of what happened between us and the role she played in it," he said mildly. "I'm sorry if that caused a bump in the road for the two of you."

"It was more than a bump in the road." Matt's jaw tightened. "It was the end of it."

"Mmm." Trace gave a thoughtful nod. "Well, I'm sorry you're hurting, my man. Truly. That wasn't my goal."

Yeah, right. Matt covered his sarcastic reply with a cough.

Trace stepped forward and laid a friendly-seeming hand on Matt's shoulder. "I never meant to cause you pain, Matty. But sometimes temporary pain is better than permanent destruction. She's bad news, and you're better off. I know you don't see that now, but someday you will. I'm just looking out for you."

Matt shook Trace's hand from his shoulder. "You mean you're looking out for *you*."

"What, you think I'm jealous? You think I still want her?" Trace smirked. "Please. That ship has sailed."

That's because you've punched your ticket for a new ship. And God alone knows how many women there were between Siobhan and Kayleigh.

The uncharitable thought rose lavalike from his chest, and in that moment the scales fell from Matt's eyes. The man before him was a lot of things to him. Pastor. Mentor. Employer. Father figure. The man who'd led him to the throne and introduced him to Jesus. He'd always be grateful for that.

But whatever Trace Jessup had once been, he was also someone who pretended to be caring and loving when he was anything but. A narcissist. Perhaps even a sociopath. Nothing beyond God's forgiveness—and with grace, Matt's own—but also something that would forever change his image of Trace. Something Matt could no longer ignore, deny, or pretend it wasn't there.

Something Matt was determined to bring into the light.

"I know what you are," he said.

"A sinner saved by grace?" Trace lifted his gaze skyward. "That's true of all of us, my friend."

"Only if the sinner repents, which you haven't," he fired back. "You're a predator, Trace."

Something dangerous glinted in Trace's dark eyes. "You're not exactly pure as the driven snow yourself."

"It's true I have a past. You know who I used to be. But thanks to Jesus, I'm not that guy anymore. He can heal you too, if you let him."

Trace stepped closer, his voice low. "Look. You and I both know that the only reason you've got a job of this caliber is because I went to bat for you. You're not even remotely qualified to be here. Keep that in mind."

"If I'm not qualified to be here, then why'd you hire me?" he shot back.

"Because I'm a pretty powerful person to have in your corner." Trace offered a snakelike smile and a brotherly pat on the arm. "Trust me, Buchanan. You don't want that to change."

Then Trace turned and strode up the center aisle, taking all of Matt's remaining illusions with him.

Trace was a danger. A menace. Matt had to do something to stop him. The only question now was how.

><

"So."

The conspiratorial note in her mother's voice put Siobhan on instant high alert. She knew that note. It meant that rather than hearing about her kid brother's college adventures or Mom's latest real estate deal, the conversational spotlight was about to shine squarely on her.

"How's life in your corner of the world?" Mom drizzled dressing over the massive salad in front of her. "Sloane said you're seeing someone?"

"Was. Past tense." Siobhan took a large bite of her bacon-and-bleu burger in hopes of fending off further questions.

"Oh no. I'm sorry to hear that." Mom put down the dressing and laced her fingers under her chin.

It was a gesture Siobhan remembered well from her teenage years. One that meant she had Mom's undivided attention, that whatever was burdening her, Mom was happy to take it on.

"What happened?"

Siobhan mopped a glob of melted cheese from her fingertips with the napkin. "Trace Jessup. He's what happened."

"Isn't he the pastor at your old church?"

Siobhan squeezed her eyes shut. "Yes. He was my pastor. He was my boss. And he's also my ex."

"I see." Mom reached for her glass of iced tea. "I knew something happened, but you never told me exactly what. Makes sense that it was a man."

"And that's exactly why I didn't want to tell you." Siobhan sighed in defeat. "Because I didn't want to disappoint you. But I've disappointed so many people—myself most of all—so hey, what's one more?"

Mom looked hurt. "You've carried this burden for three years because you thought I'd be disappointed in you?"

"My whole life you've told me to guard my heart. To be careful who I date. To make better decisions than you did." Siobhan twisted her straw wrapper into a tight little coil, the white paper wrapper rough against her fingertips. "And I thought I had. Before I found out what kind of man Trace really is."

Mom was silent for a long time. Too long.

"Mom?"

Her mother's gaze was on her salad, her fork twisting absently in leaves of dressing-drowned kale. Finally, she set the fork down and looked up. "Siobhan, I think it's time I told you about Sloane's father."

Siobhan froze, her heart leaping into her throat. All Mom had said about that time in her life was that she'd made some bad decisions, and she'd implored Siobhan to have higher standards for dating than she did.

Mom took a deep breath. "I graduated high school at seventeen. Top of my class. And I got a full ride scholarship to the College of Mount Rainier to study English lit."

Siobhan blinked. English lit? *Mom?*

"My lit professor was the absolute highlight of my time there." Mom's smile was soft, her expression fuzzy. "He was youngish. Attractive. Smart.

Funny. He loved teaching—he was so enthusiastic about it, and his enthusiasm was contagious—and there was nothing he wouldn't do to pass on his love of literature to the students. In short, he was absolutely everything you could want in a teacher. And he took a shine to me."

Siobhan's stomach churned. Was there something in the genetic code of the women in their family? Had Mom truly made the same mistake?

"Danilo—he always insisted we call him by his first name—told me I had a bright future and that he wanted to invest in me on a personal level." Mom chuckled. "I can see the red flags now, but back then the only thing I could see was him."

Siobhan got goose bumps. Oh, how familiar this all sounded. How eerily, chillingly familiar.

"It was innocent at first. Just during his office hours, and he always left the door open. It was friendly but strictly professional. Nothing inappropriate—a pat on the shoulder here, a grin and wink there, but nothing that stood out as bad. But then we started having lunch in his office. Dinner a lot of nights." Mom gave a shaky sigh. "And the week after I turned eighteen, he started shutting the door."

"You were a kid," Siobhan burst out. "Kids are supposed to make dumb decisions. Adults aren't."

"Exactly. They aren't. And Danilo was an adult. A *married* adult. He was almost twice my age. He was my professor. My mentor. He had all the power in our relationship." Mom's gaze locked on Siobhan's, dark and intense. "It took me a long time to realize this, Siobhan, but that imbalance of power means that despite the fact that I was absolutely crazy in love with him, that I wanted it too, our relationship was never truly consensual. It was abuse."

Abuse. Such a strong word. A heavy word. A loaded word.

But one that resonated in the very core of her being.

Abuse.

It all fit. The targeting. The grooming. The way Trace had plied her with lies slowly but relentlessly, insidiously and invisibly, until she was cornered like a trapped animal. She may have made the first move the night things turned physical, but in no way had she initiated the relationship. That was all Trace.

"If Trace was your pastor, if he was your boss, if he groomed you the way I suspect he did . . . then he was also your abuser."

"But I didn't say no. I didn't fight him off. I was the one who initiated our first kiss."

"Siobhan, listen to me." Mom's eyes bored deep into hers. "There is a difference between giving consent and giving in. If you felt like you didn't have the power to refuse him . . . then even if you initiated the kiss, even if you were attracted to him, it was his fault. Not yours."

"We're victims, then? Is that it?" Being a victim was just as bad. Because that made her weak. Powerless. Exactly what she'd been with Trace, which was probably why the word galled her so much.

"No, Siobhan. We're survivors. And God's going to use this for good." Mom's gaze sought hers and held it. "I know you probably don't believe me right now, and that's okay. I wouldn't have believed me, either, had someone told me the same thing. For me it took until Sloane reappeared to see it, but he promises in his Word to make good come out of even the worst things. Look at Joseph. Look at Job. Look at Mary and Martha and Lazarus."

"It's hard to see that right now, Mom."

"I know." Mom reached forward and squeezed Siobhan's hand. "But the fact that you're here, that you're on the other side of this thing, that you got out and got away and you're still standing, means God's not done with you yet. He hasn't given up. Just like you haven't given up on that busted-up old violin."

Siobhan chuckled and swiped at a tear that had managed to escape. "How'd you know I'm still working on it?"

"Because I know you." Mom propped her chin on her hand. "I know Todd's not your biological father, but you must've picked up some of his qualities anyway, because the two of you have the same gentle persistence. He met me when I was broken, and he never pushed. When I asked for space, he granted it. When I told him I wanted to take things slow, he re-spected it. But he also never gave up on me. And when I was ready for him . . . he was still right there. Thank God."

"Yeah." When Siobhan turned seven and Todd entered their world,

Mom had started smiling again. She got a bounce in her step Siobhan had never seen before.

And she sang. When Mom was happy, she sang, and when Todd came into their lives, Mom's song came back.

Just like Siobhan's song had come back about the time Matt had walked into her shop and plopped that beat-up old violin on the counter.

Maybe Matt was different.

Maybe he was the good that God was going to bring out of the mess with Trace.

She wasn't healed yet. Like the violin, she still had cracks to patch and rough edges to smooth out.

But maybe, when she was, Matt would still be there waiting, just like Todd had been for Mom.

Or maybe Matt was part of God's plan to heal her.

Maybe that was what God had been doing all along.

CHAPTER THIRTY-TWO

February 1877

DEBORAH FINISHED LETTING out the hem of one of Nora's dresses and eyed it critically. The little girl was growing faster than Deborah had ever anticipated, and the dresses she was sure would last through the winter now looked like they might not even make it until March.

"Nora? Come here for a moment, please."

But her daughter was nowhere to be seen, and the constant chatter that filled the house even when Nora was playing alone had grown curiously quiet. Setting the dress aside, Deborah heaved herself out of the fireside rocker as quickly as her burgeoning belly would allow. Though Nora wasn't the most mischievous child Deborah had ever encountered, quiet wasn't necessarily a good thing.

"Nora?" She moved toward the kitchen, where she'd last seen Nora playing with her doll. But the little girl wasn't there any longer.

Hmm. Perhaps she'd grown sleepy and gone off for her nap on her own. She'd done that once or twice. But a glimpse into the bedroom came up empty as well.

"Nora Jane." Her voice grew more insistent. "Where are you?"

As though in answer to her question, the door to the cabin creaked open.

"Nora?" Moving as quickly as the unborn baby would allow, she left the bedroom and headed for the door, then let out a quiet gasp. Nora was there, her cheeks and nose pink from the cold, in the arms of Nathaniel Martinson.

Deborah froze. Though Nathaniel's hair was dark and straight, while Nora's was red blond and curly, the two bore the same eyes. Bright, piercing blue. The genetic link between them was unmistakable. The man who murdered her family was standing in her living room. Holding her daughter. Sharing the same eyes. The same blood.

Those same arms had held Elisabeth. Restrained her. Pulled back her hair. Sliced her scalp. Ignored her screams. Left her for dead.

"Sorry for the intrusion." Nathaniel shuffled his feet. "Levi and I were feeding the stock, and this little lady decided to come help us."

She should scold Nora for leaving the house without permission. For disrupting the men's work. But she couldn't stop staring at the two of them together. At this man, this man who'd ruined her, ruined her family, standing in her home. Her sanctuary. The place where she'd finally been able to heal and let herself be loved and feel beautiful for the first time. He was here, with her child, and it was too much.

"Nora." Her voice sounded as though it came from the next county. "Please go lie down for your nap. We'll discuss the choices you made later."

"Yes, Mama." The little girl sounded both contrite and relieved to escape immediate punishment. Her feet slapped the wooden planks, and a moment later the door creaked closed and the bedsprings gave a soft squeak.

Deborah turned to Nathaniel then, the tension in the room as thick as the stew on the stove. "Thank you," she managed.

Thanking him. She was thanking the man who'd killed her sister.

"Pleasure." He slapped his hat back on his head and moved toward the door, and Deborah's heart leaped into her throat.

"Why?"

That word had been a consistent, annoying whine in her ears for the last decade. Every time her head throbbed. Every holiday meal with empty places at the table. Every time she wished for her mother's embrace, her mother's advice, her mother's love. Every time she looked in a mirror. Looked at Elisabeth. Saw the lines around Papa's eyes. Every single day. Every moment.

And now the question was out, lobbed to the one man who could answer it.

Nathaniel stopped. Took his hat in his hands and turned to face her.

"I've been asking myself the same question," he said. "Ever since it happened."

That wasn't an answer. The question increased in fury. What was a high-pitched whine, like that of a mosquito, suddenly turned into a whole horde, burning and buzzing within her until she ripped off her cap and flung it to the floor.

Nathaniel flinched. Recoiled. For the first time, she relished that reaction.

"Was this you?" She pointed toward her head. "Were you the one who did this to me?"

He shook his head. "No."

"But you did it to my sister," she pressed. "She always said it was a white man who scalped her. We thought she was crazy. But she wasn't, was she? It was you. You're the one."

Nathaniel closed his eyes. A muscle in his jaw twitched. "Yes."

The single syllable of confirmation took her right back there. Right back to that warm May afternoon at the camp. The men out on a hunt. The women bustling around, preparing for their return. She and Elisabeth playing near the creek.

She wasn't sure what tipped her off at first that something was amiss, but she and Elisabeth both had cocked their heads at the general sense of unease.

They'd heard the whoops first. The high-pitched yells, made to sound like Sioux warriors. Then the screams.

She didn't see the attack on her mother. Her siblings. But she'd heard it.

She and Elisabeth ran. They hid behind a cottonwood near the creek. And they heard it all.

They waited until it was quiet. Until the screams stopped and the war whoops faded. She'd looked at Elisabeth, and the two girls, in an unspoken agreement, decided it was safe to come out. So they crept from behind the tree.

The quiet lasted but a moment. Then came an arm across her throat. Rough cloth against her skin. The searing pain, her own screams—

"This whole time I blamed the Sioux," she spat.

Nathaniel rubbed the back of his neck. "That's what we wanted you to think."

"We?"

"William heard about this kind of thing back East. Where people dressed up like Natives and attacked settlers. The logic—if you can call it that—was that it would make the settlers think the Natives were vicious, and then they'd go after them and drive them out of the land, and it would be all ours."

Deborah's jaw slackened. "So you did this horrible thing to incite violence against innocents? Somehow that's even worse."

Nathaniel's gaze fell to the floor. "William's family was wiped out by a Cheyenne attack when he was real young. That's no excuse, I realize, but—"

"And why were *you* involved?" she demanded. "Did you have a vendetta too?"

"No. It was stupid. *I* was stupid." His hands gripped his hat, the knuckles turning white. "I was seventeen. I'd run away from home. I don't know what Levi has told you about our childhood, but . . . it wasn't the best. Our father was a drunk. A mean drunk. With the sort of consequences you can well imagine."

Deborah blinked. "He mentioned it a time or two, but not in any detail."

"I'm told it improved after I left." Nathaniel gave a bitter chuckle. "And for Levi's sake, I'm glad. From what he's told me, he got a much better version of our father than I did. But I was lost. For a long, long time."

"So you did *that*? How did you sleep at night?"

"I didn't." That sharp blue gaze came up to meet hers. "Sometimes I still don't."

"And you expect me to feel sorry for you?" She could barely hear her own voice over the pounding of her heart. "Because I can't. I won't. You chose to take part in this. Every bit of suffering you've had since then was because of a decision you made. But my suffering? My pain? My scars? My losses? My sleepless nights? None of that was my choice. *None* of it."

The word came out choked, and she willed the lump from her throat and the tears from her eyes. She wouldn't give him the satisfaction. "All we were doing was trying to get to a new home so my father could start a church. So he could share the love of Jesus with the settlers here. That's all. We were children, Nathaniel. We didn't choose the suffering you inflicted on us, and we did nothing to deserve it."

"There's nothing I can say, nothing I can do, that will excuse my actions." His voice was thick. "I've wished countless times to go back and undo what I did. To see the choices laid out before me and make a different one."

"Then why didn't you?"

"I wanted a family, Deborah." He gripped his hat, knuckles white. "I never had a family, and I wanted one, and that's what William and his gang offered me. At the time I didn't see it for what it was. I didn't realize what joining that farce of a family would cost me. I would do anything to take it back . . . because now I know what family is."

"But you and your so-called family ruined mine."

"I'm sorry doesn't make it right, but it's all I've—"

"Get out." She gripped the back of the chair. Fury made her voice tight. "Get out of my home and never return. Get away from me. From my daughter. From my husband. We are no longer your family. You don't deserve to have one. Get out. Leave my home and never come back." Had she actually thought she wanted to forgive Nathaniel? Perhaps she thought she did, in the moment, but now that he was here, standing right where Elisabeth had fallen, his soiled boots on that sacred ground.

Surely not, Lord. Surely you can't expect me to forgive him.

Nathaniel was silent for a long time. Finally, a quiet sigh escaped his lips, and he gave a small nod. "Very well."

Then he turned and left, the door creaking behind him, the chilly gust of air the only sign he'd ever been there.

Deborah sank into the chair, her whole body shaking, tears coursing down her cheeks. She'd done it. She'd confronted the man who'd ruined her. She'd told him exactly what he did, how he hurt her, the decades of damage his decisions had left in their wake.

She'd expected to feel victorious. Vindicated. As though she'd avenged the blood of her mother. Of Josiah. And Mary Catherine. And Nancy. And Elisabeth.

But she didn't.

Instead, all she felt was empty.

CHAPTER THIRTY-THREE

MATT'S FOOTSTEPS SHATTERED the 10:00 p.m. quiet in the parking lot of Pursuers. It was chilly and he was exhausted, and the last place he wanted to be was back at work. But he'd forgotten his phone—his phone, of all things—and though part of him thought it might be a good idea to break the addiction and enjoy the quiet and spend a night unplugged, in the end he couldn't be without it.

How could he have forgotten something so basic? So elemental? Then again, he'd been extra forgetful lately. Extra impatient. Extra a lot of things.

Godliness with contentment is great gain. Jesus was all he truly needed. Maybe his current heartbreak was a reminder of that. He'd heard an old saying that there was a God-shaped hole in all of us that nothing else could fill. And God filled that hole in him.

But there was a Siobhan-shaped hole too. And he had no idea how to fill that with anything but her.

Looked like he wasn't the only one here this late, though. Trace's black Jaguar sat in its customary parking space near the back of the lot.

But he wasn't alone. A gold Chevy Malibu sat a few spaces away.

Wasn't that . . .

Yeah. Kayleigh's car.

And a soft light bled from the mini blinds of Trace's office.

Stomach in knots, Matt crept up to the window, off to the side. He felt like a creeper, but he had to know what was going on in there. The blinds weren't open, but they weren't a hundred percent closed, either. And if he crouched down slightly and peered up, he got a perfect view.

Sure enough, Trace and Kayleigh were in Trace's large, luxurious office. Together. Alone. After hours. A clear violation of Trace's widely publicized purity policy.

They were just talking, at least right now. Trace stood closest to Matt, his back three-quarters turned, while Kayleigh was on the opposite side of the office. It was her face Matt could see most clearly. The bright smile. The flushed cheeks. The light in her eyes, the whole I'm-totally-into-you vibe.

Had this been how Siobhan once looked at Trace? How Trace once looked at her?

She'd looked at Matt this way. His aching heart remembered that all too well.

No. He wasn't going there right now. *Focus.*

Trace and Kayleigh talked for a bit. Too bad Matt couldn't read lips. Although maybe he really didn't want to know.

Maybe this was it, then. Maybe all they were doing was talking. Maybe it was innocent. For one wild, soul-searing second, there was a chance it was all a misunderstanding. That nothing had happened. That Trace wasn't a predator.

But Trace kept stepping forward. Inch by inch. Slowly but surely he moved toward Kayleigh. Whether she noticed or not, Matt didn't know, but the look on her face told him she wasn't about to stop it.

Kayleigh burst out laughing then, the faintest high pitches bleeding through the walls. By then Trace was close enough to reach forward and brush her hair back from her face. Tuck one of those dark-brown curls behind her ear.

Was Matt watching history on repeat? Was this how it had happened with Siobhan? Had Trace made her laugh? Had he stepped closer?

Kayleigh's laughter faded. Her smile softened and melded from amusement into something else. Her eyes fell to Trace's lips.

Matt wanted to turn away. He shouldn't be watching this. He should run in and stop it, shouldn't he? Should he? Should he catch them in the act? Should he call one of the elders right now? It was as though the forty-degree temperature had caught up to him too, gluing him here, one hand on the brick exterior. A statue of sickened shock.

Trace had turned slightly, and Matt could read his lips better. Couldn't confirm it, but it looked like he'd said something akin to "You know you want to."

Kayleigh backed up. Her lips started to form words, but nothing seemed to come out. Trace put a hand on her slender shoulder. He rubbed it a little bit, like he was reassuring a friend.

C'mon, Kayleigh. Don't fall for it. Please, God, don't let her fall for it.

She shook her head, but Trace pressed in. He brushed her cheek with his thumb, and Kayleigh's eyes fell closed.

This was how it had happened, then, hadn't it? Trace had trapped Siobhan like an animal. Through pretty words and coffee refills and gentle, subtle pressure. He hadn't forced himself on her physically, but he may as well have for all the chances Siobhan had of escaping.

Well. There had been no chance for Siobhan. But as long as Matt was here, there was still hope for Kayleigh.

Before he could second-guess himself, chicken out, or formulate anything resembling a plan, Matt tore around the corner of the building, buzzed himself in with his ID badge, and hurried toward the pastoral offices, where he pounded on Trace's closed door.

Through the thick slab of wood came a surprised gasp from Kayleigh and muttered words from Trace.

"Probably just maintenance," the pastor said, followed by some quieter words Matt couldn't make out.

"Trace." He knocked again. "Trace, you in there, man?"

The door swung open, and Trace poked his head through.

"Matty." He affixed a smile. "What are you doing here this time of night?"

"I could ask the same of you. *Both* of you." Matt looked past Trace to where Kayleigh stood near the leather sofa, her head barely visible above the pastor's shoulder.

Trace's smile widened. "Look, my man. Whatever you think is going on here, isn't. Promise."

"I don't think anything's going on in here, Trace. I *know*. I saw you guys through the—"

"You saw nothing," Trace replied easily. "We're just talking."

Behind Trace, Kayleigh toyed with a curly lock of brown hair.

"Kayleigh?" Matt met her eyes. "Everything all right?"

"Yeah." A brief smile toward the floor. "Fine, Matt."

"If you, uh, if you need a ride somewhere? You got one. Anywhere. Just say the word."

"She doesn't need anything from you, Buchanan." Trace's voice held an edge. "Now go home. It's late."

"First I want Kayleigh to answer my question." He folded his arms across his chest.

Trace turned toward Kayleigh with an exaggerated sweep of his arm. "The floor's all yours, milady."

Kayleigh's lips flickered. "I think you'd better go, Matt."

That wasn't the answer she was supposed to give. She was supposed to tell him that she needed a ride somewhere. Anywhere. *Just get me out of here, Matt.*

He frowned. "Are you sure? It's really no trouble."

Kayleigh nodded. "Yes. I'm sure."

"Kayleigh, I can—"

"You wanted her answer, you got her answer. She wants you to leave, Matt. As do I." Trace's eyes had darkened to near ebony. "And you saw nothing, because nothing's going on. Am I clear? Nothing."

"Then why not date her out in the open, Trace?" Matt flung his arms wide. "You're single. She's single. You like each other. Nothing wrong with any of that as long as you do it the right way. Just come clean, okay? Don't do it like this. Please, not like—"

But the door slammed in his face. The lock clicked shut. The lights in the office went out.

It was over.

Had he thought he needed his phone? No. That could wait until morning. He stumbled blindly through the office hallway, out into the frigid night, where his roiling stomach went into full reverse thrust and emptied his dinner beside the bushes. Matt wiped his mouth with the back of his hand, hot tears stinging his eyes. Spilling onto the skin beneath them. Once he reached the safety of his truck, he laid his head on the steering wheel and sobbed.

A little bit for himself too. For the shattering of innocence. Of illusions. For the toppling, crumbling, and crushing of the pedestal upon which he'd once placed Trace Jessup.

He'd tried to put a stop to it and come up empty. Confronting Trace directly hadn't worked. Offering Kayleigh a way out had fallen on deaf ears.

It was time to up the ante.

※

The buzz of Siobhan's phone against the surface of the workbench shattered the quiet of the workshop. She set her tools aside and picked up the phone.

Sloane was calling.

Calling? Sloane? That couldn't be right. Her half sister was a dedicated texter.

Siobhan lifted the phone to her ear. "Sloane? Everything okay?"

"Yeah. Yeah, everything's fine." Traffic noise bled in through the earpiece. Sloane must be outside the museum. "I just found something in one of Annabelle's diaries today while I was changing out the exhibit."

"Yeah? What'd you find?"

"I've been going back through the diaries to see if any of them have any mention of Deborah." Sloane's explanation was rapid, the words tumbling over themselves. "This one was in the display case, and I hadn't gotten to it yet, but I had a hunch that maybe there was some stuff in here, and sure enough, Annabelle talks about it. Apparently Deborah confronted the man who scalped her sister."

Siobhan nearly dropped the phone. "She did *what*? How was that even possible?"

"Turns out Elisabeth was right all along. They were scalped by a gang of white men dressed as Sioux to try to inflame tensions between the settlers and the tribes living in the area," Sloane explained. "And the man who scalped Elisabeth Caldwell was a guy by the name of Nathaniel Martinson. Levi Martinson's brother. Deborah's brother-in-law."

"That's insane." There was simply no other word for it. "The guy who basically killed Deborah's sister was related to her?"

"Yes. And Deborah was struggling to forgive him."

"Can you blame her?" Siobhan's jaw clenched. "Some things are simply unforgivable."

"From what Annabelle wrote, that was Deborah's perspective. But it seemed Elisabeth had a different one. Which is actually what I called about." Sloane's voice took on that higher-pitched, slightly breathless quality it did when she was excited about some new historical discovery. "According to Annabelle's diary, Elisabeth wrote a letter to Deborah about the attack and how she was able to forgive."

Siobhan nearly rolled her eyes. "Good for Elisabeth."

"Are you at work right now?" Sloane asked.

"Yeah." Siobhan frowned. "Why?"

"Do you have Matt's violin anywhere handy?"

"The glue's still drying. Again, why?"

"Oh, I don't need the violin itself." Siobhan could almost picture the harried wave of Sloane's hand. "I need the case."

Siobhan scanned the row of cases along the far wall. "What for?"

Sloane gave an impatient sigh. "Because the letter might still be in there."

"Wait a minute. What? Really?"

"Now I have your attention." Sloane sounded very pleased with herself. "According to the diary, it was in the lining of the case. I don't know much about violin cases—is that a meaningful statement?"

"Yeah." Siobhan reached for the beat-up old black case and set it on a table near the back of the shop. "I need both hands, so I'm putting you on speaker."

A slight puff of musty air greeted her as she opened the latches, and she scanned the threadbare blue velvet for any sign of a hiding place.

"See anything?" Sloane sounded barely able to contain herself.

"There's a loose patch of fabric here in the corner. Let me see if that's anything."

She worked the fabric loose enough to see the yellowed corner of a piece of paper sticking out of it. "Yeah. It's here. This has got to be it."

"Oh my word, I'm getting goose bumps. If I weren't stuck here at work, I'd be there in no time."

"Any tips on how to get it out without tearing it?"

Sloane paused. "Well, I'd say sacrifice the lining of the case before the letter, but I'm very biased."

"Hang on. I might have an idea." Siobhan reached for a purfling knife. "I think I've got something that'll get it loose enough at least for me to get a good grip on it."

"Be careful" was her half sister's warning.

"Careful is my middle name." Siobhan wedged the knife beneath the lining of the case and pulled back the fabric just enough to grasp the letter between her fingertips. "Wait, do I need gloves or anything?"

She could almost feel Sloane wince. "Probably, but it'll be fine just this once. I'm dying to know what it says."

Siobhan set the knife down and, her hands surprisingly shaky, opened the ancient paper. "Whoa. 1877."

"Read it read it read it," Sloane demanded.

Siobhan grinned. "Okay. Hold on. It's a little hard to make out." Taking a deep breath, she began to read.

To my dearest Papa and Bee-bee . . .

CHAPTER THIRTY-FOUR

March 1877

IT WAS A truly odd thing, not being able to see one's feet.

Deborah walked next to Annabelle beside the creek on a sunny but mild March afternoon.

Well. Annabelle walked.

Deborah waddled.

The baby sat low in her abdomen, making her hips and her back ache and her breath almost impossible to catch. By her calculations, the baby should have arrived a few days ago. Annabelle had said walking would help and graciously offered to walk with her. And walk they had. For over an hour now, and still nothing. But the weather was pleasant, the company more so, and Deborah found her mood lightening in response to both.

"All right, Deborah." To her left, Annabelle's voice shifted in tone, suddenly sounding a bit less relaxed than she had a moment ago. "Forgive me if I'm overstepping the bounds of our friendship, but I'm concerned about you."

Deborah shot her friend a sidelong glance. "Why?"

"You've lost Elisabeth. Nathaniel is a presence. And with this little one soon to make an appearance, I can only imagine what a burden you're carrying." Annabelle brushed a stray lock of dark-blond hair away from her face. "If there's any way I can lighten that burden, it would be an honor."

"I do miss Elisabeth." Deborah fixed her attention on the tender blades of new grass beneath the bulge of her belly. "And the baby is making me feel things differently than I once did. But the thing that feels impossible right now is forgiving Nathaniel Martinson."

Martinson. Even the name made her shudder. It had been a safe haven once. A sign that someone loved her. Cared for her. Wanted to protect and provide for her.

But the man who'd murdered her sister also bore that name, and now it felt like an intrusion. The latest in a long list of intrusions for which Nathaniel had been responsible.

"I can certainly understand why it would feel that way." Annabelle's glance was sympathetic, and there was no judgment whatsoever in her eyes.

"But everywhere I look, someone's telling me I need to forgive him." Deborah sighed in frustration. "Levi has practically begged me for it, though he understands it will take time. And Papa preached on the topic this morning in his sermon. It was the parable of the man forgiven a massive debt who then went and demanded repayment from a man who owed him only a small debt."

Annabelle nodded. "That's always such a challenging passage of Scripture. I can only imagine how difficult it was for you in the current circumstance."

"The point, of course, is that our sin is the insurmountable debt, whereas any wrong done to us is small in comparison. But . . . this wrong doesn't feel small, Annabelle."

Annabelle reached out and gave her hand a squeeze. "It isn't small, Deborah. Not in the slightest."

"And yet Elisabeth was able to forgive him. I want to do what the Bible commands. But it seems impossible. And Nathaniel never even laid a hand on me. The man who took my scalp was someone else. I don't even know his name. I've never asked. I don't much care. For some reason, he's not the one I hate."

"Likely because that man isn't your brother-in-law," Annabelle replied. "You've not seen him since the attack, and you likely never will. And because Nathaniel is responsible for your sister's death and because your grief is still so fresh, it makes perfect sense that you'd blame him more than anyone else."

"But Elisabeth had even more cause to blame him than I did, yet the second he walked into our lives, she welcomed him. And she knew, Annabelle. She knew by the scar on his wrist and the blue of his eyes. She knew before anyone else did, and she forgave him. How? How was it so easy for her? How was *everything* so easy for her?"

Tears stung Deborah's eyes, and the onslaught of emotion made breathing even more difficult. But those emotions wouldn't be denied. They rose from somewhere deep inside her, a lifetime's worth of jealousy and resentment. "Elisabeth made Isaiah fall in love with her with just a glance. I'd still be a spinster if Levi hadn't needed a mother for Nora. And Elisabeth was so sweet. So kind. She carried herself with such grace. Her scars somehow made her more beautiful. No one cared about her disfigurement. Everyone loved her. She was just so . . . so *perfect*. She was everything I could have been and wasn't. And now she's in heaven and everything is perfect, and her pain is gone, and her scars are gone, and the only person who truly knew what it was like to survive what I've survived is gone, and I'm left to struggle alone. She went to heaven quickly. Easily. Just like she did everything else. It's so like her, Annabelle. *So* like her."

Elisabeth. Her sister. Her best friend. Her constant rival. The mirror showing her how much better she could have been. Should have been. The one for whom jealousy had practically consumed her, yet the one she missed more than anything in the world. Her grief, her anger, her complicated feelings for her sister tumbled inside her, streaking tears down her cheeks. Annabelle wrapped her arms around Deborah and held her in a warm, comforting embrace until her tears stopped and her sobs stilled.

"Elisabeth wasn't perfect, Deborah." Annabelle pulled back and looked Deborah in the eyes. "I know forgiving Nathaniel was difficult for her. She worked at it."

"She did?"

Annabelle nodded. "She talked to me about it once she realized who Nathaniel was. She didn't know how to tell you. She didn't want to ruin your marriage or your family. So she came to me. And she struggled with it. She may not have shown it, but she did. And I can tell you for a fact that she didn't conjure that forgiveness on her own."

Elisabeth . . . struggle? "Then how . . ."

"Forgiveness is an act of grace and a gift from God, Deborah. Elisabeth didn't forgive Nathaniel in her own strength. She was willing to let the Lord mold her. To allow him to use the horrible thing that happened to her to shape her and mold her rather than break her."

"And I let it break me." The truth slammed into her. Once again, Elisabeth had come out ahead.

"No, my dear." Annabelle's gaze sought hers. "You're not broken. Not beyond repair, anyway. But—and I say this to you as someone who loves you dearly and would never want to hurt you, but sometimes the truth can be uncomfortable—I see someone who's weighed down by burdens she was never meant to carry. Do you need to forgive Nathaniel? I believe so. The Bible instructs it, and I know those who forgive feel lighter and more free than ever before."

That lightness, that freedom, was what she ached for. To unchain herself from Nathaniel Martinson forever and ever.

"But the first step is talking with the Lord. Giving him your burdens. You cannot summon the grace and love to forgive someone who hurt you so grievously. Only God can do that. Trust him to give you the ability to do what you need to do. To heal you. He may never heal the scars on your head until heaven, but I believe he can—and will—heal the ones on your heart."

Deborah studied the rough bark of a barren cottonwood, mulling over the truth of Annabelle's words and the light they shined on her inner life.

It wasn't Nathaniel who'd been the source of her anger all these years.

Not even Elisabeth.

It was God.

That was the difference between herself and Elisabeth. Elisabeth had welcomed God into her suffering. Sought his purpose in the pain. Allowed him to walk alongside her and sometimes carry her. Deborah had shoved God aside, blaming him for her losses. Her injuries. Her wounds to both body and soul.

She needed to forgive Nathaniel. Of course she did. But her brother-in-law wasn't the only one desperately in need of grace.

She needed it herself just as much.

A fresh wave of tears stinging her eyes, one hand on her swollen abdomen, the other on the rough bark of the cottonwood, she bowed her head.

Oh, Lord, forgive me. Please. You never left me. You've been standing here all these years waiting for me to see you. To notice you. To let you work your purposes in this pain. And despite the fact that I've kept you at arm's length, you've blessed me beyond what I deserve. You've given me a good man's love, a wonderful daughter, and this new little life. I have a home. I have a family. I have everything I need, and that's all because of your grace and love. Grace and love that has never wavered even as I've run from it.

I'm finished running, Lord. I'm finished. I surrender to your plans and your purposes. Forgive me. Let me truly embrace your forgiveness and grace you extended at the cross. Then and only then can I begin to forgive Nathaniel. And I do want to forgive him, Lord. I truly do. Please show me exactly what it looks like to do that.

Warmth gushed through her heart. Warmth and wholeness and love and healing and release. Sweet, sweet release. She felt looser. Freer. And loved. Loved, like she'd never been before or since. Not even Levi had surrounded her with such precious love.

And then warmth gushed not through her but *from* her. Warmth and wetness and . . . oh. Oh. Her belly clenched. Something soaked her undergarments and dripped down her legs.

The baby.

The baby was coming.

"Annabelle." She reached for her friend's hand, elation and anticipation and just a touch of fear coursing through her. "Thank you. My friend, thank you. I've so much to tell you about what just happened, but we're going to have to continue this conversation another time."

"Why?" Annabelle's brow creased. "Deborah, darling, are you all right?"

"Better than I've been in years." Her belly clenched again, harder this time, and she gasped.

"Oh mercy!" Annabelle's warm hands gripped her shoulders. "Deborah! The baby!"

Deborah laughed and splayed her hands across her belly. "Yes, Annabelle. Yes. The baby."

CHAPTER THIRTY-FIVE

"THOSE ARE SOME very serious allegations, young man."

The circle of faces around the table in the Pursuers conference room all fixed on Matt, and he shifted in the leather chair. The one who'd spoken was the chairman of the board of elders, a portly gentleman named Bob Hendricks, who leveled an owlish stare at Matt through wire-rimmed aviators.

"I'm aware." Matt cleared his throat. "And the seriousness of these allegations is why I've brought them before you today, following the guidelines for church discipline outlined by the apostle Paul and by our own church policies."

"Then you've taken this issue to Pastor Jessup himself?" This came from Tim Cavanaugh, the youngest member of the board. Matt felt for the guy—he was one of the lay representatives and had just been appointed to the board about the same time Matt had arrived. Doubtless he hadn't expected something of this magnitude to land in front of him at all, let alone this early.

Well. That made two of them.

"Yes, sir, I did," Matt said.

"And what was the response?" This question came from the eldest of the elders, a white-haired man named Ronald Weatherbie.

Matt looked Ronald in the eyes, his stomach clenching with the ugly reality of what had happened. The final nail in the coffin of his respect for Trace Jessup. "He informed me that I'd misunderstood what I witnessed, that his relationship with Ms. Simmons is purely platonic, and that what I saw was blown out of context."

"The two of you were kissing," Matt had retorted. *"How in the world is it possible to take that out of context?"*

"If you'd been in the room, if you'd heard what she said to me, you'd know she started it. She begged me to kiss her, Matty. Begged. And I'm a weak, sinful man. I thought I'd beaten my demons after Siobhan, but they just came back stronger. Satan wouldn't be messing with me if he weren't afraid of me."

"And you have reason to doubt this?" Bob tented his fingers.

Matt reached for his coffee mug. "Yes." Many, many reasons. So many.

Jerry Robinson, the executive pastor and Trace's right-hand man, cleared his throat two seats to Matt's left. "Would one of those reasons happen to be named Siobhan Walsh?"

Matt nearly choked on the hot sip of coffee he'd just taken. "What in the world does she have to do with this?"

"We've been told you and Ms. Walsh have some sort of personal relationship." Pastor Jerry eyed him, his gaze hawkish and piercing. "Is that true?"

Matt set the mug down and looked Pastor Jerry in the eyes. "Two days after I arrived in Wichita, I was involved in a car accident. My grandmother's violin—a precious family heirloom—was damaged. Ms. Walsh works at a local violin repair shop, and she's the one repairing the instrument."

"And that's the entire nature of your relationship?" Jerry's dark brows arched. "Because we've seen some evidence on social media that would indicate otherwise. Which, considering our history with this woman in particular, does give us pause."

Matt drew back. "Wait, why am I the one on trial here?"

"Let's all calm down." This from Weatherbie, who looked nervously from Matt to Pastor Jerry and back again. "We're just trying to get the facts. That's it. Nobody's on trial."

Hendricks leaned forward. "That said, when someone levels accusations of this nature against our highly regarded senior pastor, it does seem prudent to make certain of the trustworthiness of our witness."

Five months ago Matt sat at this same table. Looked across at these same faces.

"You all trusted me enough to hire me in the first place. You trust me to lead worship at four services every weekend. Why won't you trust me about this?" He splayed his hands across the table. "Look. I've known Trace since I was a teenager. That man led me to Jesus. He's the one who reached out to me about this position. Went to bat for me with all of you to convince you to hire me. Other than my mom and my grandma, Trace Jessup is the single most influential person in my entire life. I wouldn't accuse him of anything—much less something like this—unless I was completely convinced it had happened."

He leaned back in the chair, his skin feeling flushed, sweat pricking his hairline, his breath suddenly impossible to catch. Was this what it felt like to betray someone?

No. He wasn't betraying anyone. He wasn't Judas in this scenario.

Trace was.

Hendricks and Weatherbie glanced at each other. Cavanaugh drummed his fingertips on the tabletop, studying them as though they'd contain the wisdom he sought. Members of the pastoral staff looked everywhere but at him. All but one. Colton Devereaux. The youth pastor. Over his luxuriant beard, he offered Matt a sympathetic smile.

"I see." Pastor Jerry shifted in his chair, the leather creaking beneath his weight. "Well. Thank you for bringing this matter to our attention, Matt. Rest assured we will conduct a thorough investigation befitting the seriousness of these accusations, and any action needed will be taken. But your involvement in this matter is over, am I clear? We will take this from here."

"Sweep it under the rug, you mean. Or maybe fire Kayleigh, like you did Siobhan? Pay her some hush money, make the problem go away? It worked before." He glared across the table, heart pounding. What was he doing? What had he just said?

Jerry's mouth tightened, and his face reddened. "Pastor Buchanan, you are treading on *very* thin ice."

"So what if I am?" He shoved his chair back from the table and stood. "I know what I saw Trace doing. I know what he's done before. And if we don't do something about it, then it'll happen again."

Jerry stood, too, and met his eyes. "And in the meantime, how many souls will be doomed to hell because of it? Trace Jessup reaches dozens of people for Christ every single week through his sermons. Thousands more through his books and his podcast. Just this past Sunday we had more new decisions for Jesus than we've ever had before. Do you know how many that was?"

Matt resisted the urge to roll his eyes. "If anyone told me, I don't remember."

Jerry's face was a thundercloud. "Fifty-four. *Fifty-four*, Matt. That's fifty-four lives surrendered to the grace of Christ. Fifty-four precious souls who'll now spend eternity with the Lord in peace and perfection instead of separation and torment. And who knows how many people those fifty-four will reach? Since Trace arrived, we've had over twenty-five hundred new decisions. More than four thousand baptisms."

"You know that off the top of your head." Numbers. It was always numbers with these people.

"What gets measured gets managed," Hendricks interjected.

Matt's eyes widened. "Souls are a resource to be managed?"

"Remember the parable of the talents, Matt?" Pastor Jerry applied a smooth smile. "Pursuers is a ten-talent church. God has given us much, and he expects us to give an account for how we've stewarded what he's trusted us with."

Matt's jaw clenched. "And how are we managing Kayleigh's soul? How did we manage Siobhan's? I applaud our passion for pursuing the lost. Believe me, I'm all for it. But by sweeping Trace's pattern of sin under the rug, we're saying that those women's souls don't matter. That the harm Trace does, the damage he inflicts, is worth it if we're reaching people for Jesus. And I don't believe that's how Jesus would want us to handle this. He cared about the woman caught in adultery. The woman at the well who'd had five husbands. If we want to be like Jesus, then we need to care about the women Trace hurts just as much as we care about the lost."

He leaned against the table, shoulders tense amid the stretched-thin silence and sidelong glances that permeated the room.

Only Colton was willing to meet Matt's gaze. He looked like he wanted to say something, and his lips even moved once or twice, but then he shut them and squeezed them tight, a look of apology in his brown eyes.

"I'm going to level with you here, Matt." Pastor Jerry had regained control, as proven by a wide, toothy smile. "We like having you here at Pursuers. We think you're doing a fantastic job as worship leader, and you're a great addition to the team."

Matt could feel the *but* coming from a mile away.

"But." The smile changed. Not dramatically. Just tighter around the edges. Sinister instead of sickly sweet. "You either need to get on board with what we're doing, or you need to find somewhere else to serve."

Matt drew back as though he'd been punched. Trace was the serial predator, and yet *he* was the one whose job they'd just threatened. He glanced around the table at a series of poker faces. No judgment, but no sympathy either. Not from anyone but Colton. But everyone else? Blank stares all around.

"Be glad you have this choice, Matt." Jerry's voice was low. Tight. "Because if you keep going down this road, you might not have a choice anymore. Now. If there's nothing else, you need to trust us to handle this."

"Yeah. Sure." Matt grabbed his mug and made for the exit. "Thanks for your time, gentlemen."

He stepped out into the cool hallway and slumped against the wall next to his office. That office had once seemed like a dream come true. This whole job had. And now . . .

Well, Jerry was right about one thing.

Matt didn't have a choice. Not if he wanted to sleep at night. Not if he wanted to feel the peace of being in the center of God's will.

Not if he cared about Siobhan.

Nope. He didn't have a choice at all.

>‹‹

"Okay, perfect. Now, press up through your arms and the soles of your feet . . ."

The deceptively calming voice of the woman on the YouTube yoga video wafted from Siobhan's laptop speakers, and she glanced to the image on the screen once more before taking a deep breath.

"Here goes nothin'," Siobhan said aloud to the empty living room, then attempted to press up into wheel pose.

"Keep going . . ." said the video woman.

"I'm trying." Siobhan's voice was noticeably less calm and considerably more strained.

"Almost there . . ."

"If you say so." Then her arms gave out, and with a yelp she collapsed into an undignified heap on her yoga mat in the center of her living room.

"Perfect," said the yoga woman.

On a normal day, she'd be attempting to relax at the boxing gym, but it was raining, and she didn't feel like leaving the house. So instead she was trying one of those at-home yoga videos her mother had discovered during the pandemic and had been raving about ever since.

"This is stupid." Sitting up, Siobhan hit Pause. "Why did I let Mom talk me into this?" She reached for her phone on the coffee table to text those sentiments, but it vibrated before her fingers reached it. Maybe it was Mom, reading her mind.

But the name on the screen made her heart lurch.

It wasn't Mom.

It was Matt.

Matt.

They hadn't spoken in a couple of weeks, though he still dominated her thoughts. He was probably just checking on the violin. Truth be told, it had taken a backseat to more urgent projects. She opened the text, prepared to type out an apology with her thumbs.

> Hey, Siobhan. Hope you're well.

That was it. That was all the little gray box said.

But . . . wait. The little dots below the text. He was typing something.

It was just about the violin. That was it. That was literally the only reason he'd have to text her right now.

So why was her heart pounding way more than it had been when she was trying to figure out the wheel pose? Maybe she didn't need kickboxing today after all.

Finally, the little swoopy noise, and a thick block of text in the gray balloon.

> I know we haven't talked in a
> while, and that makes what
> I'm about to say even more
> awkward, but I'd love it if you
> would watch Pursuers online
> tomorrow. Or maybe even come.
> I know it's a big ask, and I don't
> know exactly what's going to
> happen, but I feel like you might
> need to bear witness.

Pursuers? Her? In person? No. A thousand times no.

What could there possibly be for her there? What in the world would possess him to think she should be there? What was he *thinking*?

More little gray dots.

> I've been praying for you.

She paused. Praying. For her. Even now. Even after everything blew up in their faces.

Had she been praying for him?

Was thinking about him constantly, even when she was trying to focus on other things, a form of prayer?

Another swoopy noise, another text.

> I don't know how you'll take that,
> but I have.

> Not sure how you'll take this,
> either, but for what it's worth,
> I love you.

"You *love* me?" she yelled at the phone in her hand. "And you're telling me in a *text*?"

I didn't want to tell you in a text,
but I couldn't not. It's been killing
me not to tell you.

I don't expect you to say it back.
I just wanted you to know.

Sorry for all the texts. Take care.

"Take care? You tell me to come to church tomorrow—*that* church—
and then you tell me you love me *in a text*, and then you say *take care*?" She
tossed the phone onto the couch and sat slumped on the floor, her heart
a cacophony of emotion. Forget the rain. Maybe she'd hit the gym anyway. Because how dare he? How dare he not talk to her for two weeks—
never mind that it was her idea—and then barrage her with that series of
messages?

She should be angry with him. And she was.

But part of her—most of her, actually—was elated. He'd texted her. He
loved her. He wanted her to come to church tomorrow, and why? Why?

Why?

She tapped out the word and sent it before she could change her mind.

Why what?

Why should I come to church
tomorrow?

The gray dots started up again. Then stopped. Then started again. Then
stopped. Started. Finally . . .

Because I am very confident
this will be my last Sunday at
Pursuers.

"Okay, you have my attention," she said to the phone. Because she'd been blindsided by her firing. Matt seemed prepared. Which meant he was either about to do something that would cost him his job, or he was planning to leave on his own terms.

Either way, he'd need moral support. And God knew he wasn't going to get it from anyone there.

So despite the terror and revulsion the idea of even walking into that building sent through her, part of her wanted—no, *needed*—to be there.

For him.

Maybe even a little bit for her.

But could she? Could she really walk through those doors again? Could she really face all those people? Would they recognize her with her dyed hair and different wardrobe? How would she handle it if they did?

> I can't promise anything, but I
> will try. Thanks for the prayers.
> Praying for you too, whatever's
> going on.

She sent the text. The phone buzzed in her hand with his heart reaction. And that heart made her text something else before she could think better of it.

> Also . . . I love you too.

Chapter Thirty-Six

THE LAST CHORD of the worship set rang out to a scattering of applause, cheers, and amens from the congregation, and Matt stashed his guitar pick in the mic stand. The band melded into quiet vamping over the chord changes from the chorus, and the big screen at the back of the auditorium flashed a subtle reminder that his prayer was next. That was it. That was all that was left for him to do. Just say a quick prayer over the congregation—a transition into the next element of the worship service, really—and be done until the next service. Normally, this was the part of the set when he could relax.

Instead, he was more terrified than he'd ever been on this stage. Even more than when he'd first set foot on it five months ago.

Having mentally committed to today's course of action, he thought he'd feel at peace. That sweet, subtle sense from God that, yeah, what he was about to do was a little scary, but it'd all turn out okay in the end. It had always been that way before, anyway.

But this morning, as he looked out over the sea of dimly lit faces, his stomach churned. His hands shook. Sweat beaded along his hairline. Rather than peace at his core, he felt a holy restlessness. That strong inward yank he'd come to know and dread, that inescapable pull that meant God was insisting Matt do something he didn't want to do.

And he didn't want to do this.

It would be so much easier—*so* much easier—to just stay quiet. To pray that brief prayer of transition, seat the congregation, exit stage right, and head to the green room with the rest of the band for doughnuts and coffee and some chill time before he had to do it all over again in an hour and a half.

Trace was still in his usual reserved spot in the front row, eyes closed, arms raised in a posture of worship.

God, do you really want me to do this? Right now?

Maybe Matt could wait until next week to pull the pin on the grenade. Give the board of elders a little more time to act. Maybe he wouldn't have to do this at all.

Oh, who was he kidding? If the board was going to do anything about this, they'd have done it ages ago. With Siobhan. Or the woman before her. Or the one before that. God alone knew how many women there had been.

Kayleigh stood a few rows behind Trace. Her head was bowed, dark curls draped over her shoulders. She swayed slowly back and forth with the rhythm of the chord changes.

Was it truly his responsibility to rescue her?

And was this truly the right way to do it?

God, help.

And then a shaft of light pierced the fog-machine-blurred darkness. A door opened. A person slipped in.

Matt's breath caught. He knew that slight build. That tough-yet-fragile demeanor. That plaid shirt, that quilted vest, those black Doc Martens.

She took a place along the back wall, folded her arms across her chest, and looked around. Then the door shut slowly, plunging Siobhan into shadows.

What could possibly be going through her mind right now? What memories had surfaced? What emotions? What thoughts? Was she standing there drinking it in? Or was she seized with panic, convinced this was all a mistake? Was she thinking of him? Of Trace?

Was she in prayer? In pain?

Well. Whatever was going on inside her, she was here.

She was actually here.

If ever he needed a sign from God that this was the time to act, well, here was one. A flashing neon one. Regardless of how he felt, Siobhan had to be feeling a whole lot worse.

It was go time.

"Hey, y'all can have a seat." Matt glanced toward the tech booth, where he felt more than saw the alarmed stare of Rick, the tech director.

Matt swallowed hard against the sandpapery feeling in his mouth. "I know we normally pray right now, but God's laid something pretty heavy on my heart, and I feel strongly led to share it with you."

It was true. He did have something heavy on his heart. He did feel strongly led. But his use of evangelical buzzwords wasn't an accident. He'd learned from years in church culture that those words were something of a trump card. A guarantee that he'd be given a longer leash to say what was on his mind.

Not an endless leash. He knew that. But a longer one.

Lord, give me strength.

Taking a deep breath, he pulled his phone from his pocket and, with a shaking thumb, opened his Bible app to the passage he'd marked last night. The passage that would fuel this kamikaze move.

"I have a passage of Scripture I'd like to share with you, if that's all right."

The congregation nodded, as he'd known they would. He tried not to look at Trace, but the man was inescapably in his line of sight, and Matt's heart sank when he saw his former mentor nodding right along with everyone else. *Oh, Trace. You're not gonna like this. You have no idea what's coming. But it has to be done.*

"It's from the book of Matthew," he said. "Chapter eighteen. I'll start in verse fifteen."

Trace's smile faded slightly, his brow furrowing in concentration. Doubtless he was trying to place the verse.

Matt's heart jackhammered in his throat. "'If your brother sins against you, go and tell him his fault, between you and him alone. If he listens to you, you have gained your brother.'" He looked up from the Bible at the twelve hundred gathered in the auditorium. "I have done this."

He felt, rather than saw, the heat of Trace's warning glare.

Rick piped up in his in-ears. "Hey, man, what are you doing?"

Matt ignored him and turned back to the Word. "'But if he does not listen, take one or two others along with you, that every charge may be established by the evidence of two or three witnesses.'" He looked up again. In his peripheral vision, on the big screen to his left, a larger-than-life, high-def version of himself did the same thing. "I've done this as well."

Through the dimness, he spied a few disconcerted glances between various members of the congregation. On the front row, Trace's face was a thundercloud.

Matt cleared his throat, the sound echoing through the auditorium. "And as an added step, I've also brought my concerns before the board of elders. Still, nothing has happened. This is a pattern of sin perpetuated over several years, and it won't be stopped until someone takes action." Palms damp, legs shaky, he closed the Bible app and tucked his phone back in his pocket. "I guess I'm that someone."

Trace leaped to his feet and no doubt shouted something, based on the way several people looked toward him, but Matt couldn't hear him thanks to the sound-sealing effects of his in-ear monitors. Doubtless it was for the best.

Hands, hands, what was he supposed to do with his hands? He started an absent picking pattern on the guitar, trying to find where the band was in the chord progression, but after a few strokes he realized the band had fallen silent. Either that or whatever sound they were still making was drowned out entirely by the roar of his pulse in his ears.

"Look, it brings me absolutely no pleasure to share this with you. Believe me, I don't want to do it. Like Moses, I have begged God to send someone else. But I believe he's brought me to this time and this place, and this might be my last time in this place, who knows—I mean, if it is, God bless you all—you've been amazing. I love each and every one of you, and it's been a real joy, but the Lord won't allow me to stay silent on this. And it breaks my heart, because Trace Jessup has been a friend. A mentor. A father figure."

Tears stung his eyes, and his throat closed up. Wait, what? Now? No. He could fall apart later, but not now. *Pull it together, Buchanan.*

"I love this man." His voice still sounded thick. "But he's had a long-standing pattern of sinful relationships with women. Out of respect for those women, I won't name them. But they are worthy of protection. Worthy of justice. Worthy of the redemption that has been denied them by the staff of this church."

One of his earbuds slipped just enough for him to hear the general murmur of the congregation. Each person looked to the one beside them, eyes wide, jaws slack. They truly hadn't known, and Matt's heart went out to them. How many would leave the church because of this? How many would never set foot in a church building again?

How much damage had Pursuers Church wrought in the name of the relentless pursuit of the lost?

Trace turned to the back and yelled at Rick. "Cut his mic. *Now.*"

"If you do, I'll just shout." Matt was nearly there already. "Because what Trace is doing is wrong. He grooms these women. He pursues them as relentlessly as this church pursues those outside the faith. And when the women finally give in, he blames them, he shames them, and then he sweeps them aside like garbage."

By now, the congregation was buzzing loudly, and Trace had leaped up the steps at the front of the stage. He grabbed a mic from the backup vocalist's stand and stood beside Matt, one arm looped around his shoulders. Matt's muscles tensed. His nose twitched at the overdose of cologne.

"Thank you, Pastor Buchanan." Trace gave him a squeeze, more aggression than affection, then turned loose and stepped toward the pulpit. He looked out at the congregation for a long moment, then gave a heavy sigh. "It looks like it's time for me to come clean with you all."

Siobhan. Where was Siobhan? Matt tried not to be obvious about looking for her, but she'd blended in with the shadows in the back. He had no idea where she was or if she was even still in the room.

Trace gripped the mic with both hands. "It's true. I have had inappropriate relationships with women during my time here." His voice grew husky, and tears gathered at the corners of his eyes.

But were they real, or something manufactured for effect?

And did Trace truly regret his actions? Or merely the fact that he'd been caught?

"I'm so weak." Tears flowed freely now. "I'm a sinner. I've been like this my whole life, and I'm powerless against this temptation. I wish I was strong enough to resist, but I'm not. I don't know what it is about me, but they won't leave me alone. Pastor Matt . . ."

Matt blinked as Trace met his eyes.

"Pastor Matt here believes I'm the instigator, and to him I suppose that's exactly what it looks like. But these women, they're insatiable. They won't take no for an answer. They misinterpret everything I—"

"That's not true, Trace, and you know it!"

A woman's voice rang out through the auditorium.

Not Siobhan's.

Kayleigh's.

She'd left her seat and was standing in the center aisle, staring at Trace with horrified betrayal in her eyes.

The congregation gasped, and another buzzy murmur set in. To the far right, a small group of elders huddled together, and Pastor Jerry was ascending the far steps.

"Kayleigh." Trace's voice was pleading. "Not now."

"Then when? When will you come clean? When will you admit that you have a problem? I'm not naive enough to think I'm the first woman you've had a relationship with, and I'm also not naive enough to think I'll be the last. You'll replace me just as fast as you did everyone else, and where will that leave me?"

"Kayleigh," Trace hissed. "You'll be taken care of. I told you that."

"I don't want your money." Her voice was shrill. "I don't want anything from you except what you took and can't give back."

"All right, everyone." Another amplified voice took charge, this time Pastor Jerry striding in from stage right. "I believe what we need right now is to all take a breath and invite the Lord into this situation. Matt, Trace, if you'll allow me to lead the congregation in prayer?" It wasn't a question.

Trace stepped back, and Matt turned and stashed his guitar in its stand. Would he need it next service? Would there even *be* a next service?

Would there even be a rest of this one?

Whatever. None of it was Matt's concern. He walked offstage, his legs wobbly, his muscles drained of every ounce of energy, but his head held high. He'd done what God wanted him to do. He'd trusted. He'd obeyed. The results were in God's hands now.

As for Matt?

He was heading for the green room after all.

He'd never wanted a doughnut more in his entire life.

CHAPTER THIRTY-SEVEN

SIOBHAN SLIPPED OUT of the auditorium amid shocked murmurs from the congregation and slumped against a cool exterior wall around the corner. Her head was spinning from all that had just happened—her whole body seemed to buzz.

She wasn't by herself—that wasn't truly possible, not in this place—but the handful of church members milling around in the lobby or ambling toward the bookstore paid no attention to her.

That was exactly the way she wanted it.

A trio of women spilled out the back of the auditorium, heads bent together. One glanced her way, eyes wide in surprise. Siobhan toyed with a piece of Kleenex in the pocket of her vest. Was it her they were whispering about? Or was it Kayleigh, Trace's latest flavor of the month?

Siobhan would've known who Kayleigh was even if she hadn't stepped out into the aisle to confront Trace. Long brown hair, spiraled through a curling iron and tousled just so. Clothes modest enough to pass muster at church but formfitting enough to let Trace's lecherous imagination run wild. She might as well have been Siobhan three years ago.

And now she was at the same crossroads Siobhan had faced.

What would Kayleigh do now? Doubtless her time at Pursuers was over. Would she brush it off and look for another church job? Or would she reluctantly use Trace's hush money to pursue a new dream? Would she keep her brunette locks, or would she dye them as Siobhan had? Would her wardrobe stay the same, or would she purposely choose clothes to hide those allegedly dangerous curves?

Would she contemplate leaving Wichita altogether? Changing her name?

And what would happen to her faith?

Siobhan's heart ached for the girl. It had been a long, hard road, one she wouldn't wish on anyone. But Kayleigh would survive. She'd be all right. After all, she'd been able to see what Trace was doing far sooner than Siobhan had. Someone had stood up for her. Called out Trace's sin and exposed it for what it was.

And Kayleigh had the courage to stand up for herself.

Motion out of the corner of her eye caught her attention. A flash of an olive-green jacket. Outside the large window, Matt was heading out to the sunny parking lot. Making a beeline for his truck.

Wow. Had they fired him that fast? She wouldn't put it past them.

Her heartbeat quickened. She needed to talk to him. Needed to see him. Every fiber of her being ached to wrap him in an embrace that she could only hope somehow conveyed how grateful she was, because she wouldn't be able to express it in words. The words for it probably didn't even exist.

"Matt." She whispered his name, then turned down the side hallway toward the nearest exit, her eyes locked on the figure in the parking lot. On the silver truck. On—

Oof.

She ran smack into someone. A warm, solid body whose cologne she recognized. A leather blazer she'd had nightmares about.

"So sorry. You all right?" He stepped back, and his polite facade faded. His eyes narrowed.

"*You.*"

Trace looked her up and down as he always had, but this time his expression conveyed revulsion rather than lust.

"I should've known you put him up to this." His voice was almost a growl. "Matt Buchanan was a team player before he got tangled up with you. I had such high hopes for him, but those are gone now."

Yup. They were going to fire Matt.

"And they're gone because of you." Whatever shreds of charisma and charm Trace had managed to hold on to onstage were gone now. The veins in his neck stood out. His cheeks flushed deep crimson. His dark eyes shot sparks. In the past, she'd have been terrified.

Today, she wasn't.

"You and your lies are going to cost me everything, Siobhan. *Everything.*" He shouted the word, and it echoed around the cavernous foyer. People were bound to hear. People were bound to see their carefully manufactured pastor coming apart at the seams. The thought gave her a perverse sense of pleasure.

"I spent years building this church. Building a place that'll stop at nothing to reach someone for Jesus. This place changes lives, Siobhan. It changes eternity. And now there'll be people in hell because of what you put your boyfriend up to today, and those souls are on you. They're on *you!*"

Trace Jessup was self-destructing. The monster within had burst from the carefully crafted skin of the man she once thought she loved.

And she felt . . . nothing.

She felt *nothing.*

She observed his self-immolation with the same dispassion she'd have for a football game on TV. Somewhat entertaining, perhaps worth an occasional glance at the screen, but not something to get invested in.

Somehow, someway, there was a shield around her heart now. An invisible force field that flung Trace's accusing arrows away, letting them clatter harmlessly to the ground. She wasn't the slut he painted her to be. She wasn't the woman whose beauty was too powerful for him to resist. She wasn't even a young, starry-eyed church staff member reeled in by the charm and charisma of a wealthy, powerful man.

She was a victim. A target. An unsuspecting fish who'd chomped down on bait that—thank God—hadn't proven fatal. Collateral damage in a carefully calculated attack borne of addiction or abuse or God alone knew what.

And as Mom had said, Siobhan was a survivor. God had seen her through to the other side. Even when she walked away from him, he'd never once left her. Trace had tried to ruin her, but God hadn't let that happen. And it was his peace, his presence, keeping her calm in the face of Trace's ranting and raving.

Was Trace even still talking? Sure looked like it. His mouth was moving. Flecks of spittle were flying past her. But her ears were closed to his words. Her heart was closed to his lies.

She knew the truth now, and the truth had set her free.

"Trace." Her voice was quiet. Calm. And it had the desired effect. He stopped talking.

She took a deep breath and smiled at him. *Smiled.*

"I forgive you," she said.

And it was true. She did. Doubtless many hours of counseling and therapy lay ahead. And she would probably have to forgive Trace multiple times on multiple levels for multiple things. But she'd taken the first step. She'd made a choice she never thought she'd feel like making. And she'd done it here, in this building, to the man's face.

Only God could do that.

Trace gave a bark of laughter. "You forgive *me*? That's rich."

"But it's true." Freedom zoomed through her veins, and she felt like soaring. "I made some poor decisions while I was here. I ignored that still, small voice telling me how unwise it was to be alone with you late at night. That I should've set some boundaries with you. But it wouldn't have mattered, would it?" She shifted her weight to one hip and looked up at him. "You'd have come after me anyway. You knew what you wanted, and you'd stop at nothing to get it."

"Siobhan, I can't believe you'd—"

"For three years I've blamed myself because of your lies. The ones you told to my face and the ones you told behind my back. You called me relentless." She pointed her index finger at his chest. "But you're the one who was relentless. You're the one who put a target on my back and pursued me until I broke. You're the one who made me doubt myself. Whose actions made me walk away from God."

Joy coursed through her. "But I walked back. I'm his. And he's the one you'll ultimately answer to, not me. I'm done with you, Trace. I've washed my hands of you. You don't have the power to hurt me anymore because I'm choosing to forgive you. You broke me, it's true. But God is putting me back together."

She stepped back, heart and thoughts racing. Had she really just done that? Had she really just confronted Trace? Forgiven him?

"That was a charming sermon, Siobhan." He gave a practiced smirk. "Maybe you should be a pastor."

"Maybe I should." With a shrug, she glanced out the window. Oh, thank God Matt was still there. Leaning against the side of his truck. His eyes were on his phone, his hair ruffling in the breeze, and she had never loved him more than at this moment. "But in the meantime, Trace, there's someone I need to see."

He must've followed her gaze, because he laughed again. "And when you do see Matt, tell him he's through here."

She stepped around Trace on her way down the hall toward the exit. "Tell him yourself."

"This isn't over, Siobhan." His angry words echoed around the corridor. "You'll be hearing from our lawyers. Both of you will."

The words bounced harmlessly off the walls and fell to the carpeted floors. Whatever threats Trace cared to shout, God was prepared to meet them and walk her through whatever consequences awaited.

For now, he was taking her straight to Matt Buchanan. The man she loved.

She stepped out to a fresh, crisp early spring morning. A brilliant blue sky. Dazzling sunshine.

And freedom.

Freedom.

For the first time in forever, she was finally free of Pursuers Church.

CHAPTER THIRTY-EIGHT

March 1877

DEBORAH SAT IN the rocker beside a crackling fireplace. Outside, fat, lazy snowflakes drifted down to land in grass just beginning to green.

And in her arms lay her two-day-old daughter. Her daughter, with a full head of dark hair and round rosy cheeks and little fairy lashes and the tiniest fingernails Deborah had ever imagined. The small face featured Levi's nose and Elisabeth's mouth and chin. The miniature hand reached from the nest of blankets to wrap around Deborah's finger.

It had been a difficult birth, most of which was a haze. Annabelle had summoned her uncle Dr. Maxwell, who, given Deborah's situation with her scars, had wanted to be present in case anything went awry. No one had any idea what birthing would do to Deborah, so he'd been a steady presence. Annabelle, too, had stayed by Deborah's side, encouraging, praying, and guiding her through her labor.

Mostly what Deborah remembered was blood. Blood and pain and then the sound that changed her life. The shrill cry of a newborn baby.

"It's a girl," Annabelle had said over the sound, squeezing Deborah's shoulders.

"A girl?" The fact pierced the haze. "All along I thought this was a boy." A girl. She had a girl.

"Trust me, Mrs. Martinson," boomed Dr. Maxwell, "you have a daughter. A big, beautiful daughter. Healthy as a horse."

And then he'd handed her that daughter. The precious cargo she'd been hauling around inside her, this tiny wiggly presence, the product of Levi's healing love and God's faithfulness. All that had created this. This beautiful little girl with dark hair—dark like her mother, like her aunt—and eyes squeezed shut with her hollering.

"Hush now, sweet thing." Deborah had held the baby close, tears stinging her eyes. "Mama's here. Mama's here." The baby latched on and started to suckle, and the din soon quieted. "There you are. Mama's here."

"And Mama appears fit as a fiddle." Dr. Maxwell slid a couple instruments into his black medicine bag. "A few days' rest and you'll be right as rain."

Annabelle leaned in, a tender smile curving her lips, stray tendrils of dark-blond hair dangling before her face. "Shall I send in Levi?"

"Yes, of course. And Nora too. They need to meet this new little love."

A moment later there they were. Her husband and her stepdaughter. Her other daughter.

Deborah smiled at the two of them. "Nora. Come here. Come meet your sister."

Assisted by her father, Nora crawled carefully up onto the coverlet, eyes big. "Sissy," she said. "I have a sissy."

Her face broke into a huge grin, one that warmed Deborah's heart. "A sissy! Hi, sissy! Hi!" She waved at the nursing baby, and Deborah chuckled.

While Nora's excitement was boisterous and loud, Levi's was, predictably, understated. He stared at the baby. Just stared. Said nothing.

But then his blue eyes took on a shine, he blinked rapidly, and his cheeks turned pink. He pinched the bridge of his nose and squeezed his eyes shut, and two big tears spilled down his cheeks.

Deborah's heart filled with a precious ache. The sight of his daughter had made her husband weep.

He caressed the infant's cheek. "I never knew one heart could hold so much love." His voice was thick.

"Neither did I."

Levi turned his adoring gaze to Deborah, kissing her forehead and pulling her close. His hand cupped the back of her scarred head. Her scarred, uncovered head. He'd seen her. He loved her. He'd made a daughter with her.

Oh, was this truly her life? She didn't deserve this. Didn't deserve any of it. But it belonged to her anyway, and she was grateful.

The baby opened her eyes then, and stole Deborah's breath.

Those tiny eyes were blue. So blue. Dark, piercing blue.

The same eyes as Nathaniel's.

"She has my mother's eyes." Levi trailed a fingertip over the baby's cheek.

"She has your brother's eyes." Deborah had hated those eyes since the moment she saw them. Nathaniel's eyes were what had clued Elisabeth in to the fact that this was the man who'd maimed her. Those blue eyes had always stood for evil and destruction.

But in this sweet little innocent face, the Martinson eyes weren't threatening.

They were beautiful.

God had redeemed these eyes through the blood of childbirth, just as he had redeemed her—and Nathaniel—through the blood of the cross.

And that was why she was in the rocker now, sitting by the fire, awaiting the knock at the door.

It came, and she turned. "Come in." Her heart thumped in her throat, with nerves and dread and excitement. Had God truly changed her? Had he truly done the sort of work in her she thought he had?

"It's us" came Levi's deep voice. A gust of chilly air, accompanied by a few snowflakes, stole into the warmth of the cabin, along with Levi . . . and Nathaniel.

Nathaniel. Here in her home. The man responsible for Elisabeth's death, standing a mere few paces from where she'd fallen.

He doffed his hat and held it in his hands, rotating it clockwise, his feet shuffling. "You, uh, you wanted to see me?"

"Yes." Peace bloomed in Deborah's heart, along with the smile on her face. "I wanted to introduce you to your niece."

"My niece." Nathaniel blinked. "May I . . . may I see her?"

"Of course." Her smile widened. "It's a little difficult to see her from over there, after all."

Nathaniel's smile was a tentative twitch of the corners of his mouth. He hesitated a moment, then came closer. He seemed wary, almost as though he were afraid she'd attack. She couldn't blame him.

"She's beautiful," he said.

"Yes. She is." The baby sucked a tiny fist, eyes closed in sleep, lashes casting a shadow on her silken, petal-pink cheeks. "You can't see them now, but her eyes are the most stunning deep blue. Levi says they're your mother's eyes."

Nathaniel cleared his throat. "They are. And her father before her, so I'm told."

"And they're your eyes too." Those blue eyes peered down at her now, framed by dark lashes, slightly creased at the corners and still wary.

Her heart held no hatred for those eyes now, nor for the man who owned them. Through the grace of God, it held nothing but love.

"Seeing these eyes made me realize we're all part of the same family, Nathaniel. We're part of the same earthly family—the Martinsons—but because of our faith in Christ, we're also family in him. And there can be no division in a family. Not if it's to stay strong. And I want our family— our earthly one and our spiritual one—to be strong. Elisabeth would have wanted it that way. She understood. And now . . . now I do too."

Nathaniel's dark brows furrowed. "What are you saying?"

Deborah took a deep breath. "I'm saying I apologize for the way I acted last time we saw each other. I'm saying that through God's grace alone, I am choosing to forgive you for what you did. I don't want to carry that bitterness any longer. God has given me—given us—a family. A home. And I don't want anything to jeopardize that."

Levi slid his arm around Deborah's shoulders and kissed the top of her uncapped head. She leaned into his embrace, she and the baby both.

"Deborah." Nathaniel's voice was husky, and his eyes shone. "I am truly, deeply sorry for what I did to you. To your sister. To your family. If I could change those actions, I would in a second."

"I know, and I appreciate that," she replied. "But even if you didn't regret your actions, it's my responsibility—through God's grace—to forgive you. And I have. And I shall. I shall keep forgiving you. It is a process—I know that. It might take years to truly let it go. To heal. But the God who brought me to Levi, to your family, the God who gave me Nora and this precious little treasure, I trust him to help me do it. To help me welcome you to our family. To our home. You may have intended what you did for evil, but I believe God has good intentions for it. He has brought good and will continue to bring good."

"Thank you, Deborah." Tears pooled along the lower rims of those blue eyes. "Thank you. Thank you a thousand times over."

"Would you like to hold your niece?"

Nathaniel gave a start. "Would that be all right?"

"Of course." Her heart warmed as she shifted the baby's weight in her arms and held the tiny bundle out to meet her uncle. "Nathaniel, meet Elisabeth Grace." The name had come to her in the night. A gift from God. The perfect way to honor both the past God had redeemed and the future he had planned.

A single tear streaked Nathaniel's cheek as he held the baby in his arms, his eyes shining with love. "Hello, Elisabeth Grace."

And for the first time since the attack, Deborah felt the fist that had strangled her heart finally let go.

Why did God allow such a horrible event to strike her family? She didn't know. But she was willing to trust him with it. To leave it in his hands.

Because the God who could redeem her life, who could bless her so richly, who could work in unfathomably gracious ways? There wasn't a thing in the world he couldn't do.

Finally, she was willing to let him.

CHAPTER THIRTY-NINE

MATT LEANED AGAINST the driver's door of his truck, mindlessly scrolling through his Facebook feed. The morning's service hadn't resulted in any videos yet, although they'd doubtless pop up in the coming hours and days. Not only Facebook, but everywhere else too. Maybe it'd even go viral. *Sex Pred Pastor Confronted . . . AT CHURCH! Watch what happens next.*

He'd made it to the green room and grabbed the doughnut he craved, but not the relaxation. The tension in the small space was palpable.

"Dude," Tyler the bass player had said from his spot on the couch. Chase, the drummer, hadn't even managed to summon that much verbiage. The background vocalists had been nowhere to be seen, while Jed, the lead guitarist, stood by the coffee machine, texting madly and refusing to make eye contact with anyone.

That was when Matt had headed for the parking lot. Rick would text him from the tech booth when it was time to take the stage for the closing song. If there would even be a closing song this service.

As though in answer to his silent question, his phone buzzed in his hand. Sure enough, a text from Rick.

> We've canceled the ending song.
> Jerry's just going to pray and
> dismiss. Jed has agreed to lead
> next service.

And probably the one after that, and the one after that, for the foreseeable future.

Matt clicked out of the message with a rueful smile. Doubtless his formal firing would come in the morning. And if by some miracle it didn't, his resignation letter was typed, signed, and ready to go.

There it was. His dream job. Incinerated in a matter of moments.

He wasn't even sad about it.

Just exhausted. Spent. Drained of any and all energy.

Nothing left to do now but drive home. And he would. As soon as he got the strength.

For now, he'd just stand here. Soak up some vitamin D, stare at his phone, and—

"Matt."

The familiar voice came from the back exit. Sure enough, there was that platinum hair and slight figure hurrying toward him.

His heart filled, and he tucked his phone into his pocket and met her a few paces from his truck. She flung her arms around him, and he gathered her to his chest, reveling in her. Her warmth. Her sweet fragrance. The softness of her hair against the back of his hands. The pressure of her cheek against his. The feeling of her hands on his back.

And the sheer rightness of it all. How seamlessly she fit against him, how safe and whole and loved he felt in her arms.

The tension dissolved, and his strength returned as she held him. He'd been looking for a home his whole life, and he'd found it in the arms and the heart of Siobhan Walsh.

"Thank you." Her thick whisper tickled his ear.

He tightened his embrace. "Of course." He'd do it again, a thousand times over, if this was his reward. If he could hold her in his arms forever and never let her go.

"I mean it." She pulled back and looked at him, blue eyes bright with unshed tears. "Thank you. I wish I'd had the courage to do what you did. What Kayleigh did."

"Just because you never spoke up doesn't mean you don't have courage." He slipped his hand beneath her hair and massaged the back of her neck. "You came here. You walked through those doors. You've gone toe to toe with Trace Jessup and come out in one piece on the other side. You've grown so much, and you've battled so many demons, and you . . . you inspire me. Seriously. Seeing you slip through those doors this morning was the final push God used to make me actually do what I did."

Her mouth quirked. "Any fallout yet?"

"My services are not needed for the rest of the morning," he replied. "And probably beyond that. But even if they don't fire me, I've got my resignation ready to go. I can't be here anymore. I can't endorse what this church is doing. Staying here, I wouldn't be able to look myself in the mirror."

"What will you do, then?" She took his hands in hers. They were soft and strong and still warm from being inside the building.

"No idea." His voice—and his heart—were surprisingly light. "I'm pretty sure God's got something for me, though."

She grinned. "I'm pretty sure he does too."

That bright smile, those blue eyes, they'd be the death of him.

He stepped closer. "I meant what I said in that text, Siobhan. I love you."

Her smile grew all the brighter. "And I meant what I said back. I love you too."

"Like . . . I *love* you, love you."

She grasped his face between her hands. "I know. And I *love you*, love you too."

Her thumb stroked his cheekbone, and he closed his eyes. "Man, that sounds good."

"Doesn't it?"

"I might want you to say it again."

She chuckled, low and rich. "Okay, if you insist. I love you."

He opened his eyes and smiled. "I was right. I wanted you to say it again."

And then he said it without words. His lips sought and found hers, pouring everything he had into one single kiss. His adoration for her. His hopes for the future. His dreams, all of which suddenly featured her in a prominent role.

They pulled apart slowly. Reluctantly. He pressed his forehead to hers, swallowing hard. Seeing stars.

"Listen, Matt." Her words tickled his lips. "I . . . I meant what I said. I do love you. Tremendously. In an 'I'm going to love you forever' kind of way."

Forever. That was another word that sounded good coming from her. "But..."

That word didn't. He pulled back and frowned. "But what?"

"I'm not healthy enough right now to have the kind of relationship I want with you." She peered up at him, blue eyes frank and vulnerable. "I mean, I forgave Trace just now. Which is kind of a big deal. But I've got to get some counseling, y'know. Make sure I'm okay. Make sure I don't torpedo things with you."

So much she'd just said. So much he needed to process. But one thing stood out.

"Wait, you forgave Trace?"

"Yeah. Saw him in the hallway. He was mad. He was yelling—it was this whole thing, and I didn't care." She gave a little shrug and an adorable smile. "He's not my problem anymore. I've released him."

"Siobhan. That's huge. I am so proud of you."

"Thank you." She feathered a quick kiss to his lips. "But recovering from what he did is going to be a process. I need to heal. And I feel like I need to do that on my own. Well, not on my own. With God. But..."

"Not tangled up in a relationship."

"Exactly. Not yet, anyway. Not never. But not yet."

He let out a sigh. So close. *So* close. And yet so far. "I get it, Siobhan. I mean... I'd be lying if I said I liked it. But I get it. And if I'm honest, I'm not sure I'm ready, either. I need to get through the fallout of this. And I need to figure out what my future holds. I need to be able to offer you *something*."

"All I need is you, Matt," she said. "You and Jesus."

He grinned despite everything. "Well, maybe. But I grew up not always knowing where the next month's rent would come from, or even where Mom and I would be living, and I want better than that for us. For... if we have a family. Call me old-fashioned, but I don't want to be in a serious relationship until I'm actually prepared—in all aspects—for that kind of relationship. I want to be able to pull my weight financially. And"—he gestured toward the building at her back—"I'm kinda doubting I'll get a nice severance package from this place."

Her laugh was like bells. "Yeah, trust that instinct."

He joined in with her. Man, it felt good to laugh. It felt good to be free of this place.

But when the laughter died down, uncertainty surfaced. He studied her beautiful face. "So where does that leave us now?"

"It leaves us in God's hands," she replied. "Which is, frankly, the best place to be. We love each other. We love him. We know we're meant to be together someday. We just need to trust that he'll work things out in his time and his way."

Waiting. Trusting. Matt had never been any good at either of those things.

"You should know that part of me wants to run away with you. Right now," he said. "Like, just hop in the truck and drive until we run out of gas, and then fill 'er up and drive some more."

Siobhan's eyes sparkled. "Part of me would not say no to that. But."

There was that word again.

"The rest of me knows that what you and I have together has the potential to be really special, and we need to not screw it up by bringing our damage from this place into it."

He swallowed hard. "You're a wise woman, Siobhan Walsh."

"I wasn't always. But thank God I am now."

He pulled her into his arms again, memorizing the feel of her body against his. It would have to do until the timing was right. But a small voice within him promised it wouldn't be that long.

"Take care, Siobhan," he murmured into her hair. "And stay in touch, all right? Don't just disappear."

"You forget I have your violin." She smiled against his cheek. "So I definitely won't be a stranger. But you take care too. Until the time is right."

Then she stepped back, pressed a final kiss to his cheek, and walked away.

Yet another situation where he expected to be devastated. But he wasn't. He was strangely at peace.

The timing with her wasn't right yet.

But it would be. Soon.

And then there was no telling what wonders God had in store for both of them.

CHAPTER FORTY

Two Months Later

THE PUNGENT SCENT of polish permeated the violin shop as Siobhan trailed a soft cloth over the top of the old violin. It had sure presented its challenges during the restoration process. A time or two she'd nearly given up, thinking it beyond hope, but she was glad she'd persevered. It had turned out better than she ever could have dreamed.

It had been more than a project, this violin. It had been an instrument of transformation. The story of Deborah Caldwell Martinson—her trauma, her loss, her God-given ability to forgive the man responsible for that trauma and loss—had resonated within Siobhan. Enabled her to forgive Trace. To begin to heal. To move on. The violin had become a friend, and tears pricked the backs of her eyes as she moved to polish the instrument's sides. She was really going to miss this thing.

But was it truly the violin she'd miss? Or the fact that it was her last remaining link to Matt Buchanan?

As long as she had the violin, she had a reason to stay in touch with Matt. She'd occasionally texted him updates on the repair progress, and he'd always replied with gratitude and encouragement. Sometimes memes or funny pictures found their way to her phone, and those always brought a smile. But she and Matt, by unspoken agreement, both stayed away from the heavy stuff. It was as though they were circling around the idea of each other, not wanting to be the first to make a move.

What, then, would happen when he showed up in a few minutes to retrieve the violin?

No, she wasn't going to worry about that. She was in a good place now. A healthy place. She'd been attending weekly sessions with a wise counselor, and she'd put in the work. She wasn't fixed yet—nor would she be until the other side of eternity—but she was making progress. And it showed.

Her wardrobe, for instance. Therapy had shown her that it wasn't a sin to have a womanly figure. To wear clothes tailored to it. It wasn't Siobhan's fault—or her body's fault—that Trace had lusted after her. Now she wasn't hiding behind her clothes anymore. Plaid was still a regular feature of her wardrobe, but the quilted vests she'd used to hide her curves were long gone.

She'd changed her hair too. It wasn't all the way back to her natural dark brown—she and her stylist had settled on a medium brown shade with honey-colored highlights. A look Siobhan felt blended who she'd been before Trace and who she was after.

She wasn't ashamed to be herself anymore. That was the biggest thing therapy had taught her.

And part of being herself—another part, a huge part—was playing the violin.

She was playing again regularly now. In public even. She'd started small, joining a community orchestra with a mixture of students, professionals, retirees, and hobbyists, and the weekly rehearsals fed her soul in a way nothing had in quite some time. They weren't the best orchestra she'd ever been part of, but they were definitely the most enthusiastic. They all loved music and loved making it together, and that came through loud and clear. Through their influence, and through therapy, she wasn't afraid to let people hear her play anymore.

She lifted the instrument to her chin, her traditional last step in any repair. A farewell to the instrument that had taken so many hours of her time and energy. A final send-off before placing it in the hands of its rightful owner.

But what should she play? This wasn't just any violin. And it wasn't just any client, either.

Mendelssohn? Mozart? Bach?

No. None of those felt quite right.

The answer came to her mind and heart at the same time. Something she hadn't played in a while—not since she was at Pursuers—but something that was perfect for the occasion, for multiple reasons.

Amazing Grace.

The old hymn took flight beneath her fingers as though it had never left her, and her heart soared as though it had never been silenced. God had truly worked a miracle within her, and the only appropriate response was to give that miracle back to him in worship.

The bells jangled as she improvised her way through the third stanza, drawing her eyes open. There was Matt. And rather than stop playing, startled, as she had the first time he'd walked in on her playing, she merely smiled at him and kept going. Because it wasn't her violin that had made Trace lust after her, either. It was Trace and Trace alone. He was a predator; she was his prey. But by the grace of God, she'd been rescued. Her therapist had helped her see that.

Matt. He looked . . . wow, he looked incredible. She'd never seen him in shorts before. And he had really great legs. She shouldn't be looking at those legs, not right now, but looking at his eyes, his smile, his hair, his shoulders . . . it didn't matter. All of it provoked the same reaction.

She was in love with him. She loved him.

Her cheek grazed the chin rest with her smile, and Matt was smiling back at her, standing in the doorway, watching her play. Completely differently than the way Trace had watched her.

Trace had looked at her like she was something he wanted. Something to be taken.

Matt looked at her like she was a gift. A treasure. Something to be cherished rather than conquered.

He loved her too. It shone in his eyes. Radiated from his smile. And she wasn't afraid of that anymore, either. She was ready. She was *ready*. Being with him brought a peace like almost nothing else. Matt was right, and now was right, and she couldn't wait to tell him.

She finished with a high D and a decrescendo to near nothing, at which point she lowered the bow from the string and gazed into Matt's eyes.

He broke into soft applause and a huge grin. "That sounds beautiful."

"Thanks." She lowered the violin and loosened the bow. "It better sound good. This thing took long enough."

Matt's brows flew up. "Wait, that's Grandma's violin? *My* violin?"

She couldn't resist a proud smile. "Yup."

"It sounds so . . . so different."

"Well, restoration does tend to have that effect on an instrument," she replied.

"Oh, it does sound better. It sounds way better. I mean, not that it sounded bad before—not that *you* sounded bad before, but just . . ." He broke off with a nervous chuckle and a self-deprecating grin. "Hi."

She echoed his laughter. "Hi."

"It's so good to see you." He stepped to the counter.

"It's good to see you too." She laid the violin back in its case, but she wasn't looking at it. Neither was Matt.

"I like your hair." His hazel eyes took in her new color, up the left side of her head and down the right.

She gave it a self-conscious fluff. "Thanks."

"I mean, I *really* like your hair." His dimple deepened. "Blond, brunette, anything in between. I just like your hair."

Warmth crept from her heart into her cheeks. "Thank you."

"It's all done, then?" Matt leaned in, his gaze raking over the violin's newly polished wood. The freshly repaired cracks.

"All done."

"Did you ever find out any more about it?"

"I did, and it's fascinating."

His eyes lit. "Do tell."

Siobhan leaned on the counter, her newly colored hair tumbling over her shoulders. "Okay, so remember how we found a repair ticket from John Caldwell?"

"The guy whose family was attacked?"

Siobhan nodded. "Yeah. And remember how one of the daughters got married to a guy she barely knew?"

"Levi, right?"

"Yeah. Turns out Levi's brother, Nathaniel, was the one who scalped Deborah's sister, Elisabeth."

Matt's eyes widened. "Did she know?"

"Elisabeth figured it out right before she died. She wrote a letter about it." Siobhan reached into the lining of the violin case and carefully withdrew an envelope containing the fragile pages. "About how she forgave her attacker and encouraged Deborah to do the same."

Matt leaned in, his cologne wafting toward Siobhan as he scanned the letter. "Whoa. And you found this."

"I did. And God used it to help me forgive. I mean, if Elisabeth Caldwell could forgive the man who tried to murder her, then surely I could forgive Trace."

"Did Deborah ever forgive him? Nathaniel, I mean?" Sunlight from the window glinted off Matt's stubble, turning it red gold.

"According to some old diaries Sloane found, she did. And get this." Siobhan leaned closer. "Deborah had a daughter, also named Elisabeth. And that Elisabeth inherited this violin. She ended up founding a music school in the Wichita area and teaching hundreds and hundreds of students over a five-decade career."

"Wow."

"Even more interesting? She married a guy by the name of Buchanan. Robert Buchanan, to be exact."

"Buchanan, huh?" Matt tilted his head. "As in . . ."

"As in your great-great-grandfather. Robert and Elisabeth are your ancestors."

"So it's been in my family all this time." Matt eyed the violin with undisguised awe.

"As has your musical ability, it seems." Siobhan grinned at him. "Looks like your talent comes honestly."

"Man. I love this old thing even more now."

"Me too." She straightened and shut the lid of the violin case. "Enough about me. What's new in your world?"

Matt stuck his hands in his pockets. "Well, I have a new job."

"Oh?" She was thrilled for him but suddenly terrified. Did that mean he was leaving Wichita? She'd never considered that possibility until right now, but what did he have to tie him here? No family, no friends to speak of. He'd come here for a job, so wouldn't he leave for one just as easily?

"Yeah. You know Pursuers fired me."

"Naturally."

"Couple of the guys have stayed in touch. According to them, the board of elders formally censured Trace and basically forced him to take a sabbatical, but they haven't fired him, and I doubt they ever will. They're too obsessed with the numbers. The seekers and the conversions and all those statistics that make their world go round." Matt shifted his weight. "And weirdly, all those have just increased since Trace has been on leave, so naturally they're spinning it that God is using it for good and since their pastor has been so humble and honest, droves of people are coming to Jesus."

Siobhan rolled her eyes, but her stomach didn't roil. Her fists didn't clench. What once would have been nauseating was now merely annoying. Something that didn't penetrate like before but now merely rolled off, like rain off a duck's back. "We'll see how humble and honest he is in court."

"Court?" Matt's eyebrows flew to his hairline.

Siobhan nodded, a proud smile tickling the corners of her mouth. "A couple of his other victims have contacted an attorney about pressing charges. I'm not spearheading it—Jenisa and Kayleigh are—but they might ask me to testify."

"Wow." Matt's gaze sought hers. "Are you willing to do that?"

"I . . . I think so. Yes. Forgiveness doesn't mean he shouldn't face justice. It just means I'm not bound to him anymore." Siobhan leaned in closer. "But enough about him. I want to hear about this new job of yours."

Matt grinned. "Well, Colton, Pursuers' youth pastor, didn't agree with the church's approach, so he also resigned, and a bunch of people left with him. He's joining forces with my friend Rhys from Illinois, who's moving to Wichita to plant a church. And the two of them have asked me to be the worship pastor."

"Here? In Wichita?"

Matt's eyes sparkled. "Now, the pay's not amazing, so I'm also working at a coffee shop to make ends meet. It isn't much, but—"

"Matt, I don't care. I make a decent living here at the shop, and if that's not enough, there's always Uber."

Matt blinked. "What are you saying, Siobhan?"

Smiling, she came around the counter onto the sales floor. "I'm saying it's time, Matt. It's past time. Looking at you standing there I . . . I can't be without you anymore. I can't not talk to you. Texting every few days doesn't cut it. I . . . I'm ready. I love you. *Love* you, love you. And I want to be with you."

"Oh, thank God." The words rushed from his lips, and then those lips were on hers. The kiss was fierce. Pent-up. Like he'd been waiting his whole life for this moment. Doubtless he had. So had she. His hands tangled in her hair. His heart pounded against hers. Their breaths mingled and melded into one.

When they pulled apart, he wrapped his arms around her, and she laid her head against his chest, his heartbeat thumping against her cheek. Safe. Secure. In the arms of one who would treat her like a treasure.

The one God had been planning for her all this time.

"Tell me more about this church," she said.

"Well." He pulled back to look at her. "We could use another singer."

"Could you?"

"Yeah. And maybe one who doubles on violin occasionally." His gaze peered deep. "If she's ready, that is."

Confident peace filled her heart. "She is."

She was ready for anything and everything with this man by her side. With the God who'd brought them together, against all odds and through unimaginable obstacles. He had used Matt in her healing process, and God had used her in Matt's life too. Doubtless he'd continue to do it. Even when it got difficult. Even when it felt like it wasn't worth it. It was, and it always would be.

With God in charge, there would be no stopping them.

AUTHOR'S NOTE

As with any work of fiction, some portions are inspired by true events, and some are fabricated by the author. While some of this story is definitely inspired by real history (more on that in a minute), I wanted to begin by emphasizing that Pursuers Church and Pastor Trace Jessup are creations of my imagination and are not based on any actual churches or pastors. That said, abuse within the church—be it sexual, emotional, spiritual, mental, or physical—is sadly not fictional and not a new problem. Stories like Siobhan's have happened since the dawn of church history, and I'm certain many of us can name churches and pastors who have perpetuated this sort of abuse. Fortunately, these brave survivors and witnesses have begun to bring their stories into the light. More and more, they are refusing to stay silent, calling out sin where they see it, and urging us all to be better representatives of Jesus Christ both inside and outside of the church walls.

My goal in highlighting church abuse is not, as my worship pastor friend Jerrod Byrne would say, "to punch the bride of Christ in the mouth." Rather, it is to illustrate that churches are not immune to the sin that plagues us all. My pastor from my church in Illinois, Randy Boltinghouse, likes to say that "we're a church full of sinners with a sinner for a pastor." This is not to excuse sin—by no means—but instead to illustrate that it exists even in places where we wish it wouldn't. Thank God for the gift of grace through Jesus Christ.

Wounds inflicted by the church—be it the church as an institution or individuals within its walls—cut deep. Church should be a safe place for all, and when it isn't, there are multiple layers of anger, pain, betrayal, and grief to work through. I know from my own experience that this does not happen overnight, and it frequently does not happen in isolation. I am grateful for the skilled, Jesus-following therapists who have walked me through my own healing journey, and I urge any of you who have been wounded by the church in any way to seek counseling from a trusted source.

If I may give you one further word of advice, it would be to not give up on the church. By all means, leave toxic people and places behind, but know that for every unhealthy church, there are—thankfully—many more healthy ones. I pray that you find the healing you need. And if you feel led to reach out to me in any way, I would be more than happy to provide whatever help I can. Know that you are in my prayers.

The part of my story that *is* based on actual history is the story of Deborah and Elisabeth Caldwell. This portion of the book is heavily inspired by the Corbly Family Massacre, which took place on the frontier of western Pennsylvania on May 10, 1782, near the town of Garard's Fort. As the story goes, Rev. John Corbly and his family were on their way to church when he realized he'd forgotten his Bible, so he went back to the house to get it. While he was gone, a band of warriors attacked the family, killing John's wife, Elizabeth Tyler Corbly, and three of their children: six-year-old Isaiah, two-year-old Mary Catherine, and baby Nancy outright. (These children deserve to be remembered, so I have used their real names in the story when possible. However, I did change Isaiah Corbly's name to Josiah to avoid confusion with the adult Isaiah, fiancé of the fictional Elisabeth.)

John's other two daughters, Delilah and Elizabeth, hid in a hollow log and emerged when they thought it was safe, only to be scalped themselves. Incredibly, both girls survived the attack. The identity of their attackers is, as far as I know, lost to history. It is assumed that they were attacked by Indigenous Americans, but according to family lore, Elizabeth Corbly always insisted she was scalped by a white man. (The twist of having this man reappear as part of their lives, however, is entirely my own invention.)

Much like the Elisabeth in the story, Elizabeth Corbly died at the age of twenty-one, just a few days before she was set to marry Isaiah Morris. Delilah, meanwhile, married Levi Martin, with whom she had ten children, and died in Ohio at the age of sixty-five. One of those children, Elizabeth Martin Dye, is my fifth-great-grandmother. I have always been fascinated by this story—how one could survive something that killed most—and inspired by the strength of both Delilah and Elizabeth.

Although this sort of brutal attack was not routine in Kansas by any means, there was some historical precedent for setting the story here. Robert McGee, the scalping survivor mentioned in the pages of this book, was a real person, and the details of his life I describe in the story actually took place. My original plan for this book was to set it in 1782 in Pennsylvania, but once I learned of Robert McGee, who was scalped in 1864, I made the decision to set it in frontier-era Kansas instead. This enabled me to keep the story within the scope of the Sedgwick County Chronicles theme, as well as bring back our beloved Jack, Annabelle, and Dr. Stephen Maxwell from *Roots of Wood and Stone*. I hope you, my lovely readers, will indulge this bit of artistic license and slight manipulation of history in the name of story.

The violin in the story is inspired by an instrument owned by my paternal grandmother, Laura Carter Peterson. She passed away long before I was born, so I never had the privilege of meeting her, but she was a talented musician who sang, composed and arranged music, and played both piano and violin. Years ago my mother had Laura's violin restored at a local violin shop, McHugh Violins, which inspired the violin shop in the story. As for Ian McFarland? He is inspired by our local luthier, Simon McHugh, who has faithfully served string players in Wichita and the surrounding area for decades. He is always a delight to pop in and chat with, and—like Ian—is really from Stratford-upon-Avon.

ACKNOWLEDGMENTS

EVERY TIME I start a book, I stare at the daunting task in front of me and wonder if there's any way I can do it again. And every time I finish a book, I look back and realize just how many people God brought alongside me to help me finish that daunting task and shape this book into what it is today. Specifically for this book, my deepest thanks are due to . . .

My amazing agent, Tamela Hancock Murray; my fantastic friend and developmental editor, Janyre Tromp; my rock star copy editor, Dori Harrell; and the rest of the editorial, sales, and marketing teams at Kregel Publications. My gratitude to God for bringing all of you into my life—and to all of you for your tireless efforts to make my books the best they can be— deepens with each project. It is truly an honor to partner with you all to bring stories into the world.

My sensitivity reader, Melanie Martin, whose expertise and experience were invaluable in preparing this story for publication. I wanted to write in a sensitive way that would not lead to the villainization of any Indigenous individuals or groups, and Melanie helped me walk that line. I appreciate her feedback immensely and have applied it to the best of my ability. Any mistakes are my own.

My wonderful critique partners, Theresa St. Romain and Linda Fletcher, whose enthusiasm and insightful comments are absolutely priceless. You both keep me motivated and reassure me when I'm in the weeds with a book that it is still a story worth telling. I appreciate both of you more than I can ever express.

My friend and worship pastor, Jerrod Byrne, for shedding some light on what his job involves. His insights have been very helpful in this book, and his wisdom, encouragement, humor, authenticity, and musicianship have brightened my life for the last decade-plus. Love ya, pal. It is an honor and a privilege to know you and worship with you.

My longtime luthier, Simon McHugh, whose decades-long faithful service and friendship to the Wichita string community is deeply appreciated.

My student novel-writing intern at Haven High School, Tanya Yoder, who is sitting across the table from me as I write this! I'm so grateful for the unique opportunity we've had to work together while I wrote this book, and I can guarantee I have learned far more about writing (and life!) from you than you have from me. It's been so much fun working with you, and I can't wait to see your stories take flight. My thanks also go to Megan Hett and Tara Cooprider for hatching the idea for this unique internship, and to Corri Hernandez for helping it run smoothly.

To my choir students in Haven, past and present. All of you inspire me, love me, and care for me far more than you know.

Nolan and Angie Banks, for their encouragement, snark, prayers, and faithful friendship. Your deck is my absolute favorite place to spend a Friday evening. Thank you, as always, for being yourselves.

The Quotidians, for praying me through the most difficult book I've ever written during one of the most difficult years of my entire life. I couldn't do it without you all, and I mean that most sincerely. I love you and am grateful for you.

To fellow Kansas author Sara Brunsvold, whose wonderful idea for a writing retreat in the Flint Hills helped me get going on this book. Every time I smell a skunk, I think of you, and that is far more of a compliment than it sounds. Much gratitude also to Carmen Schober; it's been fun getting to know you and having another author friend in the same state! Much love to both my Twister Sisters.

To everyone I met at Fiction Readers Summit 2023. Your enthusiasm for this book has made me even more eager to get it into your hands. You all are amazing, and I'm so happy to have had the chance to spend time with you.

Jaime Jo Wright, for taking over my social media and making it a whole lot better than it was before, and also for some very honest and much-needed conversations around the time of my dad's passing. Thanks are also due to Carrie Schmidt, Kerry Johnson, Pepper Basham, and others both near and far for providing your been-there, living-through-that insight, your friendship, and your care for me as I struggled to make sense of Life Without Dad. I'm so sorry you've all suffered the loss of a parent, but I'm grateful God chose you to help me walk this difficult road. Thank you all.

To my long-suffering and endlessly patient husband, Cheech Wen, and my three Wenlets, Caleb, Jonathan, and Selah. Thanks, as always, for understanding when I need to spend time with the fictional people and for being my biggest fans and cheerleaders. You are the absolute best family any writer could ever ask for, and I'm thrilled to call you mine. I love you more and more every day.

To my mom, Deanna Peterson, whose research into our family history uncovered the story of the Corbly family, and whose bravery in the face of the loss of her sweetheart of over five decades has been awe inspiring. You don't enjoy widowhood, nor does anyone expect you to, but you are handling it with enormous grace and fortitude. I am so proud of you, and I know Dad would be too.

To my dad, Jim Peterson. This is the first book of mine you won't read on earth, the first time I'll launch a book that you're not here to celebrate with me. But your influence is everywhere in these pages. You taught me by deed, example, and a cheerful "We can do that" that nothing is too broken to fix, nothing is too far gone to be redeemed, and nothing is beyond the reach of God's grace and love. Thank you for being such a wonderful dad. I miss you, but I know I will see you again someday.

Finally, to Jesus. Thank you for getting me through another book—this book, of all books. Losing my dad during the writing process was not something I had planned, but it was not a surprise to you. Thank you for being so faithful and helping me start to pick up the pieces. Give Dad a hug for me. I love you.

More from AMANDA WEN

Don't miss the books *Foreword Reviews* calls "satisfying, moving novels that combine ancestral stories with a new romance."

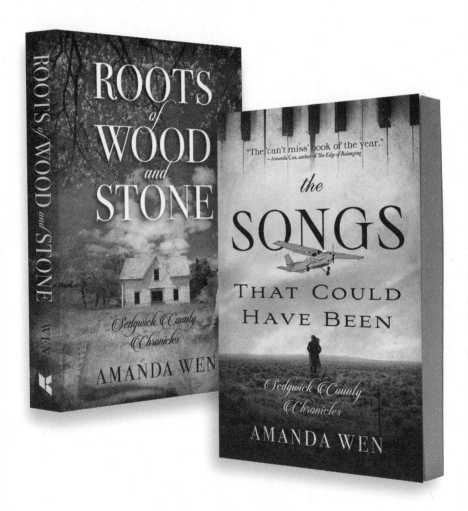

KREGEL
PUBLICATIONS

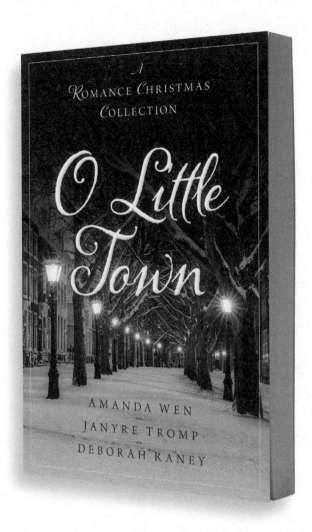

A *Romance Christmas Collection*

O Little Town

AMANDA WEN

JANYRE TROMP

DEBORAH RANEY

THIS HEARTWARMING COLLECTION of Christmas romance from Amanda Wen and two other popular inspirational authors is the perfect stocking stuffer for a very "marry" Christmas!

KREGEL
PUBLICATIONS